WE WERE STRANGERS ONCE

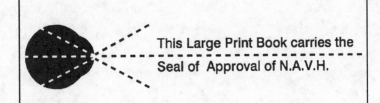

This Large Print Book carries the
Seal of Approval of N.A.V.H.

WE WERE STRANGERS ONCE

BETSY CARTER

THORNDIKE PRESS
A part of Gale, a Cengage Company

Farmington Hills, Mich • San Francisco • New York • Waterville, Maine
Meriden, Conn • Mason, Ohio • Chicago

LIBRARY OF CONGRESS CIP DATA ON FILE.
CATALOGUING IN PUBLICATION FOR THIS BOOK
IS AVAILABLE FROM THE LIBRARY OF CONGRESS

ISBN-13: 978-1-4328-4869-9 (hardcover)

Published in 2018 by arrangement with Grand Central Publishing, a division of Hachette Book Group, Inc.

Printed in Mexico
1 2 3 4 5 6 7 22 21 20 19 18

To everyone from somewhere else

My fellow Americans, we are and always will be a nation of immigrants. We were strangers once, too.

— Barack Obama

■ ■ ■ ■

PART I
IN THE OLD
COUNTRY

■ ■ ■ ■

1.

"Remember, he's a busy man. No idle talk. And don't forget to wear your gloves."

When Elisabeth looked up from the street, she could make out her mother's form, still in her dressing gown, standing behind the only unshuttered window on the street. It was early enough that there was no sun, no shadows, nothing except the familiar harsh voice ricocheting off the cobblestones and whisked away by the frigid February wind.

She wanted to shout back, "I don't have to make idle talk; my work speaks for itself," but she had long ago given up on that conversation. Besides, this morning she had no time to waste bickering with her mother. All her attention was focused on one thing and one thing only: her meeting with Germany's most famous naturalist, Professor Rudolph Schneider, who had spent the past five years compiling research on the birds of Europe. Now he was looking for someone to illustrate his work, which was, in a sense, what Elisabeth Arnstein had been doing for most of her twenty-one years.

When she had been a few months shy of eight years old, Elisabeth's father had become so ill that he'd taken to his bed. After school, she would come home and sit with him. Sometimes she'd get under the covers and lie with her head on his shoulder while he slept. It was early spring, and though he appreciated his daughter's attention, even craved it, Bernard Arnstein also felt it was unnatural for a girl Elisabeth's age to be confined to a dark room with a dying man. Knowing what a quick hand and deft mind she had, he'd said to her: "Elisabeth, take your pad and pencils outside and bring back the spring to me." So every day after school, she would go with her sketchbook to the Stadtwald, the largest forest in Frankfurt, and sit quietly in the brush, drawing the foliage and insects and birds around her. At night she would lay her sheets of sketches at the foot of her father's bed, and he would ask questions: "What did the starling's song sound like?" "Were the fawn's eyes frightened when she came upon you?" "How did the toad's skin feel in your hand?"

A jeweler by trade, Bernard Arnstein had

spent his days peering through a magnifying glass, synchronizing the mechanics of a clock or placing chips of diamond just so around the emerald centerpiece of a ring. Patience was his craft, precision his art, and he was eager to instill both in his only child. "You must make us see the light reflect off the loon's back, hear the ruffling of the hawk's feathers. Give them life, Elisabeth, not only pretty colors." Before he died, he gave her a small package wrapped in brown paper with a note inside: *Remember, fresh eyes on the world.* The gift was an old prosthetic eye made of hand-blown glass, the onyx-black pupil surrounded by a hand-painted marine-blue iris centered on a porcelain-white background. The eye had been a gift to him from his own father, and he had always kept it on his worktable. As a child, Elisabeth had been afraid to touch it because it looked so real, but after her father died, she kept it in the drawer of her dressing table, and at least once a day she'd hold it in her hand long enough for the cool glass to become warm and the memory of her father's touch visceral.

Elisabeth continued her habit of going to the Stadtwald, where she mostly drew the birds. She became so attuned to their songs and habits that she could distinguish the

13

high-pitched *tsee-tsewit* of a swallow from the sneezy *tsiwick* of a woodcock. She never tired of watching over their eggs, or waiting for the mature birds to come back from their hunt and drop dinner down the throats of their chicks. Sometimes a wren or a starling would stop at her feet and peck at her shoes. They would stare at her with their keen black eyes, and she would feel certain that something had transpired between them. She felt her father in the birds' presence. She was certain they hovered as if they were keeping watch and guiding her. How else to explain why they would stand still before her long enough that she could sketch their forms and memorize their plumage?

It was a childish habit, she knew, but this morning as she walked toward the streetcar, she checked the sunless sky for a bird, any sign of one. There was nothing. *All right,* she said to herself, *it will be Professor Schneider and me: I hope he's prepared.* Defiance was an old friend. It stuck with her when schoolmates taunted and called her birdbrain, and saw her through her mother's relentless chiding: "The birds will not put food on your table or keep you warm at night." Every evening, when she returned from the Stadtwald, her mother would grab her

14

hands. "Wash that filth from your fingers. Your hands are like a common ditchdigger's."

Elisabeth would examine the dusty colors on her fingers: the rosy gray of a pine grosbeak's rump, crimson from the crested head of a great spotted woodpecker, a yellow smudge from a wagtail's belly: her treasures of the day.

"Dirt is dirt. You and your father, you live with your heads in the clouds." Her mother never tired of pointing out the ways in which Elisabeth and her father were tethered, as if she were still trying to insinuate herself between them, even after his death.

Surely the professor shared Elisabeth's passion.

The wind picked up. For all the time she'd spent pinning her hair into a bun this morning, she could feel strands of it coming undone. She pulled her shawl tighter around her head. She had heard that the professor from Heidelberg was an elegant man, even something of a dandy. Then she remembered her mother's warning: *Don't forget to wear your gloves.* She dismissed this concern. Surely the professor had better things to worry about than her poor hands.

After a twenty-minute ride on the streetcar, she got out at Schweizer Strasse and faced a row of old stone houses with pointed roofs and smoke coming out of their chimneys. They were redbrick storybook houses, the kind of places that Hansel and Gretel might have called home. She rapped on number 916, the one with the cast-iron door-knocker in the shape of an eagle's head and was greeted by a chubby-faced woman with cheeks the color of last night's claret. "How do you do," the woman said. "You must be Fräulein Arnstein. May I take your coat? Please, sit here by the fire, you must be freezing on a morning like this."

The woman disappeared through a heavy oak door, closing it behind her. Elisabeth sat on an overstuffed chair before the fire, her portfolio in her lap. There was a worn rug at her feet, and on the walls, some of the framed original illustrations from the professor's book, *The Wildlife of Central Europe.* Published five years earlier, in 1885, it had become an instant classic, and Elisabeth had memorized every illustration in it, drawn by the professor's coauthor, an older gentleman who'd passed away shortly before the book was published. Now she rose to study the drawings up close. The colors were gorgeous, even transcendent, and the drawings were perfectly composed, but the details were muddy, and the quills on the porcupine didn't look remotely real. *These are beautiful,* she thought, *but where's the life? Mine are better.*

She allowed herself to sit with that smug feeling as she warmed her hands at the fire. There was no need to put on her white gloves, as her mother had warned. Gloves or no gloves, the professor would find her work agreeable. The woman reappeared. "The professor will see you now. Come this way." They walked down a long, dark, uncarpeted hallway. Elisabeth was aware of how her shoes clacked against the bare wood, but she had to walk fast to keep up with the woman in front of her. When they reached the office, she pushed open the door, revealing a bright and immaculate room. The stone walls were bare and painted white. The professor sat behind a long table with stacks of paper in front of him and a notebook page half-filled with his cursive handwriting. In the same cheerful voice she'd used before, the red-cheeked woman announced, "Fräulein Arnstein is here to see you, Doctor." Without looking up, Dr. Schneider said, "Thank you, Annette, you may go now."

Although there was a chair facing his table, the doctor did not invite Elisabeth to sit. Unruffled, she stood and placed her

17

portfolio on the empty chair, removing her sketches and watercolors.

"What tortures you so that you pick at your nails?" he asked, still staring down at his papers.

Reflexively, Elisabeth pulled her hands away and held them behind her back, a habit left over from childhood, when her mother prepared to use the wooden brush with its wiry bristles to clean them. Her mother would grab Elisabeth's forearms and thrust her clenched fists into a basin of hot water and soap. A frail child, Elisabeth was no match for her mother's strength and willful spite. The bristles tore at her tender skin and drew blood. After so many scrubbings, her nails were ringed with spidery scars, and her hands were as red and dry as those of a charwoman. The nail-picking was a habit that grew out of daydreaming. Her thoughts elsewhere, she'd pick at her nails as a way to process what she was seeing or thinking. Even during the times she stopped, her mother found some way to scour her hands. Sometimes they were so sore it hurt to hold a paintbrush or pick up a pencil.

No man had ever been this forward with her, and, without thinking, Elisabeth answered, "What tortures me so much is the impudence of strangers."

Taken aback by her candor, Dr. Schneider started to laugh. He was in his late thirties, with curly salt-and-pepper hair and a distracted affect. But in laughter he was present, as if an intimate part of him had escaped despite his efforts to contain it. His hazel eyes fixed on Elisabeth's. She could feel heat rush through her body and droplets of sweat collect behind her neck. Then he looked back down at the papers on his desk. "I work all the time," he said. "I have a book to finish, and another to start. This is no job for anyone looking for a holiday in the countryside."

"My work is my holiday," she said. "It's what I do. It's all I do."

He shoved his chair away from the table and stood up. "So, let's see how you spend your vacation." He was a tall man with slightly stooped shoulders, as if he was used to hunkering down. She spread her pictures on the carpet in front of the table, and she was touched by how carefully he tiptoed around them, making sure not to step on any of the corners. Elisabeth stood to the side, her hands folded under her arms, trying to read his expression as he studied her work. His face was impassive. He stopped at each sheet for several minutes, never once looking up. When he finished circling the drawings, he turned to her. "It would be an honor to work with you. When can you begin?"

Elisabeth looked at her father's pocket watch, which she wore on a gold chain around her neck. "I believe I began about twenty-two minutes ago."

Later, Rudolph claimed that even before he saw her, he felt her, "like static in the air." When he did face her, what he saw was a young girl, fresh and childlike in all aspects except for her thick brown hair, swept into an unkempt bun. And her small hands, of course: raw and scarred, with jagged nails. He wanted to cover them with his own and rub them until the wounds were healed.

He thought her drawings were beautiful. No, *beautiful* was not an adequate word for what they were. They evoked wonder and sadness in him: wonder for how animated and lifelike they were; sadness for the void of loneliness they must have filled in the young girl who drew them. As she readied herself to leave, he worried that, despite his offer, he might never see her again, and said, "I have an instinct for all kinds of natures, particularly human nature, and it tells me that ours will harmonize."

Annette led the girl back down the long

hallway and through the oak door. "He liked you," she said as she helped Elisabeth on with her coat. "He doesn't usually give people that much time."

Elisabeth smiled. "We start work tomorrow."

Slate clouds hung low in the sky, and overhead, crows circled, filling the icy air with their harsh caws. She amused herself with the thought that only a person who believed her father was among them could find promise in a day such as this.

For the next couple of years, Elisabeth and Rudolph worked side by side on a comprehensive study of European birds, *European Ornithology.* In that time, they became lovers, and they wed within a year of their meeting, settling into a spacious third-floor flat in the Sachsenhausen quarter on the south bank of the Main River so they could be near the Stadtwald. It was a large apartment with arched windows and a terrace overlooking the river. There they lived with a grand piano in the living room and an ebony table in the dining room. Most mornings they rose after dawn. If it was warm enough, they'd take their coffee and bread with butter and jam on the terrace, then head out to the Stadtwald, where Rudolph worked on his notes and Elisabeth sketched. They'd return home at noon for the lunch Annette had waiting for them and then retire to the library, where shelves were stuffed with books about plant and animal biology and the walls were covered with Elisabeth's elaborately crafted drawings. Her art had become so precise that she could reproduce a dandelion with such clarity and detail that you'd believe its seeds would scatter if you blew on it. No one could capture the iridescence of a raven's throat or map the circuitry of veins through a sawfly's wing as she did. By the time she was twenty-six, several of her drawings were featured at an exhibition in the Städel Museum.

For ten years, they followed the same routine: Rudolph would work at his oversize mahogany desk, writing his text, and Elisabeth would sit nearby at a tilted drafting table and continue with her drawing. So they passed their days, never more than a few feet from each other. *European Ornithology,* which identified more than four hundred species of birds, was published in 1900, and Rudolph and Elisabeth Schneider were becoming known as the Audubons of Europe.

Though they had many acquaintances, the

only company they craved was each other's. They talked about everything and were constantly surprised by one another, she by how much he knew of the world, he by her quick wit and beauty. Private jokes and a made-up language of their own made their world even more insular. When a Catholic family opened up an overpriced dress store down the street and called it The Golden Goddess, Elisabeth dubbed it The Naked Madonna. They had nicknames for each other: She was Gerda, he was Günther, and everyone in their orb was given a name beginning with G (Gerhard, the neighbor's cat; Gottfried, the postman; Gretchen, the effeminate mayor of Frankfurt). They used these G names over and over again, yet each time one said Gerda or Günther they would laugh as if for the first time. When Elisabeth started to pick at her nails, Rudolph would place his hand on hers and say, "Here, pick mine instead." She in one room, he in another: They would hum the same song simultaneously.

For all the hours spent together, they never lost their hunger for each other. Yet despite all the times he'd take off his glasses and she'd put down her pen, gripped with such longing that they often would not make it to the bedroom, they did not conceive a child until early 1902, eleven years after they'd married. When they discovered that Elisabeth was pregnant, they teased each other about what good collaborators they'd become, but in truth, neither had given much thought to having a child. They nicknamed their unborn baby "the surprise." By this time, Elisabeth was thirty-three and Rudolph nearly fifty.

Their "surprise" turned out to be a boy. At first, they thought to give him a *G* name, but Rudolph insisted that it wouldn't be fair to start a baby out as a joke, and Elisabeth decided to name him after her father's father, which is how Egon escaped being Günther or Gregor. They made him a perfect nursery: Elisabeth painted the walls a golden yellow and put pale orange curtains on the windows so that when the morning light shone through them, everything in the room looked as if it were lit by the sun itself.

They scrutinized Egon the way they would any new species. Rudolph made notes on his development, and Elisabeth sketched in exquisite detail the veins on his eyelids and the flecks of his fingernails. If love meant caring for and obsessing over one's latest creation, then this was a beloved child. But long before his arrival, Elisabeth and Rudolph had created their own ecosystem, thriving on each other for nourishment and breathing only each other's air. In this way Egon would remain outside their universe, a well-observed child but a child apart.

2.

Little Egon, with his father's lean architecture and his mother's wide blue eyes, had a pleasing temperament. From the time he took his first steps at thirteen months, he'd rock back and forth and sideways in rhythm to whatever music was playing. His "dancing" made his parents laugh and clap, and later, his piano playing made them sit up and listen. He spent his childhood figuring out other ways to hold their interest. While his father wrote, his mother took him to the Stadtwald and taught him about the birds. Before he said his first words, he knew how to kiss the back of his hand to make a squeaking sound that would catch the attention of chickadees and warblers. When he was old enough to hold a colored pencil, he'd sit with Elisabeth after school and draw animals. By the time he was seven, he could articulate the hook of a crane's hind toe and draw a goat's eye well enough that she framed his best pictures and hung them next to her own. She called him *"Mein schön vogel junge,"* her beautiful bird boy.

On infrequent weekends, Egon and his father would hike in the woods. Egon greeted these outings with a mixture of dread and excitement. His father would instruct him: "Follow me and be very quiet." Rudolph would clasp his hands behind his back and walk several paces ahead, keeping his eyes focused on the tree branches or the shrubs beside their trail. He could go a whole afternoon without speaking, except when they passed a grasshopper or happened to spot a white-tailed deer. Then he would become animated, reciting the Latin name of the insect or animal and waiting for Egon to repeat it.

One afternoon, they came upon a baby turtledove that had fallen from its nest. Rudolph bent down and whispered, "Sweet thing, how far away from home you are." He scooped the bird up with a handkerchief and held it in both hands, the way a child would hold a ladybug. "Don't worry, little one, we'll make you whole again and soon you'll fly away."

It was the first time Egon had heard his father use this tender tone with anyone other than his mother. In his longing to have his father address him that way, he began greeting whatever animal or insect they happened to encounter in the same kindly manner. "Hello, Mr. Dragonfly. Would you like a blade of grass for lunch today?"

His father would assume the tiny squeaky voice of a dragonfly and answer, "Thank you, I'm not a grass eater, but if you would be so good as to fetch me a plump mosquito, that would suit me fine."

Though it was an intimacy channeled through birds and insects, it was intimacy nonetheless. When they came upon a praying mantis with an injured leg or a dove with a broken wing, they'd collect the animal in a hat and bring it home to Elisabeth. Caring for the wounded animals was what they did as a family, and since Egon was an only child, the creatures' companionship took up the sibling slack.

When Egon was eight, he and his father took a train to Berlin to see the 1910 Automobile Exposition. Rudolph was intrigued by modern inventions and shared his wonder about the new autos: "I hear they can go thirty miles an hour, some as fast as forty. That's faster than a goshawk. Someday you'll be driving one of these things."

It was the first time Egon had left Frankfurt. Everything about the train was foreign to him: the plush maroon velvet seats; the brass hooks and railing; the shades you could roll up and down by pulling on a rope. The Main River and familiar cathedrals faded from his view as new rivers and strange buildings filled his window. "I don't understand why anyone would ever leave Frankfurt," he said to his father. "I never will."

His father smiled without looking at him and said, "Of course, you're homesick for your *mutti*. It's good for you to experience something new. The whole world isn't walks in the Stadtwald with your old parents." But to Egon it was.

The exhibition hall was cavernous and filled with dozens of automobiles that looked like something out of the comic strips. But what really caught Egon's eye was the brand-new Daimler model in the center ring of the hall. The way the lights bounced off that cerulean car reminded him of stars on a clear night. An odd thought jumped into his head: That car crackled and dazzled like the current between his parents. The same kind of light shone on them when his father pressed his mother's shoulder as he passed her in the hall and called her *mein schatz,* or when she'd lean down and kiss

29

his hair as he sat writing.

Egon was reminded of that exposition four years later, when he was in gymnasium. By then he was twelve, tall and graceful, with riveting blue eyes and his father's thick curly hair. After school one day, before summer recess, a girl named Leni Freedburg asked him to go for a walk with her in the Stadt-wald. She was fourteen, two years older than Egon, with breasts so pointy it was rumored among the boys that if you bumped into her, they would leave puncture wounds. She was attractive, with long blond hair, a full bottom lip, and a straight nose; only her eyes, a little farther apart than they ought to have been, kept her from being a real beauty. Egon said yes to Leni's offer because he was polite, and because she was the first girl to show any interest in him.

They walked in the woods and he pointed out the birds and insects. After he showed her a butterfly pupa, Leni turned to him and stroked his black hair, saying, "You carry so much in that pretty head of yours."

He smiled. "These are the things my parents have taught me."

She smiled and stood on her tiptoes. "I imagine this is something your parents haven't taught you." She wrapped her arms around his neck and kissed him on the mouth. At first, all he could feel were her breasts, not sharp at all but warm and soft as rabbits. He was so preoccupied with them that it took him a while to open his mouth and let in her sharp citrusy taste. The kissing, her tongue in his mouth, the breasts against his ribs, would have been enough. But Leni, perhaps sensing that she'd unearthed a wellspring, took Egon's trembling hand, ran it under her shirt, and placed it on her bosom. Tears of gratitude filled his eyes as he gently petted and stroked the yielding rabbits.

With his hand wedged deep in the promised land of Leni Freedburg's breasts, he remembered the auto exhibition in Berlin and how the dazzling Daimler had reminded him of what passed between his parents. Now, that same warmth and energy coursed through him as well. God bless Leni Freedburg. With her generous nature and rabbit breasts, she had delivered him from his otherness, at least for a few moments.

By the middle of the summer of 1914, while Egon was indulging in Leni Freedburg, the rest of the country was reveling in war against Russia, France, and Belgium. Convinced that a victory would free them from the rule of greedy bankers and industrialists, the eager warriors at the top of the German government roused the country out of its dozy complacency. Even Egon was swept up in the patriotic fervor, wishing he were a couple of years older so he could enlist in the army. Elisabeth did not share his elation and told him, "I am so glad you're too young for all this nonsense."

Late in August, right before Egon was ready to go back to school, he and his mother found a nest of sparrow eggs on a low branch of a chestnut tree near where they'd been drawing. For the next week, they came every day, waiting for the spotted eggs to hatch. When they finally did, the chicks, each no bigger than a plum, were naked, helpless, and blind, and Egon and Elisabeth hovered nearby, as did the male and female sparrows.

One morning, Egon noticed a goshawk concealed in a nearby bush. Before he could nudge his mother, the hawk swooped down and gripped the male sparrow in its toes. The flapping of the hawk's wings sounded like sheets in the wind as it tore into the sparrow's throat and eviscerated him with its sharp talons. The female flew wildly around her chicks. Her harsh chattering sounded more like grief than anything Egon had ever heard. He saw his mother's face darken as she put her pencils and pad on the grass and wrapped her fingers around the pocket watch that she wore on a gold chain. That was when she told Egon about her father, and how she always looked for him in the birds. "It's more that I feel him than I see him," she said. From then on, the birds became his family as well.

After three years, the war that had ignited Germany's spirit was grinding down. "Don't stare," his mother told Egon the first time they saw a man wearing a black patch over the place where his nose had been. It was hard not to look at first, but over time the sight of men with empty eye sockets and missing limbs became commonplace even in the Stadtwald, where some returning soldiers with nowhere else to go took refuge.

Now fifteen, Egon towered over his mother and went with her to the Stadtwald more for her company than for the birds. One day, as they strolled down a familiar path, they noticed something curious about a nest on an overhanging branch. Most nests were constructed from organic matter — thistles, rootlets, fine strips of bark or sticks. But this one was a hodgepodge of paper, string, and some vegetation. "It looks like something a child would make," he said.

"No," said his mother, studying the nest closely. "It's because of all the people who sleep here now. They leave behind their garbage and the birds scavenge."

"So they are feeling it too," said Egon.

"We all are," said his mother.

The Schneiders, like most Jews in Frankfurt, were secular. Not observant, they celebrated only the new year and Passover. The day before Rosh Hashanah, Egon went to the bakery to buy some challah. The shelves were mostly empty of the *Linzertorten* and *apfelkuchen* that always accompanied Rosh Hashanah dinners. As he left the bakery with only a loaf of yeast bread, a man approached him. He had one leg and was leaning on a crutch. His clothes were ragged and there were wounds on his face the color of pomegranates. The man extended a filthy hand. "Please, sir, won't you buy this shoelace?" The lace was brown and tattered at the edges, and because the man was missing some teeth, the word *shoelace* blew through his lips like a whistle. Egon's first impulse was to back away, but there was something about the man that caught his attention. "Please, sir, a few pennies."

Egon looked into the man's bruised and tired eyes, and the man turned his head. In that instant, Egon understood that it was

Herr Menke, his old science teacher. It was clear that Herr Menke did not want to be acknowledged, so Egon reached into his pocket and gave him all the money he had, as well as the bread.

"Thank you, sir." Herr Menke made a slight bow and turned away.

Egon was relieved his old teacher did not acknowledge him, and walked on as fast as he could.

What happened with Herr Menke was not the kind of thing he could tell his father, who was preoccupied with his new book about the wildflowers of Europe and so unwilling to believe what was happening in Germany that he had proclaimed more than once, "I will not allow talk of doomsday in this house." Normally, Egon would have confided this event to his mother, but she was busy fighting her own war in the Stadtwald, and he hardly saw her anymore.

In the Stadtwald, the wounded and homeless slept under the trees and washed in the lake and ponds but were so slapdash about their garbage and excrement that the rats and vermin threatened to outnumber the birds, deer, wild pigs, and other creatures that also lived there. Each morning, Elisabeth would go to the forest and hand out what little food she had to the hungry. She always brought empty sacks with her and would return at night, the sacks filled with rubbish. Sometimes she came home so late that the stars were beginning to disappear from the sky.

After months of this, she seemed to shrink under her burden. Weight dropped from her bones, and her glorious brown hair dulled and grew thinner. Rudolph begged her to stop. "You've done more than is humanly possible for that place, and you haven't picked up your sketch pad in months. Won't you stay here and work with me on the new book?"

She brushed aside his pleas. "I doubt that there are any wildflowers left in Europe, Rudolph. There's nothing for me to draw."

Sometimes Egon would go with her, but it pained him to watch the futility of one woman trying to save a forest of more than eighteen square miles filled with broken men and, lately, women.

One afternoon before the Christmas break, he was coming home from school when he saw her tiny figure walking up the road toward their house. When he waved and cried, "Mutti," she didn't raise her hand or call back. He ran down the road, ready to relieve her of her sacks of garbage, but when he got closer, he realized she was holding only one bag in her hand, which looked as if it contained few items: her hat, perhaps, or a pair of shoes.

"Let me help you," he cried, reaching for the bundle.

"It weighs nothing," she said flatly.

He grabbed the bag. She was right; it felt like a sack full of air.

"What a surprise that you've come home early," he said, trying to keep his voice light. "Papa will be so glad to see you."

"You'll say nothing of this to your papa. I don't want to upset him."

"Nothing of what?"

"Of what I'm about to show you." She took the bag from him, untied the rope she had wrapped around its lip, and started pulling things out: several brownish-red feathers, an orange claw, and the charred hollow bones of a medium-sized bird.

"They're killing them, Egon," she said. "The people in that forest are so starved, they're eating the birds."

Egon took his mother's arm, so tiny now that he could wrap his fingers all the way around it. She leaned against him, shivering. "I thought if I fed them I could stop it. But there are too many of them. They're freezing and they're hungry, and now the birds, they're disappearing."

Egon thought about her drawings, thousands of them, each lovingly and meticulously rendered.

At least she had them, he almost said, but realized how callous that would sound. Instead he asked, "What should we do?"

"What can we do? Look around you. Shop doors closed. No food, no money, beggars everywhere. No one's helping the people; they're surely not going to lift a finger for some poor little birds."

"Let's go home, Mutti," said Egon, who had his arm around her and was practically carrying her in the direction of their building. "I'll draw you a bath. You'll get some sleep. You look exhausted."

When they got to the front of their building, Egon hollered for his father to come downstairs. "It's Mutti; I need your help."

Rudolph ran downstairs. When he wrapped his arms around Elisabeth's waist, she collapsed against his chest. "Precious one," he said in that voice he used only with her and the animals, "you're so cold and tired. We must get you upstairs and put you to bed."

They helped her up the two flights of stairs. Once inside the flat, Rudolph took off her coat and her shoes and led her to their bed. "Egon, make her some tea," he ordered, "and bring some bread and butter with the gooseberry jam." The jam was hidden high up in a cupboard, a treasure in these times, and something they ate only on special occasions.

When Egon came into their room carrying a tray with the food and drink, his mother was lying down. Her eyes were closed and his father was sitting on the edge of the bed with her hands in his. He rubbed them against his cheek and then studied her small fingers. The old scars, though faded, still covered her hands like tiny peck marks, and her nails were still torn and jagged.

He leaned over and whispered, "What tortures you so that you pick at your nails?"

Without opening her eyes, she smiled. Then she answered, "What tortures me so? There is nothing right with the world anymore."

He kissed her eyelids. "I know, *mein schatz,* but I'll always be here. You sleep now."

His mother was already up when Egon awoke to the smell of coffee the next morning. When he came into the kitchen, he saw that her eyes were clear and her long hair was tied back with a blue ribbon. How was it possible that she looked years younger than the woman he had helped up the stairs the day before? "Mutti," he said, "are you all right?"

"I am," she said with a smile. "You and your father make excellent nurses." He noticed her sketch pad and pencils on the table. The glass eye from her father, which she usually kept in her purse or in a pocket, was lying next to them. "I've decided I'm going to work with your father on his new book," she said. "It's time for another Schneider collaboration. I've never really concentrated on the flowers except when they've served as background for the birds. An interesting new adventure for me, don't you think?"

Her gaiety seemed forced, but while he was confused about her sudden transformation, he was thrilled to hear the vigor in her voice.

"That's wonderful, but now that it's winter, how will you draw the flowers?"

"Egon, I'm forty-eight years old. I've seen enough flowers to fill a botanical garden." She tapped her head. "It's all up here. It still works."

He laughed, mostly with relief. Drawing the flowers and working with his father meant she would stop going to the Stadtwald. He kissed her cheek before he left for school. "You seem yourself again. I'm glad you're so happy, you deserve it."

She made a brushing-away gesture with her hand. "*Ach,* nobody deserves anything. It's not about that."

Later, he wished he had asked what it *was* about.

When he was called out of his history class by the headmaster minutes before noon, his downstairs neighbor, a Frau Hennig, was waiting for him in the hall. He took one look at her and thought: *She is not here to deliver good news.* She was wearing a housedress, with a kerchief over her hair. Her stockings were rolled down to her knees, and on this bitterly cold morning, she wore only a sweater that wasn't buttoned. Frau Hennig placed her hand on his shoulder. "You must come immediately," she said. They walked in silence for the twenty minutes it took to get home. Egon dared not ask any questions and tried to convince himself that the worst had not happened. He devised many scenarios: there was a fire in the building; his father had fallen ill; his mother had disappeared into the Stadtwald. And while none of these were circumstances he wished for, he intuited that whatever had happened was far graver than what he imagined. The walk seemed to go on for hours; each time Frau Hennig stopped to pull up her stockings, he wanted to run ahead, but he was too polite. She pushed her way through the small crowd that had gathered in front of their building, and Egon followed her inside. His father was sitting on the marble staircase surrounded by several neighbors. He held a cloth to his head, and Egon saw that the color was gone from his face.

Egon knelt in front of him. "Papa, what is it?"

"Your mother. Fell down the stairs." He stared past his son as if he could see it happening before him.

"Did she —"

"I don't know," his father interrupted. "We'll never know." Then he closed his eyes, and in a voice smaller than any he had used for the animals, he said, "Broke her neck."

Egon wasn't sure he'd heard him correctly. He started to say, "What?" but then thought again. No man should have to say those words twice.

3.

Everything that gives life to a man was draining from Rudolph. The color had faded from his hair, and the deep lines around his mouth had turned his face into a dour mask. His steps became heavy, and though he claimed it was his rheumatism, he walked like a man reluctant to go forward. Each day he sat at his desk working on his textbook about the wildflowers of Europe. It struck Egon that no one could have been more at odds with his subject than his father. Wildflowers were one of the earth's gentlest surprises: impulsive and gay, popping up where no one expected them, shamelessly flaunting their riotous colors. His father, who had once stooped slightly, now slumped like an unwatered plant. His prominent nose seemed beak-like against his sunken cheeks. He barely spoke, sucking the spirit from the house and leaving it in eerie silence.

Egon was no stranger to silence. At night, he would lie in bed and listen to his own breath. He'd been in the Stadtwald many times when the creatures were quiet and all he could hear was the hum of the air. But without the intimate banter between his parents and the scratchy sound of his mother's pencil on paper, the silence in the house was different from any he'd ever known. It felt as infinite and absolute as his mother's death.

The injured animals they used to collect were gone. He tried coaxing his father to walk with him. He offered to make him meals, bring him tea, buy him a newspaper, take him to see the car exhibition in Berlin. The answer always came back: no. Not a verbal no, but an annoyed shake of the head.

Nearly a year after Elisabeth's death, Rudolph was still in need of an illustrator for his wildflowers. Egon had been nursing an idea. Knowing his father would pay attention only for a few minutes, he practiced his lines carefully before approaching him at his desk late one evening.

"Papa, I wonder if you'd like me to help with your book. After all those years sketching with Mutti at the Stadtwald, I know something about how to do these illustrations. We could work together."

Rudolph looked surprised. He shook his head. "In the brain department, you're a Schneider through and through. But you're not your mother. I appreciate your offer, but frankly, your drawings are pale imitations and don't hold a candle to hers. Forgive me if I sound harsh, but you have different talents from the ones your mama and I have."

The words came at Egon so fiercely that he said the first thing that came into his mind. "Don't talk of her in the present; she's dead now and always will be."

Rudolph stared at his son as if he were speaking a foreign language, then picked up his pen and went back to work. After that, Egon packed away his sketch pad and pencils. Without his mother's company, they were meaningless. He'd always found a naturalist's life too isolated and removed from reality. It had worked for his parents because they had had each other, but it would not for him. He would be more of the world.

His father had assumed Egon would go to his own alma mater, Heidelberg University, but lately, his son had a different plan. He wanted to learn everything about how the human body worked and how to care for it. He would go to university in Berlin and study medicine. Birds and flowers were his parents' world; the secrets of anatomy would be his.

When he told his father, Rudolph put his elbows on the desk and held his hands together as if in prayer. "Why medicine?" he asked.

"Because I need something of my own," said Egon. "Because, as you've pointed out, I'm not you and I'm not Mutti."

"Okay, then," his father said, and went back to work.

Minutes before dawn on the second Tuesday of September 1920, Egon boarded the train for Berlin, carrying only what he could fit into a brown leather suitcase: essential clothing, a sheaf of his mother's drawings, the glass eye from his grandfather, and his parents' book on birds. He'd urged Rudolph not to come with him to the station. "There will be too much climbing up and down the stairs." His father, whose rheumatism had worsened, agreed, sparing both of them any last-minute sentimentality, or lack of it. As the train pulled away and the rising sun spun the Main River into gold, Egon remembered the last time he had been on this train. It had been with his father, ten years earlier — not so long ago, yet time enough for him to lose his mother and for his vigorous father to turn into a wasting old man. There was some comfort in knowing that Annette would look in on Rudolph, and it startled Egon to realize that his mother had died twenty-one months before, to the day.

Not until he walked into his new dormitory did Egon understand that his loneliness could go even deeper. The beige concrete walls were bare, and the wooden planks of the floor were warped and covered with years' worth of dirt. There was one window, so layered with soot that only a few lines of light managed to infiltrate. Although it was day outside, in here it seemed like the middle of the night. There were two wooden desks; two chairs, both nicked and scarred; and two unmade beds, each with a naked gray-and-white-striped mattress atop what looked to be a carillon of springs. The beds shocked Egon the most. He was so used to being alone, he couldn't imagine what it would be like to have another person, a stranger, share his nights or see him undressed. He placed his bag on the bed closest to the window and sat down next to it.

If his mother were here, she'd figure out how to bring life into this miserable place. The thought of her thickened his throat.

Unsnapping his suitcase, he reached into the side pocket for the glass eye and wrapped his fingers around its smoothness. He pulled out his copy of *European Ornithology* and placed it on the closer desk. At least its cover, a close-up of a red cardinal on a branch against a white background, added a speck of color. He went back to his suitcase, took out his mother's illustrations, and laid them side by side on the bed. For now, he would keep the glass eye tucked away in his bag, but it was a comfort to know it was nearby.

Egon studied the drawings until he became aware of somebody standing in the doorway. The fellow was short and pudgy, with bushy raisin-colored hair that seemed to shoot from his head as if someone were holding him upside down. "Mmm, charming place," said the stranger, stringing out the sarcasm in his voice. "And you? Are you to be my cellmate?"

Egon stood up and offered his hand. "I'm Egon Schneider from Frankfurt, how do you do?"

The young man held out his hand, soft with baby fat. "Meyer Leavitt," he said, "from the other side of the moon. Nice to meet you."

There was never a time when Egon did not wonder if Meyer Leavitt actually did come from the other side of the moon. The two boys were so opposite that they filled in each other's spaces: Egon's angles, Meyer's roundness; Egon's height, Meyer's lack of it; Egon's grace, Meyer's clumsiness. Because Egon's clothes elegantly draped his lean body, Meyer judged him to be a rich city boy. And each time Meyer hitched his pants up over his large belly, Egon thought: *I've come all the way to Berlin to end up with this hick?* But Meyer was funny and well read. He quoted writers like Mann and Rilke as if they were relatives. Egon was sociable and knew how to talk to everyone in the dormitory. Still, the friendship might never have taken had it not been for the cat.

Near the end of their second week, one of the boys down the hall snuck a black cat into the dorm. Meyer played with the cat, whom he called Raven, whenever he could. One night, when Egon and Meyer were out of the room, Raven crept in. Finding a pile of Meyer's socks and underwear on the floor, he nestled into it for a nap. The smell must have suited Raven, because for the next few days, he managed to sleep on every piece of clothing Meyer owned until, late one night, Egon was awakened by the sound of Meyer choking.

Egon had heard Meyer wheeze before. Whenever they climbed stairs or ran somewhere, he would fall behind, winded. Egon attributed this to Meyer's weight and his dislike of any physical activity. But tonight, his breathing, what there was of it, sounded different, raspy and urgent. He was struggling to say something. Egon got out of bed and rushed over to him.

"You okay?"

"The cat," gasped Meyer. "Asthma."

Egon knew little about asthma; he knew only that Meyer sounded as if something in him had closed down and needed to open up. He needed fresh air. Maybe caffeine would speed up his heart and help him breathe. Egon opened the windows. He would get him coffee, but first Meyer must calm down. Egon turned on one of the desk lamps and spoke to his roommate in a gentle voice, not unlike the one his father had used with the insects and animals. "No need to panic; you are going to be okay. Try to slow down your breathing, and stay by the window. I'm going to the dining room to get you coffee. I think the caffeine will help. Don't worry, I'll be right back. I promise, I won't leave you alone for long."

That night, as Egon poured Meyer cup after cup of coffee, the two of them stayed up talking until sunrise. Meyer told Egon about growing up on a farm in Mannheim and how his father expected him to take it over someday, despite the fact that most of the animals they owned triggered his asthma. "I never told him I was applying to university until I was accepted, with a scholarship to boot. When I finally did tell him, he flew into a rage." Meyer waved his hands and spoke in a growly voice meant to imitate his father's: " 'What nonsense! Why would you study at some fancy university when I can teach you all there is to know about farming right here?' That's when I admitted I'd never intended to become a farmer, that I was going to become a writer, and writers needed to study literature, not pig feed and crop rotation. He slapped me across the face and told me I disgusted him. He couldn't believe I didn't want his life, and I suppose he was right in thinking me a snob. I didn't want to be him, and I rejected everything he stood for. We fought all spring and summer, and when it came time to go, he warned me that if I set foot out of his house, I would no longer be a member of his family. My mother cried but did nothing. They have other children at home; I'm the oldest of four; no one will pine away for me. So, here I am." He smiled like a dog baring its teeth. "I'm all yours!"

"Well, aren't I the lucky one?" said Egon. "Are you feeling better?"

Meyer's nightclothes were drenched, and his hair was more animated than ever. "I am. Tell me, how did you know what to do?"

"I didn't." Egon told him about watching the birds and drawing with his mother, the walks with his father, and how they would care for injured animals. "It's intuitive, the healing. We never really knew if we were doing it right."

"Ah, that's why you want to become a doctor," said Meyer.

Egon nodded, and then explained about his parents. He pulled out the sheaf of his mother's bird drawings. "You've seen these. My mother drew them. She's famous." He laid them out on his desk and studied them. "Beautiful," he said under his breath. "They assumed I too would become a naturalist, but I don't really have the talent for it. That's their book." He pointed to the volume of *European Ornithology* on his desk. "She died nearly two years ago. I haven't picked up a sketchbook since. I've discovered I'm more interested in people."

"I'm sorry about your mother."

Egon looked away. "It was a terrible accident. Terrible."

"Well, I should think you'd be a very good doctor."

"Thank you. And you? What will you write about?"

Meyer seemed taken aback. "I'll write stories and essays and interpret the world through my point of view, which, I assure you, is unlike most people's. I could write about this night, for example. About how two strangers, with nothing obviously in common, are brought together when one has a crisis. You know, subjects like that."

It wasn't a thank-you, exactly, but coming from this queer duck, Egon figured it was as close to one as he would get. Two nights later, he came home late from classes and found that five of his mother's drawings had been framed and hung on the walls. On his pillow was a note: *These birds will always soar. Meyer.*

4.

In Egon's senior year, his cousin Carola came to Berlin to visit the university, where she'd be enrolling as a freshman the following year. She was a second cousin of his father's from the Polish side of the family, the poor side. Egon had met her for the first time when she and her mother visited from the small town of Kaiserslautern, south of Frankfurt, on a sweltering summer day. He had been thirteen; she had been eight. He remembered his mother telling him not to show off his expensive toys, and that, despite the heat, Carola was dressed in white gloves buttoned at the wrist and a pink lacy dress. Her skin was so pale as to be translucent, and she was difficult to engage. Egon's mother had suggested that he show Carola "the newest member of our family." He'd taken her to his room, where the box turtle they'd found the weekend before was living in a white enamel washbasin on his desk. "You can pet him," he'd said, stroking it. "He's friendly." Tentatively, she'd prodded it with her gloved finger. When it opened its mouth, she'd jumped back and run out to her mother. That was what Egon remembered about Carola. That, and her too-fancy-for-a-hot-summer-day dress.

From the moment he received the letter from his father explaining that Carola was apprehensive about leaving home and asking if he could make her feel welcome, he'd dreaded their meeting.

"Please, Meyer," Egon begged, "don't make me do this alone. I'll pay for your coffee and as many pastries as you care to eat. Come with me."

"Am I hearing correctly?" Meyer stuck his finger in his ear as if to clean it. "Herr Charming needs this slob's help in meeting a young woman?"

In their four years at the university, Egon had his share of dating success and Meyer never ceased to tease him about it. "She'll adore you. As all ladies always do. You'll have her licking your boots, and God knows what else, in no time. What do you need me for?"

"All I remember is that she was helpless and it was impossible to talk to her. And for some peculiar reason, I feel more comfortable when you're around."

"That's lovely, I'm touched. Okay, I'll come, but only for thirty minutes."

They arranged to meet at the Café Rinsler, with its black-and-white tiled floors and red Chinese lanterns hanging from the ceiling. Bottles of ruby, emerald, and amber-colored liquors filled the shelves above the bar, and the light streamed in like smoke through the picture windows. The boys were drinking *kaffee mit schlag* when Carola arrived. At first Egon didn't recognize her. She was still pale but beautiful in a way he had never seen. Her blond hair fell to her shoulders and she stood as tall and gracefully as an egret. What had once seemed fragile had become so poised and radiant that when Egon introduced her to Meyer, Meyer jumped to his feet: "Well, hello, you don't seem helpless at all."

Carola smiled as if she was used to throwing men off their pins, then turned to Egon. "You look like your father. How is he?"

"My father's fine, thank you."

"I'm sorry about your mother. I remember her well. Quick-witted, and always with a pencil in her hand drawing the birds. Your father never took his eyes off her." As they sat down, she recalled how Egon had offered to show her his turtle.

"You were terrified of it," he said.

"Well, yes, that awful creature tried to bite me!"

"It was a box turtle. They're friendly, except that —"

Meyer interjected, "Except that they are filthy and dangerous. You're lucky it didn't snap your arm off."

"Oh," said Carola, covering her mouth with her fingers. "It wasn't that bad."

Egon asked Carola what she would study at the university. "Music education. I play the clarinet — I'm not at concert level, or anything like that, but I really like it." She told them that she was nervous about sharing a room with a stranger, that her parents were still in Kaiserslautern and this would be her first time away from home. "I'm not so good with strangers."

Meyer smiled. "You do fine."

Egon said that he and Meyer would be happy to take her around the campus. "Even better," said Meyer, "we'll show you our Berlin, won't we, Egon?"

Egon glanced at his friend and then at his watch. He was amused to find that the conversation had ambled past the thirty minutes Meyer had allotted. Carola saw him look at his watch and stood up. "I mustn't take any more of your time," she said. "Thank you, I feel more at home already. I can't wait to come back and meet your Berlin." She shook Meyer's hand and kissed Egon's cheek.

After she left, Meyer sighed. "Lovely. Floated in and out of here like something from a dream."

"Forget it," said Egon. "All you can do with women like that is admire them from afar."

But Meyer could not forget her. He nicknamed her Schneewittchen after the heroine in *Snow White,* and when she came to the university, he made good on his promise. By then he was working at a publishing house for a meager salary, yet he managed to take her to exotic Italian and Chinese restaurants and to the graves of the Grimm brothers at Old St. Matthew's Cemetery. Meyer bragged to Egon that on one of their Sunday-afternoon strolls on Kurfürstendamm, Carola had taken his arm. "See, good fortune embraces those who wait their turn," he said.

"Be careful," answered Egon. "Good fortune can be a fickle friend."

But Meyer ignored Egon's warning and courted his Carola with little gifts: a papier-mâché pin in the shape of a clarinet, an onyx turtle that he promised wouldn't bite. He didn't notice good fortune loosening its grip until the day Carola, with a slight flush in her cheeks, told him she had a friend she couldn't wait for him to meet: Max Cohen.

Plump, chinless, and already balding, Max Cohen was the man who brought color to Schneewittchen's frosty cheeks.

That night, Meyer sat in their living room while Egon studied. Bathed in the light of his friend's desk lamp and his own misery, he shook his head. "What can she possibly see in him?"

Egon didn't look up until Meyer repeated the question a third time. "Don't you understand?" he finally answered. "Max Cohen comes from a wealthy family in Bonn; his father is the head of a successful architecture firm. He's studying architecture so he can take over the company someday. Architects, unlike writers, get paid good money for what they do. Women like Carola marry the Max Cohens of this world. You do want your Schneewittchen to live happily ever after, don't you?"

"Egon, open your eyes," said Meyer. "Nobody's going to live happily ever after in this country. The mark is worth nothing, and we still have veterans hobbling around in their old uniforms. Schneewittchen can marry her bloated architect, but all the money in the world won't keep her satisfied. She needs a real man." Meyer opened his arms and did a crude shimmy with the lower part of his body. "Face it, we might as well do all of our eating, drinking, and screwing today. Tomorrow will only be worse."

Egon had to laugh at the way Meyer threw in references to sex whenever he could. He teased his friend about never having even had his tongue inside a girl's mouth, and Meyer teased him back about all the women he'd imagined Egon had had. Meyer called them ladies because, in his envy, they became caricatures of women of the world, with dusted white cheeks and large breasts, and in a perpetual state of arousal. "You live in a fantasy world," Egon told him. "First of all, they're girls. They have ordinary skin and normal-sized breasts. But let's not have this conversation until *you* have something to talk about."

Meyer did not live in a fantasy world when it came to Berlin. By now, he considered himself a city boy, one who saw too keenly that awful things were going on there. More people than ever were begging in the streets, and those who weren't seemed to be living another kind of desperation. Middle-aged war-widows-turned-prostitutes had become commonplace, as had mothers offering up their teenage girls for a price to young men on the street. But even Meyer was shocked to learn that the city's most famous stripper had recently urinated on a customer's table when he booed her act.

Like many of his age and class, Egon's father lived apart from what was happening in Germany. By 1925, *Wildflowers of Europe,* with illustrations by an American artist, was nearly as successful as *European Ornithology,* but Rudolph regarded his fame as another thing to be gotten through, like paying bills. Hobbled by his rheumatism, he walked with a cane. His eyesight was nearly ruined, and he had learned to do mundane things, like fit a key into a keyhole, by touch. At seventy-two, he had become an old man, though he remained a vain one. Each morning, he massaged coconut oil into his scalp to regenerate his hair follicles, and he always wore a jacket and tie, even alone at home.

He lived in the same apartment that he and Elisabeth had moved into more than thirty years earlier, and he still took his coffee with bread and butter and jam out on the terrace. Mostly out of habit and the lack of anything better to do, he was writing a book about the trees of Europe, but with his failing eyesight, he needed his old housekeeper, Annette, to come in and take dictation. It was bothersome having someone witness his clumsy steps and awkward groping; as much as possible, he preferred to be alone.

At least this was the explanation that Egon gave to Meyer about why, after four years of college and one of medical school, his father had never been to visit him in Berlin. Not that he was in a hurry to have him come; Egon's last trip home at Christmas had left him with unpleasant memories. His father had dutifully inquired about his studies. When Egon had asked him about his work, he'd offered up generic descriptions of the "stately beech trees" and "sprawling oaks." He'd been working with a new illustrator from America who did her drawings from photographs. She'd never even seen the trees. "It's an arduous process of monthly posts going back and forth," he'd said, "but her drawings seem tidy and accurate. I couldn't ask for anything more." To Egon's mind, he should have asked for a lot more. Had Rudolph's eyesight been better, surely he'd have seen that the drawings were static and clinical, with none of the life of his wife's.

"Do you miss Mutti?"

Egon rarely mentioned his mother around his father; he couldn't bear the way Rudolph's face seemed to cave in when he did. But this time, the question had spilled out before he could catch it.

His father had stared down at his lap. "Dwelling on the past is the greatest obstacle to living," he'd said. "I try to concentrate on the present."

So it was a surprise when Rudolph wrote to say he was being honored by the German Society of Naturalists at a luncheon in Berlin on the thirteenth of April, and asked if Egon would have time to have dinner with him that evening. Egon showed the letter to Meyer and said, "You'll join us, won't you?"

To which Meyer responded, "And finally meet the famous father? Of course."

His father was already seated when Egon arrived at the restaurant. Rudolph was wearing a finely tailored black suit and a meticulously pressed white linen shirt. In the candlelit room, his eyes seemed as brooding and penetrating as ever. Even now, women turned to take a second look at the elegant gentleman with the long legs and luxurious white hair.

"Hello, Papa," said Egon.

Rudolph gripped his cane and was about

to push himself to standing.

"Don't get up, it's only me."

He sat back down.

Sometimes, when Egon was taking a difficult exam or going on a date with a girl he was eager to please, he would tuck the glass eye into his pocket like a good luck charm. Tonight was one of those times, and as he pulled his chair out, he dug his hand into his right pocket and held it. Father and son exchanged pleasantries. Egon told Rudolph that his friend Meyer would be joining them. "You two will hit it off. He's a writer. He wants to write books eventually, but for now he is a junior editor at Ullstein Verlag."

Rudolph seemed distracted, and Egon wasn't sure his father had heard what he said. He continued, "He also writes poetry and has had some essays published in *Vossische Zeitung* and a few in —"

Rudolph ordered a glass of cognac. "And what about you, Egon? Have you decided what you want to do?"

Egon touched the outside of his right pocket. "When I used to draw with Mutti, it was the eyes of the animals that interested me the most. I've been learning about them. Why dogs' eyes glow in the dark; how ducks, even though they have flat, wide-set eyes, can take in nearly three hundred and sixty degrees. Did you know that a horsefly's eye is made up of thousands of pin dot-sized lenses? It fascinates me, all this, Papa, it really does. I'm thinking that I'm going to specialize in ophthalmology."

Rudolph sipped his cognac, then dabbed the corner of his mouth with his middle finger. "I applaud your obsession. But when your mama and I worked together, we had the animals, the birds, the flowers . . . the whole world to explore. The eye, Egon, why be so specific?"

"Mutti was specific too. You know she was obsessed in her own way with the birds. Anyway, it's not as specific as you think. In order to become an ophthalmologist, I'll have to understand human anatomy, all two hundred and six bones, how each organ works. It's a world unto itself."

His father raised his hand as if in surrender. "Your mama was a genius, so that's a whole other story. If this is what you want, it's fine with me, as long as I have the money to pay for it, though it's a shame you're coming at this ophthalmology business too late to help an old man get back his eyesight."

Egon had reached into his pocket and was about to show his father the glass eye when Meyer appeared, shirt untucked and a coffee-stained manuscript under his arm. "Speaking of geniuses," Egon said, relieved to shove the keepsake back into his pocket, "here's my friend Meyer."

"Ah, the famous writer," said Rudolph, rising to his feet.

Even in his diminished state, he loomed over Meyer by nearly a foot.

"Please," said Meyer, "let's sit. I look taller in a chair."

His words made the air feel lighter. Meyer asked Rudolph about European forests and what effect the bullets and shrapnel might have had on the trees. Rudolph wanted to know about Meyer's work at the publishing house. Meyer told him about the manuscript he was reading, to which Rudolph responded, "They're Jewish, you know."

"Who's Jewish?" asked Meyer, looking around the restaurant.

"The Ullsteins. Old man Leopold was from Bavaria. Died about twenty-five years ago and left the company to his five sons."

"Oh," said Meyer. "I've only met Franz, who seems cordial enough. Even shook this lowly junior editor's hand."

Odd, thought Egon, his father had barely ever mentioned religion. "Papa, what's the relevance of the Ullsteins being Jewish?"

Rudolph turned to Meyer. "You seem like

a shrewd fellow, you tell him."

"He means that being Jewish isn't a private affair these days. We're all in the spotlight," said Meyer, raising his left eyebrow as he always did to punctuate one of his pronouncements. "Let's put it this way: When you become an ophthalmologist, you won't be Dr. Egon Schneider, you'll be Dr. Egon Schneider, the Jewish ophthalmologist."

Egon smiled. "That wouldn't be the worst thing in the world, would it?"

"Maybe not," said Meyer, "but when I become a famous writer, I don't want to be known as Meyer Leavitt, the Jewish writer, or Meyer Leavitt, the German writer. Meyer Leavitt will be quite enough."

The next hour passed in easy conversation. Meyer and Rudolph talked about Hesse's novels, Schnitzler's plays, and Schönberg's music — "like dishes crashing to the floor," said his father — as Egon listened in amazement mixed with jealousy. He knew that Meyer breathed in all this culture, but his father? What did he know of literature? When did he listen to music? It pained Egon how effortless it was for Meyer to engage his father in a way that Egon never had.

After dinner, Rudolph had a second glass

of cognac, then pushed back his chair and placed his cane directly in front of him. "A pleasure," he said, as if he were addressing the German Society of Naturalists. "I trust we'll meet again, Meyer."

Egon could see the effort it took for him to pull himself up, and he and Meyer rushed to his side. "Likewise," said Meyer. "In the meantime, I'll keep watch over this young man. Not that he needs me to take care of him. There are plenty of ladies vying for that job."

Rudolph squeezed Egon's shoulder. "It's nice to know he inherited something from his papa." There was a tremble in his touch. As they headed to the door, his father had to stop and lean against the wall in order to catch his breath. When Egon offered his arm, he refused the help: "Thank you, but I'm used to doing this on my own."

A car was waiting to take Rudolph back to his hotel. When Egon bent over to open the door, he felt a sense of loss, as if his father were fading away. *I ought to tell him I love him,* he thought. The words, so simple, formed in his mind, but his mouth refused to speak them. "Take care of yourself, Papa," he said. Once seated, his father raised his hand and waved, never turning his head as the car pulled away.

Egon and Meyer stood on the curb, their eyes following him. "Interesting man," said Meyer. "I can't imagine what it would be like to have a father who reads books and listens to music."

"I can tell you what it's like," said Egon. "He does all those things, and knows all those things, and it has nothing at all to do with me. I've never even heard of Schönberg."

"Well, whose fault is that?" said Meyer. "I guess when you spend all your free time wooing the ladies, you don't have time for books and music."

"Oh, no, not this again," said Egon, smiling.

Meyer was wrong about one thing. He didn't have to woo the ladies. They wooed him.

5.

It turned out that drawing was what capti-
vated Egon most about his studies after all:
achieving the perfect curvature of the
eyeball; identifying the nerves, veins, and
arteries; the way extraocular muscles
seemed to shoot away from it. When he
outlined the vitreous humor, the clear jelly
that filled the back chamber of the eyeball,
he'd shade it with a touch of gray to make
it look as gelatinous as it felt. Everything
about the eye pleased him. He loved how it
looked. He was fascinated by the way each
vein and membrane had a specific purpose
and neatly intertwined at the optic nerve,
like railroad lines that funneled into a single
track. The hours he spent at his medical
studies melted time away. In his absorption
and attention to detail, he drifted to the
same place his mother had gone when she
drew the birds, and often he would feel her
presence.

He chose his distractions judiciously: a pretty girl, an hour with Meyer, sometimes a nightcap at one of the nearby beer halls. Berlin of 1926 had more than enough distractions. There was the music, every night a different artist, a different cabaret; riotous dance halls; the opera; Potsdamer Platz with its overdressed baroque buildings and outdoor cafés.

Late one autumn night, Egon walked to a club two blocks from his apartment. At the bar, he ordered a port and was reading a newspaper when he became aware of people laughing and staring his way. "That's the one," said the woman onstage, who was beckoning to him. She wore a baby bonnet, white bloomers, and a pink satin bib that barely covered her nipples. "The dark one with the big blue eyes. I like him."

Egon pointed to himself with eyebrows raised.

No, he would not be part of this farce; he would leave as gracefully as he could.

He raised his arms and partially bowed to the crowd, then reached for his wallet and drew out money to pay the bartender. He blew a kiss to the woman onstage, mouthed the words *Nein, danke,* and backed himself out of the room. There were boos. As he slipped his jacket on in the foyer, he could

71

make out shouts of "homosexual," "sour sport," "Jew boy."

Though he confided most things to Meyer, Egon didn't tell him about this episode. Meyer's head was already too filled with negative images. Besides, they were Berliners now, and Egon told himself that these things came with the city. But after that night, the music sounded shriller to him. The formerly spotless streets were littered with trash. The lights that had once wooed him looked garish, and even the beautiful Grunewald, where he had walked on Sunday mornings watching for deer and fox, was barren. Berlin had become a bleak and grotesque city. He wondered if this was how his mother had seen the Stadtwald at the end.

Frankfurt seemed years away. His main connection to it was Annette, who dutifully visited his father each day and sent Egon long reports by post: *There are buds on the pear trees, and the air smells sweet,* she wrote in the beginning of May. *Your father is up to the W's. Today, he dictated the waythorn. After that, there remains only the willow, the yew, and the Ziziphus jujuba. Then Trees of Europe will be completed. He seems very optimistic.*

72

Then, on the morning of May 14, 1928, she telephoned Egon at the room he was renting. Her voice was steady as she described what had happened that morning. "When I came, I went straight to the kitchen to make a cup of coffee. I shouted to him, did he want one too, but he didn't answer. I went to the library thinking he'd already started his work, but he wasn't there. Then I checked his bedroom. That's where I found him, lying on his bed fully dressed in a suit and tie and even his shoes. He died peacefully, I can tell you that."

The news should not have come as a surprise. Two years earlier, when his father had come to Berlin, Egon had thought he would be dead within the year. Now, only months after his seventy-fifth birthday and weeks before he was to finish *Trees of Europe,* he must have finally relented and given himself up. Other than their walks in the woods, they had never been easy with each other, yet Egon found himself crying and shaking, as he had not when his mother died. He called Meyer. "You saw us together. We weren't exactly the closest father and son, yet I'm devastated."

"It's natural," said Meyer in a tone that suggested he'd given this a lot of thought. "It's the shock of the void. First your mother, now him. You spent your life trying to get his approval. It defined you and gave you a purpose. Now that's gone too. You deserve to feel devastated."

Egon thought back to the last words his mother had said to him, and repeated them to Meyer. "*Ach,* nobody deserves anything. It's not about that."

Rudolph had been the only connection to his mother. Now there was no one left who knew how she'd smelled, or the way she'd picked at her fingernails when she was nervous. For all Egon knew, the two of them were reunited somewhere: once again, without him. In that regard, Meyer was right. It was the shock of the void. He took out a copy of *European Ornithology,* and in the time it took him to page through it, the birds came alive. Their *tck-tck* calls were audible and their black marble eyes stared back at him. He could visualize the way his mother's neck would strain as they flew by or perched on a nearby branch, and he felt her breath on his ear as she whispered, "That's a blackbird." In this way she came back to him, as young and visceral as during their days in the Stadtwald before the troubles.

He remembered Carola's saying that his father had eyes only for his mother. She was the only friend he had who'd known his parents. He yearned to revisit happier moments and hoped she would be able to excavate others he'd forgotten. Had his mother smiled or touched his arm when she asked him to show Carola the turtle? Had his father ever referred to Egon as "my son" or "my boy"? When he called to tell Carola the news, she promised that she and Max would come by after work. She was completing her degree to become a music teacher, and Max was working as an apprentice in an architecture firm.

That night, Egon sat on the couch beside her. "Do you remember the first time I visited you?" Carola asked. "My mother made me wear my only dress. She didn't want us to look like the poor relations. Whenever my parents talked about your family, they would always sit up straight and say in a formal tone of voice, 'Ah, those *wundersam* Schneiders.' " She giggled at her imitation of them but saw that Egon was not laughing. "Partly, I think, they did that out of jealousy, but also out of respect. They really liked your mother. They thought she was a true artist, and very beautiful. Your father was harder to know. He was older and more standoffish, but brainy, and handsome in his day. A real ladies' man, I gather, until your mother came along." She recounted their accomplishments and how well regarded they were. "The newspapers were always writing about them, calling them the Audubons of Europe. My father said they were the royalty of Frankfurt."

Carola smiled at Egon, who seemed pleased with her recollections.

"And what about me?" he asked, immediately embarrassed by his neediness.

"You? You, apparently, were a complete surprise."

"The kind that pops out of a closet and scares you half to death?"

"No, not at all. More like the kind that arrives wrapped in pretty paper and a bow. You were apparently a beautiful child with talents of your own. You played piano. You knew all about the animals. When my mother told your mother how nice you were to me on the day we visited, your mother said, 'Egon is a big-hearted boy.' "

There it was, the gift he'd been hoping for, unopened words from his mother. Even if Carola's version of his family was overly flattering, it was what he craved on this night.

She continued: "You used to go to the forest and draw with her, right?"

"Yes, we drew the birds together."

"Did you ever think you would follow in their footsteps?" asked Max, speaking his first words of the evening.

Egon got up from the couch and went to his bedroom. He came back carrying the glass eye. "This was my mother's. Her father gave it to her with the instructions, 'Fresh eyes on the world.' My mother taught me how to observe, to study the details. I suppose, insofar as seeing is essential to being a naturalist, I follow in their footsteps."

There were so few birds in Berlin that it had been a while since Egon had given them any thought. It was not the kind of place where one stopped to take notice of a wing pattern or listen for a particular song. Even the way Berliners talked — fast and directly — was harsher than the roly-poly cadences he'd heard back home. In Frankfurt, there was space to breathe your own air and vast patches of sky where you could get lost in what was going on. Egon couldn't imagine sitting in the park for an afternoon in Berlin, as he had with his mother, waiting for a swallow to appear, or for the sun to drop low enough to backlight a loon. When you sat in Berlin it was with purpose: at a bar, in a concert hall, on a trolley; never for the pleasure of sitting. Nowadays, he found little pleasure in Berlin. Over the past years, he'd lost a part of himself here, and he felt regret for who he was becoming. If his mother knew him now, would she still think him a "big-hearted boy"?

Though he could never pinpoint the moment he made the decision to return home, he knew it was the birds that would lead him back to Frankfurt after he finished his ophthalmology studies. But not before he drew the yew and the *Ziziphus jujuba* himself.

6.

The linen tablecloth, with its embroidered diamond patterns, was perfectly ironed, as were the matching napkins. Each dish, fine Dresden china, had a garland of roses in its center and was ringed with gold filigree. The knives and forks were sterling silver with intertwined initials on their handles, as was the serving knife that sat in the center of the table, waiting to slice the crumb cake warming in the oven. Its buttery perfume mingled with the earthy smell of fresh coffee and settled like a sense of well-being over the entire apartment. This is how it was every Saturday evening at five thirty in Kaethe and Georg Schnabel's kitchen at 25 Altkönigstrasse, Frankfurt, where Egon now rented two rooms.

Outside, the building looked like the grand villa it had once been. There were recessed windows and a stone balustrade that ran across a balcony on the third story.

But inside, it had been broken up into several flats with narrow rooms and fourteen-foot-high ceilings. Kaethe and Georg's flat was filled with mismatched furniture too large for the tiny rooms. A grand piano took up the entire parlor, and the rosewood dining table in the kitchen had once been a side table in the library of their mansion. Kaethe never missed an opportunity to reminisce about their old house: "We had ten rooms, two servants, and a gardener." They kept a tiny silver dinner bell on their kitchen table, the bell they'd used to summon servants. "I only had to ring once," she'd say, shaking the tiny object as if it might still conjure up a butler. Sometimes she put her hand over her heart when she talked. "All the fruit trees and roses you could imagine, and lilacs in the spring. Those were the happy days."

Outside, it was 1932, and Frankfurt bore the ruined splendor of the depression, but inside 25 Altkönigstrasse, it felt more like the Frankfurt of Egon's childhood.

The Schnabels were in their late forties, near the age his mother had been when she died. They dressed as they might have twenty years before, he in wing-collared shirts and a homburg, she in long skirts and sturdy lace-up shoes. He was tall and angular, with sharp features that reminded Egon of a Eurasian crane. She had a round flat face with eyes as small as umlauts; although she was stout and seemed to be sinking into her frame, in the wedding photograph that hung in the foyer, she looked statuesque and self-satisfied. Her father had been a wealthy textile manufacturer, and her young husband a decorated war hero and promising barrister. Was it any wonder that Kaethe dreamed of the past and Georg, who had recently been dismissed from his law practice because it already had too many Jews, refused to accept the present? "Germany is going through a phase," he insisted. "All great countries suffer growing pains."

For only forty reichsmarks a month, Egon rented a bedroom, an office, and a surrogate family. The Schnabels included him in their evening meals, and once a week Kaethe washed his laundry and starched and ironed his white linen shirts. His medical practice had caught on quickly. The people of Frankfurt remembered the handsome and affable son of the Schneiders and were eager to come to him with their rheumy eyes and cataracts. He was also a rigorous doctor. Before any complicated procedure, he'd draw step-by-step diagrams for his patients.

He made up stories for the young ones about animals, using his father's funny voices. If a patient cried, he'd stop and squeeze her hand; those who couldn't afford to pay he'd treat for free.

"You'll never get rich taking those charity cases," Georg warned him.

"That's fine with me; this is what I love to do," said Egon. "The money will come or it won't."

By now, his reputation was such that people traveled from as far as Wiesbaden to be treated by him, and while he was still living with the Schnabels, he was able to afford a new and bigger office in the middle of town with double oak doors and a view of the river. He hung his diplomas on the wall and affixed an oval brass plate to the door with his name engraved in black script: *Doktor Egon Schneider.* When Egon described the plaque in a letter to Meyer, who remained in Berlin, Meyer wrote back, *Why make it so easy for them to find you?*

Egon was aware of a disturbance in the air, like fog rolling in, but as long as nothing had changed in his life, he shrugged off Meyer's warning as exaggerated. He was still invited to dinner parties, where he pounded out jazz on the piano, and he still had many of Frankfurt's finest women on his arm when he went to the ballet and opera. While other people his age married and produced babies, he reveled in his bachelorhood. The tall doctor was known for his gentle hands and compassionate manner. One of his patients, a middle-aged lady, said of his big blue eyes that they were the kind a woman could fall into. Mothers made sure to bring their daughters to his office, even if they weren't nearsighted or suffering from conjunctivitis. Though Egon never settled on any of them, he had his time with many of them. He was tender with them, and mesmerized by their differences. With some, lovemaking was a competitive sport; for others, a thing to be endured. Some cried out in passion, others wept softly into his neck. One smelled like rain on a summer's night, another like *lebkuchen.* In the night, they slept nestled into him or curled up on the other side of the mattress. He told himself it was the unknowable that kept him going from bed to bed; he never tired of the infinite ways a woman could be beautiful.

Of all his friends, only Meyer remained single. He was still in Berlin working for Ullstein Verlag, though now he was a senior editor and had also written his first children's book, *Die Bleiche Prinzessin von*

Preußen (*The Pale Princess of Prussia*). "I could have written *Schneewittchen*," he liked to say, "but the Grimm brothers beat me to it."

The book became a hit in Germany. Though Meyer was as plump and disheveled as ever, women began making themselves available to him. "They're like bloodhounds," Egon teased during one of their monthly visits in Berlin. "They know how to sniff out the successful ones."

Now when he and Meyer talked about sex, they did so as equals. Egon resorted to elaborate ophthalmological metaphors to rationalize his catholic tastes: "Blinking rhythms are infinite, and no two people see colors exactly the same way. If machinations of the eye can be so subtle and varied, can you imagine how infinite are the possibilities of sexual congress? Why settle for a single color when there is such a rainbow of possibilities?"

For once, Meyer was the succinct one: "I just want to fuck as many as I can before the apocalypse."

Meyer's pessimism took shape for Egon at one thirty on the morning of May 11, 1933, when Kaethe Schnabel, in her dressing gown and bare feet, pounded on his door and yelled, "Hurry, emergency phone call!"

Egon did not bother to put on his robe. He picked up the telephone in the living room and heard Meyer's ragged breathing on the other end.

"What is it?" Egon shouted. "Are you all right?"

"There was a book burning last night. At the square between the university and the opera house." Meyer couldn't get the words out fast enough. "Students with torches, they burned thousands and thousands of books. Goebbels was there screaming about the death of Jewish intellectualism, how this was the end of the old era. They called out names, then threw the books into the bonfire. Sigmund Freud. Thomas Mann. Stefan Zweig. Elisabeth Schneider. Rudolph Schneider. They burned your parents' books, Egon. All of them. And my *Princess*."

Meyer was struggling for air. "Stop talking," Egon demanded. "Breathe slowly. You've got to calm down."

"Calm down?" gasped Meyer. "Don't be an idiot. There's nothing to calm down about."

For the next year and a half, Egon continued to treat his patients behind the double oak doors. He still wore his finely tailored suits and, as always, had his Saturday coffee and cake with the Schnabels. All the things that gave him a sense of well-being were in place. But there was a sourness in his stomach that backed up every now and then.

Then, in September 1935, the Nuremberg Laws were passed, depriving Jews of their citizenship. In Cologne, Carola was fired from her job when Jews were barred from teaching in the schools, and her husband, Max, was kicked out of his company because no one wanted buildings built by Jews. Tibor Velkind, a young sculptor who lived next door to the Schnabels, was arrested because the authorities found his work to be "critical of the regime." By the new year, Egon was drinking a liter of milk a day to soothe the burning in his belly.

With newspapers under the control of the Nazi Party, there were new rules posted about Jews every day: "All jockeys and drivers of horses must be Aryans." "It is a crime for Jews to practice journalism." "The death penalty for anyone who publishes treasonable articles." "Five years for anyone distributing atrocity stories." "In public parks, Jews can only sit on designated benches painted yellow."

When Egon told Meyer, "They're making

it impossible for us to live here," Meyer responded, "Soon they'll make it impossible for us to get out of here."

In March 1936, a young friend of Carola's, a woman named Liesl Kessler, came to Egon because her right eye wouldn't stop tearing. "I'm certain I'm crying for what's happening here," she said. Even after Egon plucked the inwardly growing eyelash that was blocking her tear duct, she continued to weep.

Liesl had smoky gray eyes and wore a double strand of pearls that fell below her tanned throat. Her father, Leopold Kessler, was the president of the National Bank of Frankfurt. With her bright red lipstick and Marlene Dietrich eyebrows, she had the sheen of confidence that wealthy girls often did. Egon used his paternal voice to try to comfort this pretty child: "Come, come, it isn't as bad as all that." He heard the hollowness of his words, as did she.

"You're wrong, it really is that bad. Awful things are happening. We should get out as soon as we can."

Little by little, patients whom Egon had known since their childhood stopped making appointments with him. Some offered apologies; others disappeared. One spring evening, Egon saw a postal worker being beaten by brownshirts who were yelling that he was carrying Jewish propaganda in his mail pouch. Nobody, including Egon, tried to help him. He felt humiliated that he, a doctor, stood by so passively as another human being was hurt.

Meyer kept telling him that it was only a matter of time before Jewish doctors lost their licenses. Ever since the Nuremberg Laws, Meyer had been standing in line for hours a day at various government agencies in order to secure the visa, passport, certificate of health, financial statement, and affidavit of support — more than fifty pages of documents — one needed to emigrate.

Despite eliminating fried food, coffee, tomatoes, and citrus fruit from his diet, Egon was gulping down bicarbonate of soda every three or four hours, trusting its salty fizz to squelch the fire in his gut. His dreams were interrupted by visions of his parents' books in flames. He could see their pages igniting, hear the hiss, smell the smoke. And always, the sad mound of ashes.

On a dazzling morning in January 1937, Egon arrived at his office to find the words *Juden Doktor* written in red paint across his double oak doors. The letters were perfectly aligned. Egon locked himself inside and called Meyer, who offered no consolation:

"I'd say you got off easy. The next time they won't be so considerate."

"That's not funny."

"Not at all," said Meyer. "The only funny thing is your pigheadedness, and even that's getting stale. For God's sake, Egon, you're an ophthalmologist. Use your eyes. Look around you. The writing is literally on the wall. What the hell are you waiting for? Get your papers in order."

"I'm waiting for it to pass."

"Believe me, it's not going to."

"I see that you're still here."

"Not for long. I hope to be out of here by the end of the year."

Egon hung up the phone and went outside. He hoped *Juden Doktor* would be gone, that he'd imagined the whole thing. But there it was, its blood-red letters bold. Whoever did this had done it before.

He remembered old Frau Hennig. The day she came to call him out of class. The walk home and how he had tried to convince himself that the worst had not happened. The snag in his heart when he saw his father sitting on the steps. The way his father had whispered, "Broke her neck." The shock of those words would always be a part of him. This felt like that.

He was standing on the precipice of the

inevitable, about to spiral into darkness the way one does in the moment before sleep. It took away his breath and loosened his bowels. His office, the cherrywood rolltop desk, the Persian rug, his brass plaque, his white shirts, his home on Altkönigstrasse, the parties, his piano playing, his patients, the river, his friends, his women. If he wanted a life, he'd have to give up the very things that defined it.

It took Egon sixteen months to gather his papers — a blink of the eye compared with how long it took most people. Meyer, who had made his way to New York City, had found a wealthy friend of a friend to write the coveted affidavit of support guaranteeing to provide for Egon should he become a burden to the United States government. When the letter came, Egon had three days to pack his belongings and catch a train to Hamburg, where he would board a ship for New York City.

Kaethe cried when he told her he was leaving, and Georg insisted he was being too hasty. "You'll be back soon, when this nonsense passes." Egon gave them his treasured desk and rug from his office. He filled up a satchel with some of his mother's old dishes, silverware, and linen tablecloths, and stuffed whatever else he could into a single suitcase. As he packed, he felt himself slipping into the past tense, cherishing the scant reminders of who he'd been: two white shirts; one pair of mother-of-pearl cuff links from his father; a leather case containing a refractor, a scalpel, and a cataract knife; the oval plaque with his name on it; an envelope filled with his mother's drawings; one copy of each of his parents' books; fifteen hundred reichsmarks sewn into the lining of his black suit jacket; his mother's gold pocket watch in a green satin pouch; the beautiful old eye prosthesis; and two bottles of heartburn tablets.

Early on the morning of May 21, 1938, he shared coffee, bread, and honey with the Schnabels, then rode a streetcar to the station. He sat on the train to Hamburg, his papers neatly stored in a folder in the pocket of his suitcase, and tried to read the newspaper as casually as a commuter.

From the train station it was only a matter of catching another streetcar to the pier, where he boarded the SS *Washington*. Unlike in the movies he'd seen about sea voyages, there was no popping of champagne corks, no crowds waving handkerchiefs and blowing kisses. Passengers boarded as resolutely as patients walking into a dentist's office. Because it was raining, most went right inside, leaving Egon as one of the few remaining on deck. A foghorn bleated, and the ship lurched as it disentangled itself from its berth. Salty spikes of water blew onto his face, and a mist curled around him. There was nothing to see on this dull afternoon, no land or water. Even so, knowing that Germany was still in reach was enough to keep him outside until dark. On this night there was no sunset, only the gradual halting of light. In the moments before darkness, he became aware of a gathering cloud, one with substance and motion. As it got closer he heard a ruckus. He stared into the sky until the cloud became a swarm of birds, and the birds became familiar faces, and the faces brought him back to the Stadtwald. Then the clacking and the squawking stopped, the cloud took wing, and what was left of the light slid out of the sky.

■ ■ ■ ■

Part II
In the New
Country

■ ■ ■ ■

7.

Rose McFadden grew up as the oldest of three, and the only one of them to come to America. While her childhood was as spare and poor as those of most of the other immigrants in New York's Hell's Kitchen, she knew nothing different and would remember her first sixteen years as happy ones. Only after she met Ryan Walsh did she learn how sorrow could wear a soul down.

It was a drafty afternoon in 1904 when she first laid eyes on him. She was accompanying her mother to the emergency room across town at Bellevue Hospital. Ryan was steering the No. 3 horse-drawn trolley across Thirty-Fourth Street, wearing a black cap and a silver badge with his name on it. As Mrs. McFadden climbed the stairs, he must have seen how she limped and noticed the sores on her swollen ankle. "No need to pay," he said. "You'll ride as my guests."

Rose squinted at his badge and said, "How very kind of you, Ryan Walsh."

"And who might you be?"

"Rose," she said. "Rose McFadden."

They heard in each other's voices the dialect of County Mayo and understood that they were both immigrants. He pressed his lips together in a way that wasn't a smile exactly but made her feel noticed. When they got to First Avenue, Rose held her mother's arm as Mrs. McFadden struggled off the trolley. Ryan caught her eye and tipped his hat. "Rose, I suppose, has as many beaus as the stars in the sky and the freckles on her nose."

After that, she found any excuse to take the No. 3 trolley. Ryan wasn't anyone's idea of handsome. He was stalky and pale, his facial features were straight lines that could have been drawn with simple pencil strokes. But he had life in him that made up for his flat face and hidden eyes, and Rose found herself imagining how it would be to touch the smooth skin on the back of his neck.

They never talked when she came on board, but he'd always manage to whisper a bit of doggerel to her before she disembarked. It took him nearly two months to use up every word that rhymed with Rose. One afternoon, as she was about to step off the trolley, he turned around and whispered, "Lovely Rose, don't mean to impose, my rhymes have run out, can we talk soon in prose?" She knew what he was asking, and the next time she got on the trolley, she handed him a piece of paper on which she had composed her own poem: *My heart and head they disagree, whether you might be the boy for me. I'm not so sure that this is smart, but good-bye, head, and hello, heart.*

He smiled for real. "Will you stay on with me while I finish my route?"

For the next two weeks, after school and whenever she could get away from her chores, she traveled with him back and forth between the Hudson and East Rivers. Rose always sat behind Ryan, and when their eyes met in his mirror, they would exchange shaky smiles. After his shift, they would walk down to the water and sit on the pier. Ryan told her about his family, how they'd come over ten years earlier. "My father promised that we'd be rich in America, that we'd get new clothes and shoes when we needed them, that we'd eat meat once a day." He ran his fingers over his worn, ill-fitting pants. "Well, that hasn't happened yet."

Once, after they'd watched a seagull snap up his squirmy prey, Ryan said, "Pushy bastards, aren't they? And look at the size of those beaks. My father calls them Jew birds." He laughed so rarely that Rose, warmed by the sound of it, laughed with him.

On a late afternoon, when the fog was so solid they could only smell the water, he took her hand and said, "I never thought about marrying until I met you." He was nineteen, and although the three-year disparity in their ages seemed like a century, he said he didn't care how long it would take, that he would wait for her forever.

Forever came sooner than they'd planned. By the time she was seventeen, Rose was married and pregnant with their first child. Their daughter, Erin, was born with dimples in her cheeks, which Ryan called "God's fingerprints." She died of typhus at four.

At nineteen, Rose gave birth to a second child, with blue lips and the wrinkled skin of an old man. They called him Liam, and he lived for thirty-seven hours.

Little Kiefer was dark and fierce, and bellowed like his father. This one would survive.

Two years later, in 1910, when Rose was twenty-two, came beautiful Catrina, a perfect replica of her mother. By then, Ryan had quit driving a trolley and had taken a job as a longshoreman. He made more money at the new job, but still barely enough for them to get by. They lived in two cramped rooms on the top floor of an old tenement on Leroy Street, two blocks from the Hudson River docks. The bedroom, with only a curtain separating Rose and Ryan from their children, had one window that looked out onto an interior hallway; the other window, in the kitchen, opened onto an airshaft. The flimsy walls made daylight as scarce as money but did little to diffuse the odor of manure or muffle the sound of clomping horse hooves and bickering neighbors. The kitchen had room for an oilcloth-covered table and two chairs, which meant the family could never take their meals at the same time. Not that it mattered, since Ryan was rarely home in those days. He worked long hours, digging ditches and hauling freight on and off the passenger ships. His hands had become coarse and calloused, and if you'd asked Rose, she'd have said his soul had too.

He fought the Negroes who, he said, threatened to take his job. He raised his fists to the Italians and spat at the Jews. "Dagos, kikes, niggers"; he had names for them all, and they had ones as bad for him. Men like Ryan had to be careful where they walked at night. The first time he came home with raw egg streaming down his face, Rose said, "If you're going to bring home eggs, make them the kind your children can eat." The next time it was bruises around his eyes. "You keep this up and next thing you know, you'll walk in here with a knife between your ribs," said Rose. "Dead, you'll be of no use to us."

On his days off, Ryan took the family to his favorite place, the duck pond at Central Park. Their trip to the country, he'd call it. They'd walk the grassy slopes of a bluff called the Promontory and sometimes take the swan boats around the pond. During the winter they might splurge for sleigh rides, and once, on Rose's twenty-fifth birthday, the four of them went for a cruise up and down the East River. Rose begged Ryan to come to church with her, but he'd given up on God after Erin died.

As reckless as he was with his own body, Ryan was obsessed with keeping Catrina out of harm's way. He carried her everywhere until she was old enough to sit on his shoulders. Then he'd make it a game, bending down before her and saying, "Time to climb onto your throne." Up there, Catrina's world became his. He'd sing to her: *Have you met my Catrina Ballerina? No one's smarter, no one's keener,* and make up stories about the people they passed in the street: *Look at that woman, rich and stout, with airs like a queen, she's a Kraut, no doubt.* Up there, she was safe. She became so much a part of her father that she thought his sweat and the smell of his hair were hers.

When she was six, he told her, "You're getting too big for your da's shoulders. From now on we'll walk side by side like partners." His crusty hand enveloped her pale, freckled fingers. He still made up rhymes and called her his Catrina Ballerina, but with her feet on the ground, her world became a less safe place: Her father cursed at strangers and made sure she understood the difference between dagos and sheeneys. Rose fought him, saying more than once, "If you teach these children hate, they'll be no better than the rest of them."

He argued that the children needed to know who to avoid, even though he didn't avoid any of them. When he came home one night with three teeth knocked out and blood pouring from the side of his head, he said to Rose, "You're right, I'll sure as bloody hell get killed if I stay here any longer."

He had a plan. He was going to go to Chicago, where he had relatives from County Mayo who said they were treated fairly and that there was plenty of work in the stockyards. He promised to send for the family as soon as he got settled. "We live cooped up like cockroaches," he told Rose. "Our lives are no better than they were in Ireland, the only difference being that here no one wants us. If I see one more 'Irish need not apply' sign, I swear, I'll . . . We can do better; if not for ourselves, at the least we should give the children a proper chance."

Catrina, now seven, was sure that her father would take her with him. She'd keep house for him, boil water for his tea, and lay out his shirt and trousers and shoes each morning. She waited for him to pull her aside and tell her that it would be the two of them, partners as always. When no one was around, she'd fall on her knees and pray: "God, I will do anything you ask, but let me go with him."

In his last days at home, Ryan stopped talking to Catrina and Kiefer. There was packing to do, last-minute chores like repairing the rotten floorboard in the kitchen or hauling a winter's worth of firewood up three flights of stairs. And there was Rose. With so little privacy, she and Ryan retreated to their side of the curtain, where they had some whispered conversations but more shouting arguments.

Then one morning, Catrina and Kiefer woke up and their father was gone. No good-byes, no notes. Rose said he'd gotten an early ride and didn't want to disturb them. "We'll all be together soon enough," she promised. But it was clear from the dead tone in her voice that she didn't believe it.

"That's it, he's gone forever," Kiefer told Catrina when they were alone. "He's never going to send for us."

"Why do you have to be so mean about everything?" Catrina asked. "He'd never do that."

"He would and he did. And I'm not mean," said Kiefer. "I'm real about things. Men like him don't stick around when things get hard. That's how it is."

"I don't believe you."

"If we had money," said Kiefer, "I'd wager you a bet. But I'll tell you what. If you're right, and he does call us to Chicago, you get first pick of what room you want. But if he never comes back, and we have to help Ma with all the household chores, you have to do the cooking and the laundry."

For the previous three years, Rose had been keeping house for a rich older American woman named Mrs. Livingston, who treated her kindly, while a neighbor watched Catrina and Kiefer. Mrs. Livingston became ill shortly after Ryan left, and Rose cared for her, brushing her hair, feeding her, and cleaning her when she fouled herself. When her employer could no longer walk, Rose would carry her to the window, where she could look out on her beloved Central Park. Rose was holding Mrs. Livingston in her arms when she finally died, and it was Rose to whom she left three hundred dollars in her will, suggesting she use it to become a certified nurse. Instead, Rose used the money to buy new clothes and shoes for Catrina and Kiefer, and put the rest of it in the bank for when the four would move to a bigger apartment. After Mrs. Livingston died, Rose got a job at the only place that would employ a nearly thirty-year-old Irishwoman: the laundry in the subbasement of Bellevue Hospital.

When she came home at night, she made what Ryan used to call her "Pot of what?" Usually it was nothing more than potatoes, onions, salt, pepper, bread, and whatever meat or meat remnants she could afford. After dinner, she and the children would settle down under the red-and-white quilt on her bed. The quilt and a lace curtain were the two luxuries that her mother had brought over from Ireland. While the lace curtain covered only half the kitchen window and the quilt was tattered, they and her small shrine of two statues of the Blessed Virgin, two saints, a rosary, and a vase of artificial roses injected color into the otherwise drab apartment.

Rose deliberately kept Ryan in the conversation, assigning him tasks and coloring him into their future: "When we move, I'll leave it to your father to figure out how we'll get out there," or "I found a scarf at the hospital today. I'll save it for your father, he'll need one in Chicago." Lying under the quilt with Catrina and Kiefer, she'd spill out her daydreams. They'd gotten a map of Chicago. They drew circles around where they might live and imagined how it would be to swim in the big lake.

Ryan's letters came weekly at first. He'd gotten a job mopping the blood from a slaughterhouse floor. He'd seen an affordable house in the Bridgeport section of Chicago that had three rooms and running water. Rose hoped that they might have a backyard. "Should that happen," she told the children, "we could grow flowers and vegetables, and I think we could find our way to getting you two a pony or a horse."

Catrina asked if they could also have some dogs, and Kiefer offered that he didn't care about any of that; what he wanted was for his bed to be in a room with a door.

Rose prayed that Chicago would heal Ryan's anger and the brawling would stop. If he got a good-paying job, maybe the Lord would see fit to grant them more children. She wouldn't ask for more than that. But, after a while, the letters became scarcer. No more talk of the job at the slaughterhouse, no mention of houses. Instead, evenings spent with new friends, promises of new business schemes. Rose and the children continued writing him weekly, asking question upon question: Are there lots of Irish people there? Is it as cold as New York? Do you eat well? He never answered any of their questions. Then the letters stopped coming.

After nearly two months of silence, a thick envelope with a Chicago postmark arrived for Rose. She allowed herself a moment of hope as she tried to pry open the envelope without ripping the paper, but too quickly, unthinkable words flooded the page:

My dearest Rose,
I understand that a man doesn't leave his wife and children unless his being gone is better for them than his being

106

there. You and the children are better off without me than with the person I have become. Believe me, this causes me more agony than you will ever know. Please don't look for me but I beg that you and the children hold me in your hearts and know that wherever I am, I am thinking of you with all my love. Explain to Catrina and Kiefer as best you can, and find it within yourselves not to hate me as I am only doing the best I can. Here is twenty-two dollars. I hope that you will use some of it to take the children on a boat up the East River and they will remember the good times they had with their da. You deserve better than me. It's probably too late, but I am going to church again. I speak to you and the children through prayer, which is all I have left. That and God's mercy.

Ryan

For six days, Rose didn't tell Catrina and Kiefer about the letter. She carried it in her purse and read it every chance she got, hoping each time that it would rewrite itself. But when that didn't happen, she sat the children down in the kitchen and said, "It's time we face the truth. Unless we are granted a miracle, your father is gone. Our lives are here, and we are meant to make the best of it."

At only eight, Catrina didn't know the language of mourning, other than what she read on her mother's face. Rose stopped eating. Either she was crying or her eyes were red from the last time she had. Her cries weren't the snuffling sounds a person usually made. They were piercing and incessant, like those of a trapped animal. She stopped caring what she wore and whether or not she combed her hair; on the rare days when she did not work, she wouldn't even change out of her nightdress. Often Catrina would find her slumped on the kitchen chair or lying on her bed with both hands over her heart. When she asked, "Why do you hold your hands that way?" her mother answered, "My heart. It hurts."

"Can't you take some medicine to make it better?"

"I don't expect you to understand this kind of hurt," said Rose. "It's the kind that can't be fixed."

8.

The sound of rat claws tapping across the stone floor in the subbasement of Bellevue Hospital was misleadingly friendly. The scratchy noises they made could have been marionettes clacking across a stage rather than rodents capable of chewing through cement and carrying typhus. When the rain came, the rats took to higher ground as water trickled in. Then the only noise would be human feet sloshing around in cold water. That the light was so dim in "the dungeon" was a blessing, Rose said, because you couldn't see what else was in that water.

By January of 1918, the United States had been at war for less than a year. The Navy kept close watch over the East and Hudson Rivers, as they provided perfect cover for the Germans to snake through with submarines and torpedoes. Bellevue was on the East River, and Rose said all those patrolling naval ships made her feel safe.

Inside the subbasement, it was a different story. The walls were stone and mud, the floors granite. The space was only big enough to hold four giant washtubs and the two shifts of eight women who spent days and nights kneeling over them, scrubbing sheets, towels, and the doctors' uniforms. Lye was harsh on the hands. Sometimes the blood from Rose's hands mixed with the blood from the linens and clothes. Though they never met any patients, no one was more intimate with their suffering than these sixteen women. They saw the gangrene, smelled the vomit, and felt what death had left behind. Most of the women in the dungeon lasted a month, two at the most. They'd rather starve in the streets, they said, than live with that stench and cold. But Rose stuck it out. It was her way of proving herself a good Catholic and as brave an American as the boys fighting in Vichy and Verdun. She hoped she was a lesson to her children about endurance. And some part of her also hoped it was penance for Ryan's sins.

Catrina had to acknowledge that Kiefer had won the bet about their father. She took on cooking, mopping the floors, patching up ripped pants and worn blankets, and, of course, the laundry. Her brother earned

110

extra money by selling newspapers before school. He was clever, like his father, and listened well, but unlike his father, Kiefer fought back with wits rather than fists. One morning, a gang of boys confronted him and his friends as they hawked their newspapers. The leader, a squat freckled boy, stood a foot away from Kiefer and shouted, "Get the fuck out of here!"

Kiefer stepped forward and said in a stage whisper, "If I got the fuck out of here, you'd be gone, wouldn't you?" The kid stood silent as his friends laughed.

Physically, he and Catrina were opposites: Kiefer was short and thin with dark skin and straight black hair; she was tall and big-boned, like her mother, with the same raging red hair and islands of freckles. Handsome Kiefer was sought out by the girls and respected by the boys, but no matter how hard he tried, he couldn't pull his younger sister out of her own little world into the aura of popularity he enjoyed at school.

Catrina was the largest girl in her class. As there were two Catrinas in her grade, she was known as Big Catrina. Until her father left, the name had never bothered her. Catrina Ballerina, she imagined, was beautiful at any size. But in the logic of an eight-year-old, her father's leaving had everything to do with her. She wasn't pretty or clever enough to keep him home.

Rose insisted that Catrina and Kiefer come to the Church of the Guardian Angel with her every Sunday, and every Sunday, Catrina wore her one "church dress," a hand-me-down pink frock with puffed sleeves and a high round neck. They'd sit in the same pew in the same dark church that never had enough heat and say the same prayers: "Sacred heart of Jesus and Mary, protect us . . ." Jesus and Mary had always felt like kin to Catrina: Jesus with his big blue eyes and forbearing smile; and serene Mary, shy and loving with perfect skin. It had never occurred to her that they wouldn't protect her. But when her father disappeared, so did her trust in Jesus and Mary. Despite her prayers and devotion, they'd let him vanish, and eventually she took off the cross she'd always worn around her neck and hid it away.

Catrina had seen her mother's hands and understood how lye could eat away at anything it touched. On one of her laundry days, she crumpled up the pink dress, stuck it in a basin, and covered it with lye. When she took it out, it was full of holes. An accident, she told her mother. Besides, it didn't matter; she wasn't going to church anymore. Rose wouldn't hear of it. For months afterward, she dragged Catrina off every Sunday morning wearing an old skirt and blouse. Catrina would focus on anything but the paintings of Jesus and Mary. She swore she'd never look at them again, nor would she ever say their names out loud. Rose understood that though she could make an eight-year-old go to church, she could not force prayer or comfort into a heart that had closed. But she never gave up trying.

One snowy afternoon, Catrina headed down to the river. It was cloudy, and there was a yellow cast to the sky, making it not quite day or night. Her daydreams sank into that peculiar nether light, and she must have dream-walked ten blocks before a noise jarred her back into reality. Howls they were, as unworldly as the awful sounds her mother had made after her father left. That's when she noticed a man lying on his stomach leaning over the river. He was holding on to a rope attached to a small crate with bars that made it look like a prison. Inside the crate were dogs, eight or ten of them, packed so tightly that it was impossible to make out their forms, just their muscular necks craning and the horrible sounds of their cries as the man lowered the crate into the water. Catrina caught the bulging eyes of one of the dogs before he went down. She had to do something, she thought, but she couldn't figure out what. The dog sank out of view, and the barking stopped. Only a few bubbles floated to the surface. The man held on to the rope and turned his head when he noticed Catrina. "Rabies," he said, as if that explained everything. Catrina shook her head. She didn't believe him. "A menace to the city," he added.

So that's what they do with the dogs no one wants, she thought. It was harder to get rid of unwanted people. Catrina never forgot those eyes and the realization that dogs could cry without tears. After that, she did what she could to take care of the strays. The cat was her first. She found him on the side of the street. At first she thought he was a dead pigeon. He was dirty and so scrawny that his vertebrae felt like the teeth of a comb. She carried him home and put out a bowl of milk. He lapped it up and then hid under the bed. Over time, she nursed him back to health until his coat was so white and shiny that she named him Spooky.

After Spooky came another cat, and a turtle she rescued from the park. Catrina trusted animals, and they her. She could look in their eyes and know if they were sick or had been mistreated. Even the irascible ones who initially growled or hissed could feel the kindness in her touch. The stiffness would go out of their backs and they'd allow her to handle them.

With her father gone, Catrina retreated into her own world, which her schoolmates misread as snobbish and odd. They ridiculed Big Catrina, the fatherless girl who always had the faint odor of animal piss about her. "It takes a stray to know one," they teased. Catrina turned away from their taunts, and after a while they ignored her. The animals were kinder. They were hers alone: them and the memories of her father. The latter she parceled out in meager bits, only occasionally allowing herself a thought about those visits uptown to Central Park or reciting the rhymes he'd made up. Swallowing rocks: that's what loneliness felt like to Catrina. It constricted her throat and weighed down her arms and legs.

On a cloudless afternoon in July, not long after her tenth birthday, she felt those rocks bulging out of her. Taking the trolley up to Central Park suddenly seemed the only thing that might contain them. She walked through the shrubs and white ash trees that muted the traffic sounds on Fifty-Ninth Street, then up to the duck pond. Folding her long skirt over her legs, she sat on the bluff overlooking the water. The swan boats sputtered around the rim of the pond and Catrina let her thoughts float behind them.

Her father. He'd been around her age when he'd come to this country. She could picture him: pale, skinny, licorice-black hair. Scared? Shy? No, he wouldn't have been either. She remembered his walk, how he led with his chest, fists clenched, sleeves rolled up above his elbows, as if something was about to happen. His calloused hands with ridges of scars, so big for his size. Her hand in his. A duckling under its mother's wing couldn't have felt safer. His voice. How he stretched his syllables so *can't* became *cahn't* and *church, chaaarch.* She knew that he'd stuttered as a child. The stutter had mostly vanished by the time he came to America, but he was always frightened that it would slip out of him like a *faart.* That's why he talked in short blasts of words. Maybe that's why he talked in rhyme. To make the sentences go faster. So fast that sometimes he'd gulp in the middle of words, his voice surprisingly soft for a man of his ferocity. She could almost hear it. Catrina closed her eyes. *Concentrate,* she told herself. *Listen.*

She stretched out on the bluff and let the

sun beat down on her. With her eyes closed, she saw the colors of fire. Warmth trickled through her, filling her with a kind of peace she had rarely known. The edges between her body and the ground blurred until she felt as if she had melted into the earth. She no longer summoned her thoughts; they flowed into her. *Catrina Ballerina.*

Catrina Ballerina. Have you seen her?

It was his voice.

Catrina Ballerina. Have you seen her? I'm her father.

Catrina Ballerina. Have you seen her? I'm her father, only farther.

Catrina Ballerina. Have you seen her? I'm her father, only farther, never further, always near her.

Had anyone looked down at the young girl lying on the bluff above, they would have seen her arms stretched out by her sides and her palms turned up to the sky as if she'd surrendered. And in a way she had. Her father was gone. She would never see him again.

The rocks had gone out of her, the loneliness filled up.

Rose tolerated the various strays that Catrina brought home. By 1922, five years after Ryan had left, Rose had enough money

117

to afford a four-room tenement on Tenth Avenue and Thirty-Sixth Street. Kiefer, now fourteen, had his own room with a door, and Catrina slept on a couch in the living room. The rooms were small, but the kitchen was wide enough to fit a table for four. The living room window faced the street, and Kiefer's window looked down onto a back alley. With his door open, there was a cross-breeze through the apartment.

Unfortunately, the breeze was not strong enough to unseat Sunny the rabbit's stink. Catrina had nabbed her newest pet by the neck one afternoon in Central Park, stowed him in her book bag, and brought him home. A squirrel was really what she had been after. Lots of people kept squirrels as pets, but they darted so quickly through the underbrush that the closest she'd ever come to getting her hands on one was the swish of its tail through her fingers.

Sunny was Catrina's first rabbit. Until Sunny, she hadn't known that rabbits could burrow through couches and nest in their cushions, and nothing prepared her for his smell. The moment anyone opened the front door, their eyes would sting and they'd put their hands over their mouth. Rose finally put her foot down: "This place stinks. Get rid of the stench or the rabbit goes."

Catrina promised she'd fix it. The next morning before school she shredded up the newspaper from the day before and put it in a corner of Sunny's crate. When she came home that afternoon, the paper was soiled, but the house didn't smell as bad. Kiefer supplied her with spare newspapers for the next several weeks, until his boss complained that he wasn't returning enough papers for pulping. She decided to seek out one of the newsboys who hawked the *New York Evening Journal* and ask for his leftovers. It gave her an excuse to walk down to Madison Square Park on Twenty-Third Street and Broadway and look up at one of the tallest buildings in the world. The new Metropolitan Life Tower was fifty stories high and had a white marble tower with an ornate four-faced clock that told time in all directions. Accustomed to the weather-beaten shutters and drab red bricks on the walk-ups of her neighborhood, she thought this skyscraper was as modern as a rocket.

According to the clock, it was nearly five p.m. when she spotted the newsboy standing beneath a streetlamp next to the subway station. She asked if she could have some of his unsold papers; he told her to come back at six and he'd give her what he had.

The next time she came by for the papers,

he asked, "What do you do, eat them for dinner?"

"No, they're not for me." She explained about the rabbit.

"I know a little about rabbits," he said earnestly. "What are you feeding him?"

"Any scrap I can find, pieces of bread, cheese, like that."

"Rabbits love to eat grass," the boy said. "They also like lettuce. The vegetable stand on Thirty-Second and Eighth dumps their brown lettuce leaves in the street every night after nine. It'd be a feast for him."

The boy, James Harty, was taller than Catrina and just as fair-skinned. He had cat-green eyes and wavy blond hair, and was fourteen, two years older than she. He promised her his leftover newspapers if she'd meet him under the clock each day at six. The third time she met him, it was raining. She hadn't realized how eager she was to see him until she found herself running down Tenth Avenue without a hat or umbrella. By the time she reached Madison Square Park she was soaked and out of breath, and her red hair trailed down her neck. "I'm here," she said, standing before him.

He looked startled. The way he stared at her made Catrina worry he didn't recognize her. "You're pretty, and you're shivering," he said, pulling off his jacket and throwing it around her shoulders. "Let's get you to a dry place." With his hand on her back, he led her to a luncheonette on one of the side streets. She could barely feel his touch, but there was something about him — maybe his height or the way he'd looked at her — that made her want to nestle under his arm. At the luncheonette, he ordered an egg cream and told her she should get some hot barley soup. Though the soup was too salty, she liked the feeling of being taken care of and drank it down without a word of complaint.

Whenever she could, she'd meet James under the clock at six. In time, she told him about her other pets, and about her family. On weekends, they took walks around the city, and on the first warm day they strolled up to Central Park and lay in the grass by the duck pond. She recited some of her father's limericks and a few of the stories he'd made up about people. "He's gone and he's never coming back," she told James. "He lied to my mother. I should have known by how mean and quiet he got right before he left that he was never coming back. She cried for days and days. I don't understand how you could do that to another person."

James put his hand on her arm. "I'd never do anything like that."

"I didn't think he would either," she said. "Tell me about your parents?"

"My father worked in construction. Two years ago, he fell off a ladder while he was putting up a window in some building on Broadway. He broke his leg in four places. It never healed right. We thought it would only be a matter of time before his leg got good again, but it stayed bent. Now he can only walk with a crutch. He can't do much of anything with a crippled leg, so my mother has to work. She's a teacher. She loves children. Well, she'd better love children, she has five of us. Anyways, I hear she's really good at it. Sometimes my father gets so mad at her for no reason any of us can see. His face goes pale. He'll curse and his voice gets different from his real voice, high in a scary way. Then me or one of my brothers has to grab him before he hurts her." James turned to Catrina. "I can't make up limericks, but I like to write stories and things."

In the bubble of their world, Catrina was beautiful and smart, and James was a magician who made her feel safe and promised her a forever. He knew how to make shadow

122

puppets with his hands. By holding his fingers a certain way, he could cast a swan or giraffe on a wall. Love in itself was dizzying. Adding shadow swans to the equation launched Catrina out of time and place. Her days at school were hours to be gotten through, the portal to afternoons with James. She knew that girls whispered about the things boys wanted them to do with them, but she and James never spoke about those things. Kissing and touching came naturally to them. At first, he would fumble when he tried to undo her brassiere, but Catrina thought it was sweet. Together they learned what to do and where.

They married in 1926, when Catrina was sixteen, and James moved into her room at Rose's house. By the time she was nineteen, James was dead. All she had to show from him was a stack of letters. He'd leave one under her pillow each morning: her name written one hundred times, a short poem, random thoughts — anything that reminded him of her, which was everything. The letters were hopeful and so filled with the promise of their forevers that even when his fever sweat soaked through the bedclothes and he stopped taking food and water it never occurred to her that he might die.

When he did die, he took whatever joy was

left in her. She yearned for the darkness of night and hid herself from daylight and other people as best she could. She let her hair run wild and her face get puffy. Ringed with sadness, her eyes seemed to recede. She tried to make herself believe that James was watching over her, but mostly that fantasy unraveled before she opened her eyes in the morning. She took to talking to Spooky, her only surviving pet. She'd ask him whether she'd need an umbrella when she went out, and read to him from James's letters. "He's never coming back. They never come back," she'd whisper. Spooky's pink ear would twitch, and his soft breath on her neck was as reassuring as things got in those days.

Often Rose and Catrina, with matching untamable cinnamon hair, were mistaken for sisters. They were built the same — as Ryan used to say, "generously constructed" — both had milky complexions that blotched with the slightest emotion. But their hearts were made of different stuff. Rose was as set in her ways as she was in her opinions. Even after Kiefer moved out and James died, she wouldn't be budged from the old apartment on Tenth Avenue and Thirty-Sixth Street.

At forty-two, she still worked in the laundry at Bellevue and kept the same shrine on her bedroom windowsill that she'd had on Leroy Street. There was sad-eyed Saint Benedict and kindly Saint Anthony, along with two statues of the Blessed Virgin, all of them bleached by the sun. Every morning before work, she went to the Church of the Guardian Angel, where she sat in a pew in the third row on the left side of the organ. On her knees, hands folded and eyes closed, she gave herself to prayer. She prayed for the souls of her two lost babies. She asked God to look after Kiefer, now a detective in the police department, and to heal her grieving daughter and bring her back to the church. She even prayed for the patients at Bellevue, but she never prayed for Ryan. It had taken her two years to stop mourning him, but when she had, like Catrina, she had shut him out as if he were dead.

Rose wasn't one to criticize God, but in the matter of her unanswered prayers about Catrina, she felt he was being obstinate. No matter how hard she prayed for her daughter to come back to the church, it never happened. A typical argument between the two of them ran like this: Catrina would say,

"The church was no refuge for me when Da disappeared, and all your praying and devotion didn't help James stay alive. I have no use for a God like that." And Rose would remind her, "You're a girl from the church, like the rest of us. The world sees you that way whether you wear a cross around your neck or not." But as in all things, Catrina went her own way.

Rose prayed that she would become a teacher when she finished high school, but Catrina had no interest in that either. Now that James was gone, the only place she could find the kind of absolute love he'd shown her was among the animals, and she was determined to work with them. It wasn't hard to find the ones who needed help.

The stray dogs lived off the garbage in the streets, and people often dumped water on them to shoo them away. The law protected the ones with collars and licenses, but the collarless ones were rounded up and faced the same fate as those Catrina had seen down by the river, only these days they were gassed instead of drowned. Catrina looked after as many of them as she could. She'd bring them home, wash and feed them, and try to find a place for them. In that regard, Rose was helpful and would offer the strays up to coworkers at Bellevue or to the parishioners at her church. When a neighbor's German shepherd, Sasha, got hit by a car and lost the use of her back legs, Catrina took her before she could be put to sleep. At first, Catrina tried tying a rope around Sasha's hindquarters and letting her use her front paws to walk. Sasha never complained and gamely hobbled alongside Catrina. But she could see how it tired the dog, and eventually she jerry-rigged a Radio Flyer wagon with a pillow and a leather strap so, secured by the strap, Sasha was able to sit on the pillow and pull herself forward with her front legs. The dog thrived for years in that Radio Flyer and could even romp with the beagle puppy and the stray terrier that came later.

Four months after James died, Catrina went to the offices of the ASPCA to see if she could find a job. Their headquarters were on Twenty-Sixth Street and Madison Avenue and overlooked the park where she'd first met James. Inside, the smell of urine, feces, and unwashed animals smacked into her with such force, she thought she might be sick. When the urge to vomit subsided, she walked up to the man sitting at the front desk and said, "My name is Catrina Harty and I've come to apply for a job."

The man was balding, with sad brown eyes and the defeated posture of someone accustomed to delivering bad news. "You say your name like I'm supposed to know you." He squinted at her. "Do I know you?"

"No, but I'd like to work here. I'm very good with animals."

The man snorted as if she had told a bad joke. "This work isn't suitable for everyone."

"There's nothing about animals that frightens me," she said.

"Oh yeah?" He took a deep breath as if savoring the punchline he was about to deliver. "How about dead animals? Anything about them frighten you?"

Catrina stiffened. "No, sir," she lied. "I'm willing to take whatever work you might give me."

"Don't say I didn't warn you." He gripped the arms of his chair and pulled himself up. "This way." He led her to a room that looked like a stable and smelled even worse than where she'd been before. There were overcrowded pens with straw beds for dogs and separate cages for cats and other small animals. "Here's where we keep 'em. We hope some of them will be adopted, but it doesn't always work out that way. When the pens get so full that we can't fit another dog, we take 'em across the hall. We use gas. Chloroform. It goes quickly and they don't feel nothing. You still interested?"

Catrina nodded, not trusting herself to speak.

"So it would be your job to walk these dogs and, if you can, find homes for them before they're, you know, put to rest. We got two other gals in there. You'd rotate with them. You'd also have to clean up the shit and piss and scrub down the floor." He studied her pale, soft hands. "As I said, not the kind of work for everyone."

Catrina thought about her mother and all the years she'd worked in that awful basement in Bellevue; how her father's hands had been calloused from working at the docks. She looked at the animals, crammed together so closely that it was difficult to see them one by one. "I'm not scared. When do I start?"

Susanna and Iris were the other two gals. Both were older. Susanna had worked at headquarters for a year and a half, Iris for only three months. "You never get used to it," Susanna told her. "It just becomes bearable."

There were so many dogs that sometimes

they weren't walked for days, and no matter how many buckets of water the women poured on the floor, nothing could obliterate that smell. Catrina kept a change of clothes at the shelter: trousers, a pair of shoes, and an old shirt of her father's. At first she washed them every day, but they'd be shit brown by the time she went home, so after a while, she didn't even bother.

As much as she loved the dogs, Catrina wasn't the kind to murmur to them, "Who's the best dog?" and expect them to answer. Yet, taking them on their last walks felt like a sacred duty. She'd sit down on the street beside them and let them burrow their heads into her shoulder. Long after she went home at night, the sound of their barking rang in her ears.

Only once did she allow herself to get attached to one of them, a white terrier with tired legs and a worried expression. Whenever Catrina came into the shelter, the dog would greet her with a round, high-pitched cry. Catrina named him Felix and brought him pieces of ham from home. She wanted to take him in, but Rose said enough was enough, absolutely no more pets. Catrina tried to keep Felix separate from the other dogs in the pen, but it was impossible. When his time came, she walked with him across the hall and watched through the glass window as he and the other dogs were chloroformed. The sickeningly sweet smell of it seeped under the door. Felix fell on his side and weakly tried to kick back the gas. His eyes seemed to find Catrina's. "I'm sorry," she said as she watched the fight go out of him. She was reminded how dogs never cried with their eyes.

9

Rose was concerned that her daughter's infatuation with the animals would keep her entombed in widowhood. "I'm worried that you've let yourself go since James," she said after Catrina came home from work one night reeking of God knows what. "Nobody wants a girl covered in dog hair."

"That's fine," Catrina shot back. "I don't want anybody who *isn't* covered in dog hair."

Rose recognized in Catrina her own intractability, and Catrina saw in her mother a familiar willfulness. It made for a contentious relationship, but also one of grudging respect.

They got up at six thirty every morning and had breakfast together before Rose headed to the hospital. Catrina fed and walked Sasha, then headed crosstown to the ASPCA. The two women divvied up the cooking and shopping and ate supper together. On Fridays, when Kiefer came for dinner, they'd cook some fish. Kiefer always brought fresh fruit and on very special occasions a bottle of wine.

On weekends, Rose and Catrina walked to Herald Square, where Rose would urge Catrina to at least look in the shop windows. But Catrina had no interest. "We can't afford these things anyway, so why bother?" she argued. The only thing Catrina enjoyed on those outings was traveling up and down the modern wooden escalators at Macy's. Rose would stay outside with Sasha while Catrina gripped the handrail and studied the electric stairs unfolding and folding into themselves as many as four or five times in a morning.

In the afternoon, Catrina took Sasha for walks down to the river. On a sunless Saturday in January, the two of them were making their way back to Thirty-Sixth Street when a man strode up to Catrina and asked, "Is this dog an athlete of some sort?"

She laughed. "Not at all."

"Then it must be that you use her wagon to haul home your groceries — am I correct?"

"No, you aren't." She told him about Sasha's accident and how she had rigged the Radio Flyer for her.

The man was older, and handsome. His eyes, nearly black, went well with his white teeth, black hair, and dark skin. He looked like a movie star, though Catrina couldn't figure out which one. He crouched down beside Sasha and rubbed her chest. "Well, look at you, what a pretty girl you are; you are some girl." Sasha licked the man's hand.

"She likes you," said Catrina.

The man continued to scratch Sasha. "It's not me, it's the chicken I was handling this afternoon. I'm very good with chicken cutlets." He winked at Catrina.

"So you're a butcher then?" Catrina was disappointed that he wasn't a movie star.

"Nooo," he said, cracking a toothy smile. "I run a restaurant and cabaret east of here, on Thirty-Eighth between Fifth and Madison, the Blue Moon. Maybe you've heard of it?"

Catrina shook her head. "Truth be told, I don't get out very often."

"I hope I'm not being too nosy," he said, "but what do you do when you're not walking Sasha?"

"I work at the ASPCA. Mostly I take care of the animals who are about to be put to death." Catrina thought of her mother's warning about men not wanting women covered in dog hair and realized that she didn't want this handsome man to think of her smelling like shit, so she turned the conversation in another direction. "Someday I'd like to work for a veterinarian, but right now, I don't think any will have me, a woman with limited experience."

"I'm sure lots of veterinarians would have you. You haven't found the right one." The way he looked up at her, sideways with a half smile, made her smile back in an equally provocative way. She couldn't remember the last time she'd had this much conversation with a strange man. When he stood up, he shook each leg as if to make sure his pant cuffs were even. He wore a blue-and-white-striped shirt with a white collar and red braces under a camel-colored coat. She could see that the coat label said Brooks Brothers. His clothes fit well, and their fabrics seemed soft and expensive.

"I'm an animal lover myself," he said. "Do you mind if I walk with the two of you for a while?"

"Suit yourself."

His name was Walter Bianco. He told her that he'd grown up with three dogs and two sisters in Mount Vernon.

"I've never been there," she said. "Is it far from here?"

"Far enough. We had our own house, a

backyard, a porch, you know, the whole kit and caboodle. How about you? I hear a little brogue. Are your people from Ireland?"

His smile was like the sun in her eyes. She noticed how soft his lips were and wondered if he had more teeth than other men.

"My people, yes, all from County Mayo. I'm the first American girl in my family. My parents came over as children. In fact, I grew up close to here." Her whole kit and caboodle was a far cry from three dogs, a porch, and a backyard, so she decided to leave it at that. Besides, they'd arrived at her building. "Well, here I am," she said, planting a foot on the front stoop. "You must be very busy at the restaurant. I've taken too much of your time already."

"You haven't taken anything," said Walter. "You and Sasha here have given me great pleasure. I often take a break from the restaurant at around this time, so maybe we can take another walk together soon."

Catrina considered her answer. "I see no harm in that."

"Good." He drummed his fingers on the wrought-iron banister. "Now I know where to find you."

The next time they met, a week later, it was not by accident. Walter was sitting on the stoop of her building as Catrina and

136

Sasha came down the stairs. "Ah," he said, "I thought this was the right time. Mind if I walk with you?"

"Would it matter if I minded?" she asked, lifting Sasha onto the wagon.

"If you told me I was the last person in the world you would ever walk with and that you found me repulsive and annoying, it would matter."

"And why would I tell you that?"

Walter smiled. "Do they teach girls how to be sassy in County Mayo?"

"My da," she said. "He brought it with him."

They headed downtown and talked about Sasha and the spell of cold weather they were having.

"Do you ever get a break?" Walter asked.

"A break from what?"

"You know, your work, Sasha, this neighborhood? Do you ever get away from it?"

Catrina laughed. "I work very hard to be in it, my life, my work, Sasha. Why would I want to get away?"

"I don't mean forever," he said. "I mean a distraction. For instance, have you ever been to a show on Broadway?"

"No."

"Would you like to go with me to see *The Band Wagon*? It's supposed to be a wonderful revue with Fred and Adele Astaire. I could sneak out of the restaurant for a few hours Thursday night."

"A Broadway show?" she asked. "And what does one wear to a Broadway show?"

"When one is as beautiful as you, it hardly matters. Any old dress will do."

"That's good, because I happen to have only one dress, and it's old."

That evening, Catrina told her mother that she'd met a man in the street who'd been friendly to her. "I was friendly back," she said. "I didn't realize it until after, but I was definitely very friendly back. He invited me to see a show on Broadway, something with Fred and Adele something-or-other. I said yes."

"An Irish man?" asked Rose.

"He's very handsome and he owns a restaurant uptown."

"Yes, but is he Irish?"

"Almost certainly not," said Catrina.

Walter Bianco was forty-one, Catrina was twenty-one. He wooed her with raw oysters and thick steaks. He took her to the circus and to the Metropolitan Opera House. He bought her expensive silk suits and hats with stitched-on labels that said *Made in France.* When the air was cold enough to form breath clouds, he bought her a silver fox jacket with squared shoulders and flared sleeves. It didn't take her long to understand that the Blue Moon was one of New York's most deluxe restaurants and cabarets, and slim Walter Bianco, with his lantern jaw, big smile, and glazed black hair, was the man of the moment.

It seemed to Catrina that he knew everyone in New York. If people didn't already know Walter, something about him made them think they did. When she walked down the street with him, she saw how men nodded at him, and how women nudged whomever they were with and then turned away, probably thinking, as she had, that he looked like some movie star. People were forever touching his forearm and saying, "Oh, excuse me," or brushing up against him, though probably not by accident. By his side, the world was a prettier and more exciting place, the way it had been on her da's shoulders.

On Valentine's evening 1932, they were invited to the opening of a new nightclub in Times Square. Walter told her he wanted her to be the sexiest girl there and gave her a midnight-blue dress made of clingy silk jersey that was slit up the side. It had a low back, décolletage, and long sleeves that came to a point right after her wrist. She'd never worn anything so glamorous or expensive, and it felt liquid against her skin. That night, she pinned up her hair and wore the faux-diamond drop earrings he'd given her a few months earlier. Rose was still at the hospital when Walter rang the bell. Catrina opened the door and watched as he took in the sight of her. "You're magnificent," he said, holding out his arms.

In that dress, under the gaze of that man, Catrina took his hands in hers and pulled him toward her. It had been a long time. He kissed her neck. She turned away and locked the front door. He kissed her back. He didn't fumble when he unzipped the dress and carried her to the couch. He stroked her in ways and places that made her cry out. In turn, he took her hand and showed her where her touch was welcome. He called her "baby doll" and "sweetheart," and she called him "my beautiful man." When they were finished, she asked him, "Are you this attentive to all your chicken cutlets?"

"No," he answered. "Only the ones I intend to eat."

Walter said of himself that he'd been around the block a few times, and Catrina knew he hadn't traveled alone. He taught her things and made her feel desirable and beautiful. It was different from being with James. James and she had been the same. With him, she'd felt safe and understood. She had loved him purely; sex had been sweet. Walter was anything but safe; sex with him was not sweet. There was something dangerous about him that she found arousing: the way he scattered vulgarities through his sentences, the company he kept, how he held her by the wrists when they kissed. He was nothing like James, and with him, she was nothing like the girl she'd been then.

She took care with how she looked for him. For the first time, she wore lipstick and chose clothes that showed off her natural curves. She styled her hair with waving lotions and wore it tied at her neckline. After work at the ASPCA, she'd scrub down and splash 4711 cologne on her neck. These days, she spent less time commiserating with Iris and Susanna, as she was eager to get home and prepare for her time with Walter.

Rose saw the change in her daughter. "I'm not blind to how good-looking he is," she said after Walter had joined them for dinner the first time. "And it's nice that he has a lot of money. But I worry that he's filled your head with highfalutin notions." That evening he'd brought an expensive bottle of wine and called Rose "sweetie" at least twice. "Imagine him calling me sweetie." She shook her head. "Nobody's ever called me sweetie."

A few days later, Rose watched her daughter zip herself into a tight new evening gown as she prepared to go with Walter for an evening at the Stork Club.

"This man who has swept you off your feet, what do you know about him? Is he a kind man? Is he honest? Aside from his good looks and big wallet, what do you really see in him?"

"I have *fun* with him," Catrina said. She knew how that word, with its frivolous and sexual overtones, would sound. She said it again. "I haven't had *fun* in a very long time. I know he isn't Irish and I know that makes you uncomfortable. I married one of us and he died. Da was one of us and he left. Walter Bianco is here. He takes me places I've never been and introduces me to interesting people. What's so wrong with that? You don't have to worry, I still am who I am."

Rose's eyes traveled up and down her daughter's body. The two women had the same broad hips, large breasts, and winter-pale skin. She remembered why Catrina's schoolmates used to call her Big Catrina. Her daughter was what men would call ripe. Rose had been ripe once. She knew from her own body that ripe turned flabby soon enough. She scrutinized her daughter one more time before asking, "So tell me this, what does Mr. Romeo see in you?"

"Believe it or not, he thinks I'm pretty. He says I'm different from the other girls he's known. He finds me funny and charming and, you know, other things."

"What *other things* would those be?" asked Rose.

"You met Da when you were very young, right?"

"Yes."

"He was different from all the other boys. He was exciting and made you feel a certain way, didn't he?"

Rose flushed. "I suppose he did, but that was so long ago —"

Catrina interrupted, "Surely Ryan Walsh was not your mother's cup of tea. She would have wanted you to wait until you were older, to marry a professional man, maybe even an American, but Da was charming and made your world bigger. So what if he had a temper and used bad language; you loved him and nothing would have stopped you from marrying him."

"Honestly, I can't remember."

"Of course you can," said Catrina. "That's why you worry about Walter so much. He reminds you of your own bad choice."

"And if he does, is it so wrong to worry about you?"

"No, but at least my bad choice can keep us fed."

Walter had courted bosomy blondes with tiny waists and made-up faces, and black-haired girls with dark skin and full features like his own, but he told Catrina that with her red hair and whiskey-colored eyes, she was more beautiful and exotic than any woman he'd ever known. "You're gorgeous in an uncommon way," he told her. "We make an eye-catching couple, like Jean Harlow and William Powell." He taught her how to hobnob with the fancy patrons at the Blue Moon. "Be natural. Talk about what you know. You're so direct and unpretentious, they'll be charmed."

Whether it was her looks or the frankness with which she dealt with people, Blue Moon customers took to her. Walter convinced Catrina to quit her job at the AS-PCA and made her the hostess. Soon she was on a first-name basis with actors, financiers, and members of Governor Roosevelt's family and inner circle.

"You're my greatest asset," Walter told her. Even years later, she'd be walking along Fifth Avenue and be startled when some fancy East-sider gave her a second glance and asked, "Don't I know you from the Blue Moon?"

It seemed as if Rose was the only person in New York City whom Walter didn't charm. "He's a sly one," she said to Kiefer, when he asked what she thought of Walter. "Your sister's so blinded by his fancy life, I hope she knows what she's doing. I have a funny feeling about him. I don't trust him. I wish I knew more about him." She gave her son the hard stare he knew from childhood, the one that meant she wanted something.

"Why don't I hang around his restaurant and see what I can find out about him?"

Rose patted his hand. "That's my good boy. Of course, we won't tell Catrina."

"Of course not."

Kiefer started going to the Blue Moon late at night, after Catrina had left. Mostly he sat at the bar and watched. He noted Walter's slick hair, his dazzling smile, and the Cuban cigar he kept in the front pocket of his suit. He saw how the young girls ogled him and how he kissed the hands of older women and sometimes patted their behinds.

Men of every age slipped him bills and whispered in his ear. As far as Kiefer was concerned, the showgirls who danced in their feathers and sequins were naked.

After a while, he became a regular. He'd talk with the bartender or other customers and make casual inquiries about Walter. "I gather he's a family man from Mount Vernon, two sisters, dogs. Sounds nice," he said to Tony the bartender one night.

"Are you kidding?" Tony laughed. "Me and him grew up in the same neighborhood. The Bronx. No sisters. No dogs. Nothing like that. Always had a lot of girls, though. With a puss like that, hell, even I'd kiss him."

Kiefer laughed. "Sure seems like he has a lot of friends, though — all those actors and politicians who pass through here." He purposely didn't mention the loan sharks, bookies, and occasional toughs from one of the city's criminal gangs he'd also observed. He'd watched Walter in nervous conversations with one or the other of them, and noticed how, when talking to them, he would take the cigar from his pocket and finger it like a rosary bead.

"Sure, he's got lots of friends," said Tony. "Not exactly the kinds you'd take to your mother's house for dinner. But friends of a

146

certain sort, yeah."

On another evening, Kiefer struck up a conversation with a reporter for the *Evening Journal,* a regular at the bar. They talked about the beautiful women and all the famous people who came to the Blue Moon. "You ought to do a story about the guy who runs this place. I hear he's quite a character."

The reporter took the bait. "Bianco? He's a character right out of a Dashiell Hammett novel. Rumor is this place is backed by Owney Madden and that Bianco is always late on his shipment payments. I'll tell you this: His story won't have such a happy ending if that's true. Too bad, he seems like a nice enough guy."

Kiefer raised his eyebrows. Madden was a known bootlegger and gangster who'd also muscled his way into a piece of the Stork Club. He wondered how much of this to tell Catrina or Rose.

On the following Friday night, Rose, Catrina, and Kiefer had their usual dinner together. Catrina was talking about the party that she and Walter were planning to go to that weekend. "It's in Great Neck," she said. "Great Neck. What a funny name. I wonder if there's a town called Not Such a Great Neck or Pain in the Neck?"

Kiefer interrupted her. "I've been hanging around the Blue Moon for a couple of weeks. Been watching your fellow." He shook his head. "He's not who you think he is."

"What? You've been spying on Walter?" Patches of red blossomed on her neck.

"Not spying, exactly," said Kiefer. "Looking out for my little sister." He told her about the rumors: the bad company Walter kept, the pandering to his customers. "He didn't grow up in Mount Vernon with sisters and dogs," he said. "He's from the Bronx. He lied about that. Who knows what else he's lied about?"

"Listen to him," said Rose.

"So the two of you have become experts on Walter because Kiefer's been playing big-shot detective for a few nights? You have no idea who Walter is."

"I have some," said Kiefer. "Look, I'm not blind. He's rich and good-looking, I'll grant you that. Guys like that know how to sweep gals like you off their feet."

"What's that supposed to mean?"

"He's like Da. Charming, handsome, but a cad at heart. You live in a daydream. Have you forgotten what it was like when Da walked out?"

Rose looked down at her plate as Catrina

shoved her chair away from the table, stood up, and called to Sasha. "I may be living in a daydream," she shouted at Kiefer, "but this is a damn nightmare!" When she was halfway out the door, Catrina leaned back in and called to both of them: "You'd better get used to this cad, because I'm going to marry him."

10.

Everyone said it was good luck the way the harvest moon shone on the night Catrina and Walter married. He closed down the restaurant and invited nearly two hundred of his close friends. Harry Hopkins, a crony of Governor Roosevelt's, presided over the ceremony.

A red carpet covered the walk down the long hallway from the front entrance to the main room. As the band struck up "Blue Moon," Kiefer took Catrina's arm. With her upswept hairdo and made-up face, Kiefer thought she looked older than her twenty-two years. "Ready?" he asked as they headed down the hallway.

"I guess," she said.

They walked silently and slowly. He figured she was nervous and that was why she looked so dour, but as they were about to enter the main room, cameras popped and the band switched to "Always." Catrina licked her lips, took a deep breath, and switched on a smile as if a director had yelled "Show time!"

"You okay?" Kiefer whispered.

"I'm perfect," she whispered, still smiling.

Catrina wasn't lying. Everyone in this room had to see how perfect it all was. Didn't Susanna and Iris envy her as she walked down the rose-strewn aisle in her ivory silk and Chantilly lace gown with its three-yard-long veil? Kiefer was certainly taking it all in: the rich ones, the famous ones. He liked to talk about taking care of his little sister, but his little sister was doing fine taking care of herself. Even her mother, for God's sake, must be impressed by Walter in his perfectly cut tuxedo, by this world and the role that Catrina was about to play in it. The image of James standing next to her came into her mind, but she pushed it away. *Not here. Not here.* She almost laughed when she imagined her father mingling with the Jews and Italians in this room and the Negroes in the band. His voice seemed to breathe in her ear: *I can see her, Catrina Ballerina, a beautiful bride, her da by her side.*

Catrina felt exhilarated, the same way she used to as a kid when Kiefer would dare her to jump into the Hudson. The icy water always shocked the breath out of her, but she'd rise to the surface and shout triumphantly, "I did it!" She shivered now as she'd shivered then. Her eyes welled up as Walter slipped a ring on her finger, and Hopkins pronounced them man and wife.

I did it, she thought.

The band played "Star Dust." Catrina and Walter danced for a while, then Catrina asked Kiefer to dance and Walter asked Rose. "No, thank you," Mrs. Walsh said. "I'm not the dancing sort." For the rest of the evening, mother and son sat apart from the guests, whispering back and forth.

"No priest, no nothing. You'd think she never saw the inside of a church," said Rose.

"Walter looks tanner than usual. I don't know how he does it; it's been cloudy and rainy for the past week," noted Kiefer.

"Have you noticed the size of the diamonds these women are wearing?" asked Rose. "I swear, if they cashed in all the jewelry in this place, they would have enough money to feed the entire country."

"Half these guys would hock that stuff tomorrow morning if they could," Kiefer said with a laugh.

There were slipper orchid arrangements on every table, and even if the country hadn't been in the midst of a depression, the food would have been considered extravagant: turtle soup, steak, lobsters from Maine, roasted potatoes with sour cream and caviar in mother-of-pearl shells, hearts of palm au gratin, and, as a private joke, chicken cutlets. The chocolate wedding cake had a likeness of the newlyweds piped in yellow buttercream icing, and there were ice buckets that stayed filled with Champagne bottles until the last guests stumbled out at two thirty in the morning.

Walter decided they would walk to the Plaza Hotel, where he had reserved the ten-dollar-a-night honeymoon suite, facing north onto Central Park. It was early September, and the leaves on the trees were still heavy with summer. When he asked if she'd ever had a bird's-eye view of the park, Catrina answered, "I've been in the park many times, but never over it."

Walter put his arm around her and squeezed her waist. "Well, Mrs. Bianco, it's only one of many treats I have in store for you!"

By the time they got to their room, it was after three. Walter had drunk more than his share of the Cristal Champagne and fell into bed without removing his tuxedo. Catrina lay next to him and watched him sleep. He breathed through his mouth as tiny bubbles escaped his lips. With his eyes closed and his face slack, he looked his age. She didn't know this Walter: this old man of forty-two, her husband. Dutifully, she turned on her side, wrapped her arm around his chest, and sank into the boozy smell of him.

When she woke up a little before ten, Walter was still asleep. As this was her first stay in a hotel, she was glad to have time to explore by herself. In the bathroom, she ran her fingers along the rim of the smooth porcelain tub and the faucets, which had gold handles shaped like swans. On the marble sink were two packets of soap wrapped in white paper. They had the words *The Plaza* written in blue, and each fit perfectly into the palm of her hand. No one would notice if one were missing, she told herself as she slipped it into her handbag, aware of the irony of Mrs. Walter Bianco wanting to steal soap. Then she went and looked out at Central Park.

Across the street, men in top hats were feeding their carriage horses from tin buckets. She could hear the barking of the sea lions at the zoo. Making no noise, she lifted the chair from behind the desk and moved it to the window, where she sat and stared out at the children playing, the green that seemed to spread out forever, the duck pond where she and James had gone on weekends. The thought of James, his young body, the surprise of him, made her eyes water. She visualized them on the other side of this window, walking hand in hand through the park. She wished for a moment that she were that girl again and wondered how she'd become this one: a rich woman with her husband asleep in a bed in the Plaza Hotel, a husband twice the age James had been when he died. God's injustice, she thought, was immense and cruel. So caught up was she in her thoughts that she barely noticed that Walter was awake and calling out for her.

They stayed in bed until early afternoon, making the kinds of plans for their future that couples make when their bodies are sticky and satisfied. He stroked her hips and told her she was built for motherhood. "You'll give me beautiful children," he said. She promised him as many as he wanted. He held out his hand for her to shake it. "You've got yourself a deal, sister." He vowed to always take care of her. Money was not an issue, he said. They'd continue to live as they had been living. She'd have to stop working at the restaurant when the kids arrived, of course, but they would have all the domestic help they needed — Irish girls, if she wished.

He'd seen a brownstone on 185th Street in Washington Heights. "In this market," he said, "I can get it for a song." They were living in Walter's apartment, near the restaurant, a world away from Washington Heights. It would be a long trip downtown to the restaurant, but he thought the building was perfect for them, one of a row of houses with chocolate-colored turrets that hovered over the street, he said, like a cluster of witches. He described the mahogany trim on the parlor walls and how there was a skylight latticed with wrought iron on the top floor. "It has four floors, including the basement, and that's about ten rooms. We'll fill each of them with a little Bianco."

The brownstone sealed the deal. Walter would have his children, and Catrina would finally have her forever.

Two months after the wedding, they moved into the brownstone. They filled the rooms with cane chairs and brass beds and tables with Florentine marble tops and carved oak legs. Catrina found a stray terrier who got along fine with Sasha and Spooky, and a new beagle puppy. They bought a Pfaff sewing machine and installed a Steinway baby grand on the parlor floor. He called it their music room and said that this would be where they'd hold their parties.

On Rose and Kiefer's infrequent visits, Catrina would stash the most ostentatious crystal decanters and Tiffany lamps in a closet. Rose always greeted Catrina with a kiss on the cheek, and Walter shook Kiefer's hand with a polite "Nice to see you again." They'd sit in the parlor, Rose and Kiefer on the powder-blue velvet settee, Walter and Catrina across from them on the white Louis XV sofa. Walter would try to engage Kiefer in talk about Babe Ruth's latest homer for the Yankees or the fluctuating stock market, but her brother wasn't a willing conversationalist and would come back at him with two- or three-word answers, all the while jiggling the keys in his pocket.

Rose usually came straight from work, wearing her old drab green coat over her hospital uniform. She sat stiffly and claimed she had just eaten when they offered her food. Catrina would ask her about her trip uptown, or they'd discuss neutral subjects like the new Empire State Building. Before long, Rose would look at her watch and then at Kiefer, who would mutter, "It's getting late. I gotta get Ma home." Although Catrina offered Rose money, Rose always refused. Catrina worried that her mother looked shabby and wondered if Walter found Kiefer boring, then felt embarrassed that she'd had these thoughts at all.

After a year and a half, no kids had arrived, and no parties had happened. The rooms gathered dust. Sometimes one of the dogs wandered upstairs, but mostly the house remained unlived-in. "We can't make babies with a menagerie in our bed," Walter declared, and from then on the dogs were locked in the kitchen until morning. When there was still no baby, Walter and Catrina's lovemaking became less frequent. He spent less time at the restaurant. He began coming home late at night, or sometimes not until early in the morning. In the past, he'd invited her to go to parties with him. These days, he didn't bother.

"Where do you go when you don't come home?" she asked after another absence.

"Here, there, anywhere," he said.

"And what about home? To your wife?"

"My wife?" His voice became hoarse with anger. "My wife promised me babies, that was our deal. My wife got the big house, the fancy clothes, the jewelry, and what did I get? Where are those beautiful babies we were going to make? All I've got here is a house full of animals. My wife should stick with the dogs, because she's not suited to be any man's wife."

Then one night, he did not come home at all, nor did he show up at the restaurant the next day or at home the following night. Catrina told the folks at the Blue Moon that Walter was sick. She tried convincing herself that he was probably out with a business associate and couldn't get home. *People don't disappear into thin air,* she told herself. But she knew better. That's exactly what they did. They died. They moved to Chicago. Who cared where they went, they were gone. She wanted to leave Kiefer out of this and called the local police station instead. The cop who came took out a pad and asked her a series of questions: "Does he often stay out late at night?" "Does he like to drink?" "Can you give me a list of all of his friends and their phone numbers?"

She laughed at that one. "You don't have enough room in your notebook for all of them," she said.

When he snapped his pad shut, he gave Catrina a wary smile. "I wouldn't concern myself too much with it, ma'am; he's probably sleeping it off somewhere."

But after a few more days, when Walter still didn't show up, Catrina called Kiefer. "Okay, Mr. Detective, I'm sure it's nothing, but . . ." She tried to sound jaunty.

"Sure thing, I'll look into it," he promised. Her heart stopped when she heard the worry in his voice.

At the Blue Moon, people acted as if Walter had never existed. When Kiefer asked Tony the bartender what Walter did in his off hours, Tony put down the drink he was preparing and leaned across the bar. "Are you a cop or something?"

"I am," said Kiefer. "But I'm also Catrina's brother. So this is personal."

Tony's face softened. "I'm sorry. Catrina's a fine lady. Anything I can do to help?"

"Yeah, tell me anything you see or hear that sounds out of the ordinary or pertains to Walter, even if it seems beside the point."

A few nights later, Kiefer came back to the bar around midnight. "Got anything for me?" he asked Tony.

Tony looked around before answering. "Let's just say I don't think Walter's friends are too happy with him right now. Please, give my best to the missus."

For the next week, Kiefer checked the missing persons reports and found no hint of Walter. Catrina's calls to him became more frequent. "I'm working all ends," he reassured her. "I'm sure he'll show up soon enough."

Another week went by before a call came into a precinct in the Bronx from a chimney sweep who'd gone to clean the flue at a large apartment building and found a corpse in the chimney; the rope was still around the torso. When Kiefer got word of the unidentified body, he went up to the Bronx morgue to examine it. It had a head of thick, shiny black hair and was wearing a jacket with a Cuban cigar in the inside pocket.

Kiefer called Catrina. "I think we found him," he said in a professionally calm voice. "I'm afraid the news is not good."

Catrina fell into the nearest chair and covered her mouth so as not to scream. Kiefer kept talking, and though she heard his words, none of them made sense. "It looks like a murder. We can't be sure until we do some tests. Unfortunately, we can't do any tests until you identify the body. I'll send a car for you. We're at the chief medical examiner's office on Worth Street. I'm sorry, Catrina. I know this is hard. Whatever you need, I'm here."

She remembered the strange noises her mother would make when she'd sit alone in the kitchen after her father left. The sounds that came from her sounded like those. Although Walter had been cruel to her lately, there had been happy times and promises of more to come. He was her life and security and now he was gone. She wept for the losses — for her father, for James. But mostly she wept for who she'd become: a childless, used-up woman who, like her mother, would pay the price for her bad choices.

Kiefer and Rose tried to be comforting and swallowed their *I told you so*'s, but their suspicions about Walter were confirmed when it turned out that the brownstone in Washington Heights was all he'd had in his own name.

Several weeks after he died, Catrina went back to the Blue Moon. She walked in tentatively, wearing a long skirt with a brocade cape, not one of the revealing dresses she usually wore there. She waved at Tony the bartender, who floated his dishrag in the air and said, "So nice to see you, Mrs. B." But when it became clear that he wasn't going to invite her to have a drink, and no one was going to ask her to sit at their table, she decided to go home. About a month later, a new owner took over the restaurant, a former banker from Westchester. He did away with the dancing girls, the opulent menu, and the ornate banquettes and changed the name of the place to Child's.

At home, Catrina removed all traces of Walter. She sold most of his possessions, though not the grand piano. She packed up the cocktail dresses and evening gowns she couldn't imagine she'd ever wear again and donated them to the Red Cross. She kept the silver fox, not because she had use for it but as proof to herself that she'd once been a girl with a reason to wear a silver fox. She figured that her time with men was finished. Between James and Walter they'd used up her sex and her body and exhausted her spirit. She felt older than her twenty-four years. The parts of her where a baby might have nested felt hard and cold. She'd never questioned whether or not she'd have a child; it was a matter of when. She'd hoped it would be with James, though had there been one with Walter, maybe the marriage would not have faltered. Although she'd long ago given up her belief in the church and its retributions, she couldn't help feeling that being barren was her punishment for the life she'd led.

With Catrina on her own, Rose came around more often, though never without offering a reminder of how right she'd been about Walter. "He thought by dressing you in fancy clothes he would make you into someone more appropriate for who he was. But all the fur coats in China couldn't erase the fact that you are the daughter of Rose and Ryan Walsh from County Mayo."

Catrina let her mother think what she wanted about Walter. She never admitted to her inability to have children, figuring it was too cruel a thing to tell someone who had lost two of her own. "One thing has changed," said Catrina the third time Rose brought it up. "I have this big house now. You don't have to live in that tiny apartment anymore. You could come live with me. You'd have the whole second floor to yourself. I know you'll say no, but think about it before you do."

Rose bristled. "I don't belong up here. I've lived so long in that tiny apartment. You can't uproot an old tree just like that."

"Even if I rent out the other floors, this place is too big for me. Besides, for better or worse, you and I know how to live together. And this time we wouldn't be living on top of each other. I'd like it if you came to live here."

Rose looked away from her daughter, embarrassed by how moved she was by Catrina's words. "I'm not promising I'll stay, but I suppose we could try it for a while."

"It's you and me again," said Catrina.

"Thank God."

Rose laughed. "You may thank God, but frankly, I'm going to ask him to help us."

Catrina changed her name back to Catrina Harty and returned to her old job at the ASPCA, where the strays bounded to her, and Iris and Susanna embraced her as if she'd never left. Even the familiar smell of shit felt like a homecoming. At night, she slept with Sasha curled in the crook of her arm, Spooky on the other side of her, and the beagle and terrier by her feet. One evening, as she and the girls were cleaning up to go home, she overheard Iris singing "But Not for Me." Her voice was girlish and not the least bit mournful as she sang about the memory of his kiss and clouds of gray. Catrina knew Iris was a spinster in her late thirties and had had one serious romance. "Do you ever miss the company of men?" she asked.

Iris ran her hand through her hair, and Catrina could see the beginnings of gray at her roots. "I used to think it was sad, being one of those women who thought of animals as their children," she said. "But now I come home late at night. I make myself a cheese sandwich. I sit on the couch and read a magazine with a dog's head in my lap. No one asks anything of me. It's quiet.

It's not a bad life, really it isn't."

So that's how it would be, Catrina thought. She wondered what her father would have to say about his Catrina Ballerina: an old maid covered in dog hair.

Catrina and Rose fell back into their old routines. Catrina would stop by the A&P on Fort Washington Avenue on her way home from work. She'd pick up whatever meat was on sale that day and a can of peas or wax beans. On Friday nights, Kiefer would come for dinner often with a bottle of wine. They'd roast a chicken and some potatoes and talk about their lives as if Walter Bianco had never happened.

On a rainy Thursday afternoon in April 1939, Catrina realized there was no food for lunch. The A&P was four blocks away, so she decided to dash out to Art's Grocery Store, which was slightly more expensive but only two blocks away.

"May I have a half pound of Swiss cheese and a quarter pound of ham, please?" she asked the man behind the counter.

"Perhaps you would like to try a slice of our American cheese," said the man.

"I'm sorry? I asked for Swiss cheese."

"I understand that, madam, but perhaps you would like to try a slice of our American cheese. Free, compliments of Art's."

"No thank you, I've come for Swiss cheese and I'll pay for Swiss cheese."

"Of course."

The man hunched over the slicing machine as he prepared the Swiss. His hands were thin and knotty. He was attractive despite his messy apron and formal way of speaking.

When she came back to the store later that week, she bought a can of peas and a loaf of bread and watched him from afar. He was older, probably Walter's age. He was polite to the customers yet seemed distant. If it was possible that blue eyes could fade, then his had.

She didn't think about him for the next week, though every now and again the image of his black hair and light blue eyes would scrape her memory. It had been nearly five years since Walter, and she'd not given much thought to men. Older men in particular.

So when she returned a few days later, she told herself that she only needed a few things and Art's was more convenient.

"Hello again," said the man. "I would offer you some cheese, but I know you will refuse it."

Catrina patted her hair and looked away

from his eyes. "Sir, do I look to you like someone who needs a handout?"

"Not at all, madam, but it's the policy of the store. And please, I am no sir." He pointed to the name tag affixed to his apron. "My name is Egon Schneider."

11.

Because the apron absorbed the mustard and bloodstains, Egon was able to wear the same shirt and pants several days in a row.

He worked behind the delicatessen counter in the back of Art's Grocery Store on the corner of 187th Street and Overlook Terrace in Washington Heights. The store was long and narrow. There was sawdust on the wood-planked floors and about two feet between the gray cement wall and the refrigerated case filled with white and yellow cheeses and cold meats. Egon was one of four employees: a cashier, a stock boy, Art, and himself. The other three were Americans. Short and round and the color of liverwurst, Art Able, in his late forties, was the oldest by far. He told Egon that he'd hired him because he was a doctor. "We could use some brains around here," he'd said when Egon told him his profession. "Also, it doesn't hurt that you speak

169

German, with all these refugees swooping in."

Art had taught him the English words for ham, salami, bologna, turkey, roast beef, cream cheese, Swiss cheese, and American cheese, then handed him an apron that tied around his neck and waist. "This one's for free. Keep it clean. Lose it or mess it up? There goes a buck fifty out of your paycheck." He showed Egon how to use the slicing machine and the way to wrap meat or cheese in brown paper, folding it around the edges as if wrapping a gift. "You don't need to say much; 'Thank you' and 'How may I help you?' will do. Oh, and the men like to be called 'sir' and the women 'madam.' It makes them feel important. Be friendly, but don't talk too much, and don't bring up any of that stuff that's going on over there. You're here to sell meat, not teach world politics."

Egon considered the fact that he'd gotten this job six weeks after arriving in America to be a miracle.

It wasn't the only one.

There was a fan in the back of the store that blew hot air on him, but at least it was air.

When Art wasn't looking, he sliced pieces of bologna or cheese and shoved them into his mouth. Sometimes it was all he ate in a day.

The sawdust made standing for eleven hours easier on his back.

Carola and Max had come to America four months earlier and gotten an apartment ten blocks up from Art's. Egon spent his first months in New York sleeping on their pullout sofa. From their living room window, he looked out onto Our Lady Queen of Martyrs parochial school. There was a statue of the Virgin Mary in a niche above the entry. A shawl was draped over her head and body, and pigeons took refuge on her outspread arms. He stared at her finely honed face and downcast eyes, certain that, though he was not a Catholic, she would shelter him as she did the birds. When he couldn't sleep, he'd whisper to the dark, "I am alive and in America." These were the things Egon Schneider was grateful for in the summer of 1938. He recited this litany to himself. It became his prayer of hope, his lifeline from the outer edges of despair: the apron, the fan, the free cheese, the sawdust, the job, the statue of Mary. He was alive.

When a customer asked for turkey, he answered as slowly and clearly as possible, "How much of this would you like?"

"What?"

"How much of this would you like, sir?"

His *h*'s stuck to the back of his tongue and his *th*'s hissed. His *w*'s slipped out as *v*'s.

"Can't you speak English?"

"I try, sir."

He'd learned some English in school, but none of it came back to him at times like these.

He used hand motions.

Some made sour-milk faces, others cursed: "Go back to where you came from."

At those times, he reminded himself of the apron, the fan . . .

In the mornings, before the customers came, he unpacked boxes, stocked the shelves, and stamped prices on the dry goods.

. . . the free cheese . . . .

At night, when the store closed, he swept the floor and emptied the garbage. He rummaged through the rotten tomatoes and broken eggs until he found stale rolls and cracker remnants and collected them in a bag.

. . . the sawdust, the job, the statue of the Virgin Mary.

By the time he got home, Carola and Max were usually asleep, so he undressed in the hall, folded his clothes and left them at the foot of the pullout sofa, then got under the covers and lay in the dark waiting to fall into a bothered sleep. Always an early riser, he awoke at five thirty, before Carola and Max. He showered and brushed his teeth, made his bed, and boiled water for tea. He was conscious of not eating their food, knowing that they, like he, lived on a crimped budget, so he'd eat one of the rolls he'd bagged the night before, then head off to Fort Tryon Park, where he'd sit on a bench (none of them yellow) and scatter the crumbs from the previous night's scavenging on the ground. He never figured out where the pigeons came from or how they knew, but within moments there would be a horde of them at his feet, waddling like old men, cocking their heads and *bru-u-ooo*ing as they gobbled up breakfast. Egon found them drab and inelegant, nothing like the sleek warblers and mottled woodcocks in the Stadtwald, but then again, perhaps buried inside them was the link to something grander.

Every Sunday afternoon at four, he would meet Meyer at Nash's Bakery uptown on Dyckman Street. Sometimes Max and Carola joined them, but on this gusty fall afternoon it was the two of them. At Nash's they ordered éclairs and *Linzertorten*. The small wicker chairs and round marble-topped tables reminded them of the *kaffeehäuser* back home, and, because most of the customers and all of the waiters were German Jews, they could speak German without feeling self-conscious.

Washington Heights was filled with German Jews, most of them from the smaller cities in Germany, particularly Frankfurt, because they'd heard that this fifty-block aerie at the tip of Manhattan had a new park with winding paths and, beneath it, a sweep of the Hudson River. It was as similar to the Stadtwald and Main River as they were likely to find in America. In truth, they found little of the gentility of home. The streets were lined with red and white brick apartment buildings, none of them higher than six stories. While many had fashionable art deco–style mirrors and tiled floors in their lobbies, most were walk-ups with small rooms and low ceilings. The three main shopping streets were wide but littered with newspapers and candy wrappers, and streams of people crowded the sidewalks. There were so many automobiles that Egon felt he was taking his life in his hands every time he stepped off the curb.

Meyer had been in New York for a year and was eager to try out his Americanisms on Egon. "So how's the tricks?" he asked Egon as they sipped their coffee.

"If you mean how am I doing at the grocery store," said Egon in German, "then the answer is not so good." He talked about the long hours, about how Art was always watching him, and about the customers, some of them so rude and cruel. "They use words like *Kraut* and tell me to go back where I came from. It scares me, like it is happening all over again." He told Meyer that no matter how many Tums he took, his stomach always burned. "I have become so bashful in the past four months that I cannot even look people in the eye anymore. Think of it, looking in people's eyes was my job. Now I keep my head down and wait to be spoken to. Sometimes I feel as if I am becoming invisible."

"That's how it is with horses," said Meyer. "When we would have a new horse on the farm, at first you could never look it straight in the eye. They're nervous animals, and if you stare right at them, they see it as a sign that you will hurt them. Once they trust you, they're completely friendly and affectionate. You'll see, these people have to get to know you."

"That is very nice of you to say," said Egon. "And so unlike you, Meyer. Are you feeling sorry for your old friend?"

"Ha," said Meyer as he slapped whipped cream onto his éclair. "Why should I feel sorry for you? At least you get to work inside all day."

For $1.10 an hour, Meyer walked up and down Seventh Avenue between Thirty-Fourth Street and Thirty-Fifth Street, wearing a sandwich board advertising Kallen's, a clothing shop for men. When people asked what he did for a living, the author of *The Pale Princess of Prussia* would answer, "I am fortunate to remain in the print business."

Egon studied his friend's wild hair and jumpy brown eyes and saw the same eager boy he'd met in Berlin nearly twenty years earlier. Here he was, one of Germany's most promising young writers, trudging up and down the street hawking men's suits. How could that be?

Egon put his elbow on the table and rested his chin on his fist. "We're like fledglings fallen from our nests onto the cold pavement."

"Oh, for God's sake," Meyer snapped. "We're the lucky ones. May I remind you that in gay old Deutschland, those thugs are beating up Jews on the street and burning down synagogues? We got out in time. Would you really rather be *Doktor* Schneider working in your tidy Frankfurt office waiting for the knock on the door? Look at us. Here we sit in a bakery shop in New York City eating our favorite desserts. It could be worse. Well, it was worse a moment ago, when you talked about the fledglings falling out of their nests. Please, from now on leave the metaphor-making to me."

Embarrassed, Egon stared down at the cake he had dunked into his coffee. "I admire you, I really do. Of all of us, you probably have the worst job, yet you manage to remain so kind and upbeat," he said, trying to sound ironic. "Tell me, how do you do that?"

"*Ach,* Egon," said Meyer, sliding his chair closer to his friend. "You are amusing when you try to be sarcastic, but I must give you credit for trying. If you really want to know the secret of my unique personality, I'll tell you."

Sparring with Meyer was one of the few things that still felt normal to Egon. "Of course; I'd give my eyeteeth to know what makes Meyer Leavitt tick," he answered with mock enthusiasm.

"For one thing, I never thought I'd make

it this far. I don't mean to America, I mean in life. I come from a family of farmers, and the fact that I'm not a farmer means I've already exceeded my highest expectations. The rest of my family, they're so caught up in their lives over there that no matter how many times I beg them, they won't even consider leaving," said Meyer, shaking his head. "I've written a book, and I intend to write more books. These crappy jobs we have and the shitholes we live in, this won't go on. Take yourself out of our little world and out of 1938. Look five and ten years down the road. In five years, we qualify for American citizenship. Will you be working in a grocery store? Will I be walking up and down Seventh Avenue selling men's pants? Will Max still be selling wrenches in a hardware store? You bet your boots we won't. Even if you want it to, life doesn't stand still. So imagine what happens when you will change and work hard. We were successful in Germany and we'll be success-ful here. I'm not going to stop writing; you're not going to stop being a doctor because some maniac kicked us in the nuts. Now we get up and we begin again." He raised his left eyebrow to let Egon know he was finished.

How like Meyer to turn friendly repartee

into serious exposition. Yet Egon inhaled his friend's determination, felt buoyed by it. He was the one who suggested they walk the fourteen blocks back down to Meyer's new apartment on 186th Street.

As was typical for this time in late November, the sun set at four thirty, and the air smelled of rotting leaves. A raw chill whipped off the Hudson, and Egon blew into his hands to warm them. "Overcoat season, eh?"

"So begin the meager days," Meyer said. "The sun is thin and the city turns a grimy gray. The cold can be punishing, and you feel as if you'll never see green or be warm again. And then comes spring, which, if you believed in God, you'd swear was his atonement for winter. It's like a miracle, you'll see."

But Egon had trouble seeing beyond the dread of tomorrow. He'd become one of those people who hung a calendar on his wall and made pencil slashes through each day as he finished it. Sunday afternoons were the worst. That's when the image of Art's pudgy face would start to hover and the odor of meat would fill his sinuses. He tried to push back fears of what was happening back home and the terrifying possibility of it happening here, and the words

179

of his litany became meaningless. By the time they reached Meyer's apartment, he felt the familiar burning in his stomach.

They stood in the foyer as Meyer searched for his keys. The hall smelled moldy. Except for the splints of light from under the neighboring doors, it was dark. When Meyer finally did unlock his door, he switched on the overhead light and shouted triumphantly, "Home sweet home!"

The apartment was the size of their dormitory room in Berlin, and about as handsomely furnished, with a bed, two folding chairs, and a metal card table. In the corner was a small icebox; next to it, a food-stained stove and an overhead shelf that held two plates, two glasses, and an eggcup. There were no pictures on the wall, no rugs on the floor, only a tower of books beside the unmade bed. The grimy window above the kitchen sink looked as if it hadn't been opened in years, and the place smelled of stale cigarette smoke.

"Your asthma, it is all right here?"

"As long as there are no cats, I breathe perfectly," said Meyer.

Egon offered a thin smile and leaned against the dim white wall, his arms folded in front of him. An ambulance was passing, and he held his hands to his ears, still unaccustomed to the insistent sound of it.

"How do you do it, Meyer?" he asked when the awful sound stopped. "I mean, really, how do you do it?"

Meyer took off his jacket and hung it behind the door.

"I do it because I have to do it." He shrugged. "Really, Egon, what choice do we fledglings have?"

Meyer was right about the New York winter: It was angry and merciless. Trees shed their bark, birds hid in their hollows. People bent against the wind as if fighting a crowd, and the sky seemed always to be the nameless color of phlegm. Only the brick buildings stood resolute, impervious to the snow and bluster.

Egon had been living in his own apartment on Bennett Avenue since the end of August. It was a one-bedroom on the sixth floor of a typical six-story building, though this one had an elevator. The kitchen had a partition that created a separate eating area, and if he stood at a particular angle and looked north through the living room window, he could see the edge of Fort Tryon Park and a slice of the Hudson River. He would stand at that window with his binoculars and watch the birds. Out of habit, he wrote down the names of the ones he recognized and sketched the ones that sat still long enough to be captured. He hung his mother's framed pictures on the bedroom walls. The rest of his furniture consisted of four folding chairs, a green velvet armchair that someone had put out in the trash, and a used oak desk, on which he placed his parents' books and his mother's gold pocket watch. He rested the brass plate with *Doktor Egon Schneider* engraved on it against the telephone. It felt good to put out the little things that used to shine. In the back of his dresser drawer he kept the artificial eye.

Though the building's incinerator was in the basement, seven stories below him, he had to open all the windows when he came home each night to air out the smell of burning garbage. The radiators never spit up enough heat, so at night he wore a sweater over his pajamas and covered himself with a quilt and two blankets. Even then he had trouble getting warm. At the grocery store, the door was always swinging open and shut; the cold inside was almost as relentless as it was outside. By mid-January, the streets were covered with snow, and customers tracked in gray footprints, turning the sawdust into mush. Egon wore a jacket over his shirt and slipped on gloves when he wasn't helping customers. The tips of his fingers were always white and bloodless.

Determined not to give in to winter, Egon kept up his morning routine of feeding the pigeons in Fort Tryon Park. The only other people there were those walking dogs. Occasionally he threw a stick for a Dalmatian or stopped to pet a schnauzer, but mostly he kept to himself. He always sat on the same bench overlooking the river, and even before he poured out the crumbs, the birds would gather as if they were expecting him.

On one frigid morning in January, he didn't linger. As soon as he finished, he crumpled the bag, threw it in the trash, and headed up the hill. Ahead of him, obscured by a clump of holly bushes, he heard a dog howl and a woman scream: "Speedy! Stop, Speedy! Oh, Christ." He ran and caught up with the woman, who had reached the animal and picked him up; a Chihuahua, he guessed, with a pointy rat face and blood streaming from his left eye.

"Stupid squirrel!" she said to Egon. "I tell him, 'Don't chase the damn things,' but does he listen? Never. Now look. He finally catches one and the SOB rips his eye out. My poor baby." For a little dog, Speedy was making sounds as long and low as a bull in heat.

Egon hesitated for a moment. "I am a doctor," he said. "The eye is my area of specialization. Perhaps I can help you."

Ophthalmology was one of the few medical disciplines that applied to animals as well as to humans, and in Frankfurt, Egon had successfully treated a few of his patients' dogs. He suspected that Speedy might have a scratched cornea, which would need to be cleaned up as soon as possible so infection didn't set in.

"Yeah, sure, a doctor," said the woman. "It's gonna cost me a small fortune, isn't it?"

"It will cost you nothing, madam."

"Well, if you're kidding, this sure is a bad time for a joke, 'cause I gotta tell you, I got nothing. Me and Speedy, that's it." Her nose ran and mascara zigzagged down her cheeks. Egon wasn't sure who was the sorrier sight, she or Speedy.

"I can assure you, I am serious. Come."

"What've I got to lose?" she said, sizing up Egon. With the bleating dog in her arms, she followed him until they came to his building. By then, he had figured out how to explain to Art why he was late. "A small boy was injured and bleeding, and I was able to treat him." Not a complete lie. Speedy was small and male. So what if he was a Chihuahua?

He told the woman to have a seat at the dinette table and took Speedy into the bathroom. With a towel soaked in warm water, he tried to dab at the black swirls of blood under the dog's eye. Speedy bared his teeth and kicked his scrawny legs. Egon picked him up, sat on the toilet seat, and placed the dog on his lap. "Of course you are scared," he said. "I would be too." He rubbed the animal's stomach and started to sing *"Hänschen Klein,"* a song about Little Johnny, a boy who leaves home but comes back because his mother is so heartbroken. Speedy splayed his legs and relaxed into Egon like a chicken waiting to be stuffed. Egon cleaned the wound, then shone a light into the dog's eye. The light didn't bother him. No corneal damage. A relief. The squirrel had missed its mark by a hairsbreadth. Egon kissed Speedy's belly and whispered in German, "You are a lucky dog." Egon felt lighter than he had since he'd come to America. For once he was visited by happy memories: his father's sweet voice when he talked to the animals, sitting and drawing with his mother in the Stadtwald.

Somehow, the dog's good fortune seemed to portend his own. He spied a bottle of Kreml Hair Tonic in the medicine chest, which he'd bought at half price when he first started working at the grocery store. The Kreml was a luxury he used sparingly. Now he poured a generous gob into his hands and rubbed it through Speedy's mussed coat until it was shiny. He tucked him under his arm and opened the bathroom door.

The woman was still at the table. She'd combed her hair and put on lipstick. The mascara tracks were gone. "He is fine," said Egon, hoisting Speedy like a trophy. She snatched the dog and held him to her breast. She called him Speedo, Speedling, Sweetie Dog, and Speedattle, and told him he was a beautiful boy. She rubbed her nose in his neck. "You smell good too." Only then did she seem to remember that Egon was also in the room. "You saved his life. I must owe you something."

"Nothing, you owe me nothing."

"I don't understand." She shrugged.

He raised his hands as if in surrender.

"Well, I'll tell you this," she said. "You sure do give refugees a good name. There must be something I can do for you."

That word again. He'd come to despise it.

Refugee. It sounded like something used up and thrown away. It even looked ugly when he read it in the newspaper. *Re-fug-ee. Re-fuse.* Forbid. *Ref-use.* Worthless.

But the woman had offered a favor, and he would not *re-fuse* it.

"Yes, there is something you can do." He spoke tentatively. "I am a doctor. Maybe tell your friends in the neighborhood they can bring their animals to me." He took a piece of paper and printed his address and phone number under his name: *Dr. Egon Schneider.* It was the first time he'd written those words in more than six months. He knew he was taking a risk, but he would only take in neighborhood animals.

In Frankfurt, he really was Dr. Schneider. In this country, where his license and medical degree were not recognized, they were a deception. But at this moment, Speedy and his owner gave life to the old reality. The woman studied the paper. "Hmm, Dr. Schneider. Okay, I'll do that. Lotsa luck."

Meyer might be right, he thought. He wouldn't work in the grocery store forever. In five years, he would become a citizen. Maybe it was possible that he might practice medicine again, maybe this time, veterinary medicine. He would find out what was required to get his license. If he could afford it, maybe he'd take some night classes.

He started to accumulate books: some in English, a few in German: *Veterinary Practice; A System of Veterinary Medicine; An Illustrated Guide to Canine Pathology.* Using his American dictionary, he eked out the basics. The illustrations were so poor, nothing like the precise details of his mother's drawings.

The first call came two weeks later, on a Thursday night. Cat, hit by a car, broken leg. Then dog, shot with a child's BB gun, four stitches. Another: hamster with red lumps on its backside; rabbit, scratched bloody. Egon came home from the store one night to find a large brown bag at his door. Inside was an emaciated mongrel, an older dog. His white fur was filthy and matted, and he was missing a chunk of his right ear. Worse, he smelled like rotting pumpkin. Egon washed the dog and clipped his fur. He fed him rice and, in the days to come, scraps of salami and ham from the store. At first the dog seized up when Egon tried to pet him. He'd take his food from the bowl, hide it in a closet or under a piece of furniture, and eat only when Egon was out of sight. He slept in an old carton lined with a blanket at the foot of Egon's bed. Egon named him Johnny, after the boy in the song, but when he called, "Johnny, come," the dog backed away.

With time came trust. After several weeks, Johnny ate out of Egon's hand and slept in his bed with his head on Egon's leg. Egon figured Johnny was around ten or eleven, but he looked like a puppy. There was a slight ridge on the top of his head, which Egon would rub: "We stick together, eh?" He started practicing his Americanisms on Johnny. Hands on hips, he would say, "I will teach that so-and-so a thing or two." Or he'd put to words feelings he couldn't admit to anyone else: "I have an aloneness I could not imagine." No matter if Egon bent his *o*'s or mixed his tenses, Johnny looked up at him and thumped his tail against the floor. Egon determined that Johnny was part bulldog and part poodle, and it was Johnny who reminded him that animals don't care where you come from. Love them well and they love you back. It was as simple as that, even in America.

Art had many theories about the retail grocery business. In February he told Egon that when women or children came to the counter, he should offer them a free piece of American cheese. "Make it an end piece. Slice it as thin as you can. People get stuff for free, they think everything here's a bargain." In March he gave Egon a button to pin on his apron with THE CHEESE MAN in big capital letters, and his first name beneath it. "It becomes personal. They think they know you. Their children see you as a friend." Art laughed. "I like it."

The button invited new humiliation. He had always hated his name. *Ee-gon.* It sounded like a cricket's call, or the last sound a person might make after falling down a flight of stairs. In America, no one could pronounce it. *Eh-gong? What kind of name is that? Egg-on?* Immediately, it branded him as a foreigner. *A-gong?* It made coming to work each day even more onerous. Meyer didn't help. "The Cheese Man, that's wonderful," he said, imitating Egon's broken English: " 'Please, you should take a free slice of this, Ms. Fitzenheimer. Certainly, Ms. Blahblahfeld, for you a fat and juicy piece of roast beef.' "

Weeks earlier, Egon had been waiting for a subway train when he noticed a pigeon trapped inside the station, trying to find its way out. The sound of its aimless flapping echoed through the tunnel. Egon knew the bird would never get out, and it made him want to weep. He felt like that bird every morning when he put on the button and stood behind the counter. But unlike most of Art's theories, this one worked.

12.

Egon thought about that woman with the
red hair. There was something about her
impudence, and the way she said his name
without mispronouncing it. He promised
himself that if she came in again, he would
talk to her about something other than
cheese.

On the first Thursday in May, she showed
up this time with a German shepherd seated
atop a red wagon.

"How are you, Egon?" she asked, squint-
ing at his button.

"I am fine, and how are you?"

"Fine, thank you. And while I don't have
a name tag, I'm Catrina Harty."

"How nice to meet you, Catrina Harty."
She wore a tan cape and was neither graceful nor slim. Her red hair was windblown
and fell dramatically against her dove-white
skin. "What can I do for you today?"

"A half pound of ham, please."

"And who might this be?" he said, looking down at the dog.

"This is Sasha."

"I know something about dogs," said Egon, slicing a piece of American cheese. "You will not turn down my offer, will you, Sasha?" he said, stepping around the counter and kneeling to give the dog the cheese.

"Do you have a dog?"

"I do. His name is Johnny. But I also work with animals."

"I do too."

Egon glanced around and saw that Art was standing nearby in canned goods. Art frowned on conversing with the customers. "A polite give-and-take is one thing," he'd said many times. "Any more than that, you do on your own time."

Egon got up and went back behind the counter. He ran his hands down the side of his apron before slicing up the ham and wrapping it in brown paper. With Meyer's imitation of him still fresh in his memory, he crafted his words carefully: "I hope you will not think it too forward of me, but we could perhaps have a cup of coffee one night after I leave here." He looked over at Art. "Here it is hard to talk, and I think maybe we have much to say to each other."

Sasha sat staring at Egon, her tongue

193

hanging out. He quickly cut off another piece of cheese and gave it to Catrina. "If such a thing can be considered a bribe, then please give this to Sasha with all my good intentions."

Catrina smiled. He'd never seen her smile before. It was as if someone had lifted the shades and let in sunlight. "Why not?" she said.

"Tomorrow, then," he said under his breath. "Eight o'clock at Nash's Bakery on Dyckman Street? I hope that is okay for you." And then, in a voice loud enough to carry to canned goods: "Will there be anything else, madam?"

"Not at this moment," she said before turning on her heels and heading toward the cash register.

The next morning, he studied his face in the mirror. He hadn't noticed the new currents of gray running through his black hair. The jawline was still strong and angular, but those lines under his eyes and the parentheses around his mouth, when had they gotten so pronounced? Did he look older than his thirty-seven years? The ladies of Frankfurt used to say that his blue eyes were the kind a woman could fall into. Was this still true? At home, he had taken his looks and status for granted. Now he wondered how a man could explain to a woman who he once was without sounding vain or pathetic. He slipped the glass eye into his pocket. It wouldn't help, but it would be there.

He arrived at Nash's promptly at eight. Catrina was already settled at a table in the back corner. She stood up and he gave a slight bow. "Nice to see you," he said, aware of how formal his gesture and his speech must seem. "Nice to see you too," she said. She was wearing a black cardigan and a gray skirt that fell way below her knees. They sat down and the waiter brought them a menu. He could see her moving her lips as she read it. She looked up at him and shook her head. "I don't know what any of these things are."

Of course she didn't. They were all German pastries. What a mistake it was to bring her here, where all the waiters had accents like his. *Idiot,* he thought, *do not let her see how embarrassed you are.*

"Do you like chocolate?" he asked.

"I do."

"And peaches?"

"I do."

"Then, if I may, I will choose something for you."

He ordered in English, then asked Catrina

195

to tell him about her work with animals.

"I work with the strays at the ASPCA."

"The ASPCA is an organization for animals?" he asked.

Catrina smiled. "Something like that. It's the American Society for the Prevention of Cruelty to Animals, though I'm afraid my job there borders on cruelty."

"I do not understand," said Egon.

Catrina explained how she readied the animals for their deaths, and how she and Iris and Susanna tried to save as many as they could. "It's heartbreaking, and I come home every night smelling like shit — pardon my French. But I love them. Everything I don't like about people, I like about dogs. There's nothing dishonest about them. They're grateful for your attention. Slobbery, but grateful. I don't like slobbery in people" — she smiled — "but I love it in my strays. I take some in, but it's never . . ." She stopped midsentence. "I suppose this isn't the kind of conversation you want to be having over coffee and cake."

"No, on the contrary, this is the conversation I most enjoy." He started to tell her about Speedy when the waiter came with coffee and a piece of chocolate peach cake for each of them. Catrina took a bite and then another. She let the cake sit in her mouth for a while before swallowing. "I don't mean to interrupt you," she said, "but this cake! I used to work in a fancy restaurant downtown, the Blue Moon. Have you heard of it?"

"No, I have been here a short time only."

"Well, in my time at the restaurant, I tasted every delicacy you can imagine — caviar, foie gras, lobster Newburg, crème vichyssoise — but I have never tasted anything this delicious." She took small forkfuls and chewed slowly, sometimes with her mouth open. In Germany, this would have been considered bad table manners. But now, the eagerness with which she ate seemed delightful. When she finished, he asked if she'd like another piece.

"I certainly wouldn't turn it away."

He continued to tell her about Speedy and how he'd been treating animals at his apartment on weekends. "It seems I am easier with animals than with the people. My dog, Johnny, he is also a stray."

Catrina put down her fork. "I guess you could say I'm a stray myself. I've been widowed twice, and my father left when I was seven." She nodded slightly as if she'd suddenly resolved something within herself.

She was beautiful. Such an intelligent face. That skin and exuberant hair. But mostly it was her eyes that drew him in. They were amber, the rarest of colors. In all his years as an ophthalmologist, he'd never seen eyes this color. "I suppose in this country, I am a stray too," he said. "Not, how you say, a sloppery one, I hope."

Catrina laughed. "There's nothing slobbery about you."

"Thank you, that is very kind. I am from Germany; maybe this is obvious to you from the way I speak. In Germany I was an ophthalmologist. I loved my work. Because I have no license to practice here, now I am in the grocery store, but I do not intend to be the Cheese Man forever."

"Is there anything you would like to be forever?" she asked, licking a piece of chocolate off her hand.

He thought about his office in Frankfurt and what it was like to be unafraid. "Yes, to be who I was before . . . all this. And you? Is there something you would like to be forever?"

Egon knew he'd pronounced "something" *some-sing*. Those damn *th*'s. He repeated the question slowly, making sure that the tip of his tongue curled around his front teeth ". . . *something* you'd like to be forever?"

Catrina closed her eyes. "Many things."

"Such as?"

"Oh my, such a question." She swallowed the last of her cake and gulped down some coffee. "That's a conversation for another time. Right now, I'd like to be home. It's late and I have to be at work early tomorrow. Thank you for introducing me to your chocolate peach cake." She took her wallet from her purse. "How much do I owe you?"

"Do I look to you like someone who needs a handout?" He caught the waiter's eye and asked for the check.

Catrina crossed her arms. "I meant no offense. Where I come from, we never assume anyone will pay for anything."

"Where I come from, when a man and woman go for a cup of coffee, it is unheard of for the woman to pay anything." Egon thought he sounded sterner than he'd meant to.

"Then I'd rather come from where you come from," she said with a laugh.

"No, you would not." Again, he heard the harshness in his voice. It was difficult enough translating words from German to English. To also have to worry about how you sounded when you said them was too much to think about. Catrina's speech had a cadence to it that he found pleasing. Meyer had a sense of timing and a way of saying things that made people laugh. Egon thought his own voice was dull and heavy.

"Well, thank you," said Catrina, after he paid. "I've enjoyed talking with you."

"And you. Such sympathetic conversation one does not find often."

Catrina said nothing. She stood up and brushed the crumbs from her skirt. They walked outside, and in the light of the streetlamp he noticed that her lipstick had worn off, leaving only streaks of red in the places where her lips were dry. There was a crumb of chocolate on her bottom lip.

He started to put his finger to her mouth; she moved to take his hand. Neither of those things happened, but each saw the intention in the other. "Good night," she said, extending her hand for a handshake.

"Good night," he said, extending his. "Will I see you again?"

"No doubt. Sasha loves your American cheese."

13.

Young Liesl had come to Egon back in 1936 with crying eyes. She'd claimed that they were crying for what was happening in Germany, and she'd been the first person to tell him that they should get out as soon as possible. Now, three years later, in the spring of 1939, she was standing on the bow of a ship staring ahead at the water. If you kept your eyes fixed on the horizon, the ship's steward had told her, the nausea would subside. She glanced over at the young man a few feet away from her, long enough to see that his blue-eyed gaze was aligned with hers. In his cashmere coat, fine-twilled pants, and spectator shoes, he wore money well. Wealth and clothes were beside the point now, but she enjoyed drifting into the comfort of her old world.

The boat scaled a wave and landed with force in the lap of the ocean. The movement was lurching and the water hard as bones. Liesl felt the bottom of her stomach drop away before she vomited. Chunks of forgotten food, slippery pieces of beige and yellow, splattered all over her pearl necklace and gray silk blouse. The deep and sour taste stayed with her for the rest of the thirteen days it took her to cross the ocean to America. She wondered if this was the taste her father carried with him.

Months earlier, two members of the Gestapo had shown up at her father's bank, demanding to see "the Jew, Leopold Kessler." When he presented himself, they stood him on the head of the gold-inlaid eagle, the symbol of the bank, in the middle of the floor. The one who kept wiping his nose said, "Jews eat money like candy, don't they, Herr Kessler?" The tall one slapped him when he refused to answer. Then the one with the handkerchief in his hand repeated, "Jews eat money like candy, don't they, Herr Kessler?" He finally nodded. The sniffling one stuck his hand in his pocket, pulled out a wad of reichsmarks, and held them up to Leopold's face. "We have a treat for you. You can eat as much as you want, like candy." He crumpled the reichsmarks one by one and stuffed them into Leopold's mouth. "Chew," he demanded. "Feast on your beloved, worthless money." It went like that until they had made him swallow so much that he gagged and vomited on his shoes. They both moved aside. "No Jews will work for this bank, is that understood?" said the tall one. "Should you show your face here again, Herr Kessler, we won't be as kind to you as we were today." He pulled the handkerchief from Leopold's breast pocket and held it out. "Clean up this mess and get out."

Her father said he never lost the taste of vomit. He knew they should flee, go to America, but her mother said to leave behind her house, garden, and friends would be a knife to her heart. Her father argued, but not with do-or-die conviction. Liesl could see he was slipping. He'd always been fastidious about his appearance, but with no place to go and no work to do, he laid his hand-tailored suits aside and didn't worry whether his shirts were freshly pressed. He stopped clipping his beard and mustache. Untrimmed, hair crept over his lips like ants. Sometimes his wife would pick bread crumbs from his beard.

He was fifty-five, too old, he said, to start all over in a new country. But Liesl, their only child, was not. Her parents insisted, begged, and finally demanded that she leave, but she could not bring herself to abandon her father, not in this condition. Leaving was barely an option after November 9, 1938, when the Nazis burned down nine hundred synagogues and killed hundreds of Jews. But the Kesslers still had connections. In the three months it took for them to use them in order to find Liesl a sponsor and get her papers in order, she urged them to start gathering their own. "We will follow," they promised, "after you are settled."

They promised her many things. That in New York City she'd find the gentility of Frankfurt. That her sponsor, a former business associate of her father's, Flora Einson, would meet her at the boat. That she could stay with her close friend Carola and her husband, Max, in their beautiful apartment in the hills of Washington Heights. That people would recognize that she was a pretty girl from a well-to-do family and be generous to her, as they were at home. That luck had always been on her side and there was no reason to think it would leave now.

The sway of the sea apparently knew nothing of luck. Liesl's stomach heaved and her head swirled, causing her to hold on to the bulkheads when she walked from one side of her cabin to the other. Still, she had the presence of mind to wash her hair on the

204

morning of the landing. Having heard what happened to people arriving in America with lice or jaundice, she put on more lipstick, powder, and rouge than usual.

It took nearly two hours for her to clear inspection, only to wait another hour and a half for customs officers to go through her luggage. As she stood in line with the rest of the people whose last names began with *K,* an announcement came over the loud-speaker: "Liesl Kessler, identify yourself to the agent at Gate Five." Her legs were still wobbly, and her head was filled with the noises of the street. She worried that they had called her because her papers weren't in order, or because the doctor had heard something amiss with his stethoscope. She swallowed her dread. The announcement came three times before she found the nerve to come forward. She ran her fingers through her hair. *Remember, you are Leopold Kessler's daughter.*

She walked up to the agent and in her best English said, "Please, sir, I am Liesl Kessler." The customs official checked her passport. He looked at her picture and studied her face. "So you are," he said with an inappropriate smile. He pointed to a policeman wearing white gloves with a whistle around his neck who was directing

205

people through the crowd. "Tell him who you are." She found the officer and again presented her passport. "Please, I am Liesl Kessler."

He checked her papers, then held up his hand and led her to a street where automobiles were lined up. He blew his whistle and waved to a black man wearing a gray cap and navy jacket. "Hey bud, I've got your gal."

The man came forward, pressed a bill into the policeman's hand, and took Liesl's luggage. He led her to a cream-colored car with black trim and opened the back door. There sat a striking woman wearing an aubergine suit, her legs crossed at the ankles. The feather in her stylish hat picked up the color in her suit, as did her matching pumps. "You must be Liesl Kessler," she said in perfect German. "I'm Flora Einson. Welcome to America."

Liesl got into the backseat with Flora. The leather was soft and smelled rich. Flora's fingernails were blood red and perfectly manicured. Liesl touched her pearls and took her first easy breath in weeks. Flora said something to the driver in English, then told Liesl in German, "Today we'll take the scenic route."

They drove through a white tunnel and

turned left, heading to Thirty-Fourth Street. The driver stopped the car at Fifth Avenue, and Flora told Liesl to get out and look up. The Empire State Building. She'd seen it in photographs but never imagined any structure could be so tall. Even on her tiptoes, she couldn't see to the top. "How far does it go?" she asked Flora.

"Farther than any building in the world," Flora answered. "Come. We shall see more of New York." Back in the car, the driver turned up Park Avenue and slowed as they approached a commanding limestone and brick building with chrome-capped towers. "The Waldorf-Astoria Hotel," announced Flora. "The finest hotel there is."

Liesl nodded as if taking measure of the place for future reference.

They drove on. Flora asked Liesl about her father. Liesl told her about the incident at the bank and about how her father had been dismissed.

Flora shook her head. "They have to get out. What are they waiting for?"

"It's hard for them," said Liesl. "They have their friends, their house. They promise they will come soon."

"Soon is not soon enough," said Flora. "Do you understand?"

The urgency in Flora's voice jelled in

Liesl's stomach. *"Natürlich."*

"Good," said Flora brusquely. "Now, let's talk of more pleasant things." She pointed out some tall apartment buildings. "This is where wealthy New Yorkers live."

Liesl wondered if Flora lived here, but she was too shy to ask. "So big," she said, straining to see out the window. "Do people ever get lost in them?"

Flora smiled and pointed to the uniformed doormen who stood outside each of these canopied buildings. "No, that's what these gentlemen are for."

At Seventy-Second Street they took a left and then a right onto Fifth Avenue. "Now I'll show you where the millionaires live." Here were the mansions with elegant courtyards and limestone facades that looked like the French chateaus Liesl had visited as a girl. Flora rattled off names: Astor. Vanderbilt. Whitney. Warburg. They meant nothing to Liesl, but she liked the way they sounded: solid and gilded, as she imagined everything in America to be. "And this," said Flora, pointing to one of the grand homes with its heavily curtained windows, "this is the Woolworth mansion. Which brings me to the subject of work. I have secured a job for you at the five-and-ten-cent store on Fourteenth Street. You'll be a clerk, but a job is a job."

A job? Liesl had never had to work before. She thought about the clerks at the bank: tidy older women with soft-heeled shoes and tightly rolled buns. She couldn't imagine being one of them.

At Ninety-Seventh Street, they turned left again and drove across Central Park toward the Hudson River, where they headed north on Riverside Drive. The road twisted and the air smelled fresh and earthy.

"How do you like it so far?" asked Flora.

"I like it very much. Very much," said Liesl, thinking this was how her America would be.

The car followed the Hudson uptown until they passed the George Washington Bridge and took a right turn at a sign that said FORT TRYON PARK. They rode through streets filled with stubby apartment buildings and children playing, nothing like the limestone palaces and sparkling sidewalks they'd seen on Park Avenue. Liesl assumed the nicer homes were up ahead, like the half-timbered ones in which she had grown up. But there was one apartment building after another, until the car came to a stop in front of one made of red brick, and Flora announced, "Here we are, Three Fifty Pinehurst Avenue. Your friends' apartment."

The driver unloaded Liesl's bags from the trunk and placed them on the curb. Flora wrote the address of the five-and-ten-cent store and the name of the woman who would be Liesl's supervisor, Audrey Holmes, on a thick notecard that had *FE* embossed in gold letters. "Miss Holmes does not expect you until next week. Call me if you need anything." She jotted her phone number down on the card. "And please, tell your parents to hurry. This is no time to dillydally." Flora waited in the car until she was sure Liesl was at the door.

Liesl saw Carola standing in the building's cement courtyard. She was hugging a sweater around her shoulders. In the late-afternoon light, the tulips in the planters on either side of the wrought-iron doors looked faded. Carola's face too looked drawn in this light, but it brightened as she embraced her friend. "Thank God you're here." It was the first time since she'd left home that Liesl had touched or smelled a familiar person, and the first time in more than a year that she'd seen Carola.

"Rosewater," said Liesl, burying her head in Carola's neck.

"You remember," said Carola. "You look as beautiful as ever."

The two had been close friends since they had met at a summer youth group in Frankfurt. Liesl had been fifteen at the time; Carola was eight years older and one of the leaders, but the two paired up, as pretty girls often do. Aside from their beauty, they seemed to have little in common. Liesl was an athlete who won swim competitions and beat the boys in tennis; Carola never went out in the sun. Liesl loved parties; Carola was happiest playing clarinet alone in her room. Carola liked quiet, bookish boys and married one; Liesl went for handsome types who dazzled on the tennis courts and brought her ivory edelweiss from St. Moritz. She never settled on any one of them, but according to the gossip slept with all of them. Despite their differences, Carola and Liesl were easy with each other, and shared confidences and private jokes.

From the letters Carola had written about the heather garden in Fort Tryon Park and all the wonderful shops and bakeries in their neighborhood, Liesl and her parents had been certain that the Cohens were thriving in America. In reality, their small apartment was overrun with whatever furniture they'd been allowed to bring over. A mahogany china cabinet filled with porcelain figures and some of Carola's mother's cherished

Spode china, their bed with its massive headboard, her dressing set, a ponderous foldout sofa, and a muted Persian carpet swallowed the floors. Liesl felt everything in her body contract, as if she were trying to fit herself into this space. Flora Einson had made her feel small, Carola's pinched face even smaller. And now, in this mishmash of the old furniture and bare walls, it was conceivable that Liesl might disappear entirely. "You've done such a lovely job of making this feel like home," she said.

Carola put her hand on her friend's shoulder and pretended to shove her. "Dear Liesl, we have known each other too long to pretend. You do not have to use your good manners with me. Max and I do not intend to stay here forever, but it is a start. This is nothing like *heim.*" The way Carola said the word "home," *heim,* with its embracing vowels and familiar accent, brought tears to Liesl's eyes. "It's all so strange, this," she said. "America. It's not how I thought it would be."

"I know," said Carola, her arm around Liesl. "We all thought it would be different."

During her first four weeks in America, Liesl slept on the sofa. Though she fell into bed exhausted by the end of the day, rest did not come easily. The mattress was worn and each spring pressed against her. Outside, cars honked, neighbors talked. Flora Einson's icy voice when she said, "This is no time to dillydally," filled her head.

Liesl started wearing her pearls to bed at night. Her parents had given her the double strand when she turned sixteen. They were the finest, they said, from the South Seas. "You're a young lady now," they'd told her. "Wear them like a lady." What they meant, of course, was: "This is jewelry worthy of Leopold Kessler's daughter; don't embarrass us." The pearls shimmered like wet sand and sounded like plops of water when they bounced off one another. Many men had run their fingers over them, commenting on their beauty while managing to skim the arc of Liesl's neck. Lying in the darkness, she imagined the men, and how it used to feel to be Leopold Kessler's daughter.

Home. *Heim.*

At home she'd been lulled to sleep by the evening breeze against her window or her parents' voices in a nearby room. Here, it comforted her to close her eyes and take inventory of her old house: her mother's satin robe hanging on the back of the bathroom door, the bronze lamp in the shape of an upside down bell in the library, the starchy feel of clean linen sheets against her skin, the two loose floorboards in the parlor. And if this didn't quiet her, she turned to food, recalling the black bread with butter, the *teewurst* and cervelat, the flourless chocolate cake with walnuts her mother made for special occasions. Night after night, she'd call up these memories, and like a child's favorite bedtime stories, only they could soothe her.

At home, she had never arisen much before eight. Here she had to get up at six thirty and wait her turn to use the bathroom. Then the subway to Fourteenth Street. A new kind of hell. So many people, too close and pushing. Squeals and rumbles that echoed in her belly. Curves taken at such a speed she thought she might fall over. Holding on to straps with strange hands touching. At work, no one even tried to pronounce her first name. They called her Lee, though she overheard her boss, Audrey Holmes, call her "the Kraut" when she thought she was out of earshot. Audrey ordered her to do things like clean up a mess left in the ladies' room. If one of the customers cupped his hand around her behind or whispered something in her ear that she was grateful not to understand, she didn't complain.

After all, a job was a job.

14.

Trips to greet old friends at the Hoboken pier had become commonplace. Egon persuaded Meyer to keep him company when he went to pick up Kaethe and Georg Schnabel. It was late May, warm enough to wear the new camp shirts and plastic sunglasses that Liesl Kessler had brought them from her five-and-ten-cent store. "For my American men," she'd said when she gave them these gifts.

As always, the wait at the pier was long and the crowds dense, but eventually Egon spotted the Schnabels in line under the *S*'s. "There they are," he said, pointing. Georg had his trouser legs tucked into his boots and was leaning on a walking stick. Kaethe wore a brown felt hat and a long brown skirt with a matching vest.

"That's them?" asked Meyer incredulously.

"Yes, I told you they were older."

"You did, but you didn't tell me they were characters out of *Heidi*. *Mein Gott*, they look ready to climb the Tyrolean Alps."

"Please, Meyer, be nice. Coming here was a hard decision for them. They swore they'd never leave."

"So why did they?"

Egon took off his sunglasses and wiped the lenses with his handkerchief. "*Ach*, why did I invite you?"

"Because you're trying to be a good boy and do the right thing for your landsmen even though you find these people silly and you'd rather be spending the day walking in the park with your friend Meyer. So instead, you brought him along to cheer you up and say things about these batty people you're too polite to say yourself. Any other questions?"

"Only one," he answered. "How does it feel to always be right?"

Meyer smiled. "It feels like the moment when you put your hands between a lady's legs and you can tell she's ready and you're almost home. That's how good it feels."

Egon shook his head: "And when, may I ask, was the last time you were that close to a lady?"

"Ha! Do you think I tell you all my secrets?"

"Seriously. When you don't work, you are with me. I have seen your apartment. It does not exactly look like a love nest."

"If you really must know, I plan to invite the luscious Liesl Kessler to dine with me next weekend in what you so touchingly call my love nest. She's a looker. I think we'd make a perfect couple." He stuck his chin out and lowered his eyes.

"Do not," said Egon.

"Do not what?"

"Do not start with her."

"Why not? Have you already lured her to Noah's Ark on Bennett Avenue?"

"It is not that. For one thing, she is Carola's best friend, and I do not think any of us can go through one of your Schneewittchen obsessions again. For another — well, she is too young and too . . ."

"Too what?" Meyer interrupted. "Too rich? Too pretty? Too well bred for your hick farm friend? Well, not anymore. America, the great equalizer, has seen to that. She's one of us now: willing to take any kind of shit work, embarrassed that her English isn't good enough, nearly broke. I'll bet you anything she'll be grateful for a free meal — even at my disgusting love nest. And what about you, Mr. Cheese Man? Surely there's some beautiful woman who thinks she's the one. Tell me, who is it?"

"You know, sometimes I wonder why I have stayed friends with you all these years. You are so . . ." Out of the corner of his eye, Egon saw the Schnabels wave at him. "*Oopa*, here they come. We can continue this brilliant conversation later. And please, try to act civilized."

That weekend, the Schnabels were the guests of honor at one of the Saturday afternoon *kaffeeklatsche*. This week, it was at the Cohens'. Carola set the table with the linens and serving pieces she and Max had managed to bring out with them. There was *apfelkuchen* and coffee with heavy cream in a silver pitcher, and cubes of sugar in a matching bowl. Talk inevitably turned to the possibility of war and President Roosevelt. "He is probably the greatest president America has ever had, and I believe he's the only one who can defeat Hitler," said Egon.

Meyer tucked his hands under his armpits. "Roosevelt is a bloated snob, an anti-Semite, like the rest of them. Another one of those Harvard boys who think they own the world."

"I disagree," said Egon. "For the Jews, he is our only hope. Look what he has done for other groups. His work programs —"

"For crying out loud," Meyer interrupted. "Roosevelt could give a shit about the Jews. Do I have to remind you about the quota system? That even after Kristallnacht, he continued trade relations with the Third Reich? If it were up to him, we'd be back in Frankfurt quaking in our boots. Roosevelt or no Roosevelt, they can turn on us here as easily as they did there."

It always came back to the same fear: that it could happen here. Carola, whose parents were still in Kaiserslautern, placed her hands over her ears. "Please, can we take a short vacation from all of this?"

"Amen," chimed in Max.

Meyer shrugged. "I surrender."

They talked about Joe Louis's latest fight, the Clark Gable–Carole Lombard marriage, their favorite bakeries in Frankfurt — anything but what they did during the week. The Cohens had a piano, which Egon loved to play. Dutifully, he banged out the familiar songs with all the oom-pa-pa he could muster, but on this Saturday, Liesl brought the sheet music to the Cole Porter song "You're the Top." She sat next to Egon on the piano bench and beamed as he said, "This next song I play to welcome our new friends Kaethe and Georg." Carola and Liesl tried to sing along, but they stumbled

220

over the lyrics: *You're a Bendel bonnet, a Shakespeare sonnet / You're Mickey Mouse.* Max and Meyer tapped their feet. Only the Schnabels, he in a three-piece suit and she in a long skirt and lace-up shoes, sat impassively. Afterward, there was schnapps and more talk until it was late enough for them all to go home with the feeling of having been out on the town.

Egon invited Kaethe and Georg to come with them on the following Sunday. It was another of their rituals: They would meet at Nash's and then go window-shopping up and down Dyckman Street. The Schnabels, he figured, would find this comfortingly familiar, like their weekly *spaziergänge* back home.

Georg showed up with his walking stick, Kaethe in her felt hat. "You two are dressed for an expedition," said Meyer. "We're only going so far as éclairs and *apfelkuchen.*"

"This is nothing to laugh at," said Kaethe. "We dress as we dress at home."

"This is home," said Meyer. "You're in New York City, not Frankfurt."

"For now," said Georg. "When things get better, we go back. Until then, we dress as we please." The others stared at Kaethe and Georg as if they'd just declared that Hitler was their grandson.

"Fine, but until then, we eat cake," said Meyer, digging into his napoleon.

After Nash's, they strolled down Dyckman Street, Max, Meyer, and Egon with their hands clasped behind their backs, Carola and Liesl with arms laced. They nodded at familiar faces and exchanged gossip with old acquaintances, only these days their gossip was of urgent matters: who was looking for work, who was missing back home, would Roosevelt bring America into the war. On this afternoon, they ran into Frieda Bauer, an old friend of Liesl's family, who asked about her parents.

"They still haven't gotten their papers in order," she said. "I keep writing for them to hurry, but they don't."

Frieda told them of two other mutual friends who had arrived from Frankfurt this week and needed a place to stay. Did they know anyone who could take them in?

This was always an uncomfortable situation, as no one had space. Kaethe and Georg were staying with Egon until they could find an apartment. Liesl was still with the Cohens. Meyer, who lived in the smallest place of all, finally said, "For God's sake, send them to me. I must have extra room on my kitchen floor."

With time and money so scarce, nights

out were a rare and big event. On an evening in June, they paid twenty-five cents each to go to Lewisohn Stadium and hear Oscar Levant play piano. Liesl sat beside Egon in the bleacher seats. The bright lights bathed her in a way that cast a bronze glow on her skin, making her look clean and classic. Only when the audience began clapping did Egon turn away from her.

Levant took his seat at the piano without a smile. He flexed his hands and lowered his eyes, then attacked the keyboard like a man getting even. He started with Chopin's "Étude in C-Sharp Minor." When he finished, he sat with his fingers poised over the keys. There was the sound of an ambulance approaching. People looked around. As the wailing became a fixed melody, they realized it was the sound of a clarinet, the startling prelude to "Rhapsody in Blue." The pace became urgent and the notes more rhythmic. Car horns, subways, people yelling in the streets — everything that frightened and amazed Egon about the city — exploded from this piece. He looked at the others, expecting to see his excitement reflected back. Carola bobbed her head along with the clarinet; Meyer tapped his index finger in time to the music. Georg slept and Kaethe sat upright, staring straight ahead.

Only Liesl squeezed his arm in a way that made him think she felt what he did.

He remembered when Liesl had come to see him in Frankfurt, a pretty young girl with bright red lipstick and watering eyes. When she'd said her eyes were crying for all that was happening in Germany and that "all of us Jews" needed to get out as soon as possible, he'd said something foolish, like "It's not that bad," and tried to comfort her in a fatherly sort of way. Now he was feeling anything but paternal. His heart raced, and his foot swung back and forth as he tried to keep pace, but Levant's fingers were gymnasts, and Egon couldn't begin to follow, so he gave himself over to the melody and let himself be taken up by the ruckus and sweetness of it. When he thought back on it, he realized that this was the moment when New York City finally entered him.

As they headed downstairs into the subway, Liesl stayed by his side. Her face still glowed, even in the dim light of the station. The train was crowded and the seven of them huddled together around a single pole. Liesl let her body slide against Egon's. She smelled fresh, and he could feel her eagerness through the thin rayon dress she wore. "Tonight, I come home with you," she whispered to him in German. She spoke with the confidence of a woman who had never known rejection. He imagined what it would be like to have her in his bed. It had been a long time since he'd had anyone in his bed. She was beautiful, young, slender, and familiar. She had known who he'd been when he was Dr. Schneider. He thought about Catrina. A fantasy floating on impossibility. An American who knew him as the Cheese Man. So far away. The music still filled him with elation, and so did the thought of making love to Liesl Kessler.

Even before he nodded yes, he saw Liesl whisper in Carola's ear, and Carola shake her head and whisper back. Carola, in her gentle mocking way, probably said something like "You naughty girl, you're at it again." He also saw Meyer watching it all and knew that come tomorrow, there'd be hell to pay.

Sure enough, Egon's phone was ringing when he came home the next evening. "So that's why you steered me away from her! Too young, my foot. Greedy Egon wanted little Liesl Kessler all to himself, so he played holier-than-thou and warned his friend away." Meyer spoke in the singsong cadence he used when he was being sarcastic. "Tell me this, does she taste like money? When she cries out in ecstasy, which she no

225

doubt does with the Cheese Man perform-
ing his remarkable feats of lovemaking, does
she yell, 'Ooh, Camembert!' or 'More
Roquefort, please, more Roquefort!' " His
voice got serious. "Honestly, Egon, the least
you can do is give me details."

Egon tried to explain how this had caught
him by surprise, how spontaneously it had
happened. "I am sure the music had something to do with it," he said, which piqued
Meyer even more.

"Really? Do you think if I'd been sitting
next to Liesl Kessler during 'Moonlight
Sonata' or one of the Brandenburgs, she'd
have started nibbling on my ear and ended
up back in *my* love nest? Details, Egon,
that's the least you can serve up to your
starving friend."

"Okay," said Egon. "The details are sweet
and simple. As you may imagine, she is
athletic and experienced in that department.
Let me say this: She knows her way around
men. Her physique, or how you call it, is a
fine one. When I told her she was beautiful,
she took the compliment like it is one she is
used to getting. She does not demand
conversation, so it was easy. It was lovely
and fun, if you must know."

"What I must know," said Meyer, "is what
you're not telling me."

"Ah, always the writer. I'm not not telling you anything, I swear it."

That was a lie. What Egon didn't tell Meyer was this: Liesl kept her pearls on while making love. When he suggested that she might remove them for fear of their getting damaged, she told him she never took them off. They looked luminous against her bare skin. More than once he let his lips glide over them as he kissed her neck and stroked her back. Once inside her, he was seized with the thought that those pearls held the memory of the brass plate and cherrywood rolltop desk in his old office, and in his passion, he grabbed both strands and shoved as many pearls as he could fit into his mouth. They were soft against his tongue, like chocolate before it melts. He cried as he came, then hid his head in her neck so she wouldn't see his tears.

Meyer's questioning became relentless. "Tell me about her breasts," he demanded two weeks later. "Is her red lipstick all over your *schwanz*?" he asked on the phone one evening. Egon fended him off as best he could, until one Sunday in Nash's, Meyer whispered, "Really, what does she taste like?"

Egon put down the fork he was holding.

227

"Enough. These questions of yours are perverse. Find your own romantic life and get your nose out of mine."

"Fair enough," said Meyer. "Only one more question: When I expressed interest in Miss Kessler, you told me it was a bad idea, she was too young and Carola's best friend. Yet none of these matters seem to concern you, which leads me to think one of two things: that because you are the better-looking one of us, what applies to me in this area does not apply to you, or, more simply, that you have betrayed me."

"This is nonsense," said Egon.

"Then you admit it's a betrayal."

"You never *had* Liesl."

"But you knew I wanted her, and that makes it a betrayal."

"No such thing," said Egon. "It is more what I would call a moment of weakness."

"Once would be a moment of weakness; now it's been nearly a month of Liesl and Egon. I call this a betrayal."

"I am sorry you feel that way. I did not purposely mislead you."

"Then we call it a small betrayal?"

"Maybe a very small betrayal," said Egon.

"Small betrayals add up," said Meyer.

Egon bought himself a phonograph, and

Liesl brought him records: "Rhapsody in Blue," the Dorsey Brothers, Glenn Miller, Duke Ellington, anything that was new. She was sweet that way, always bringing presents for the group: a comb for Carola; colored pencils for Max; New York City maps for the Schnabels; the shirts and glasses for him and Meyer. Egon worried that she spent too much money on these gifts. When he told her this, she made light of it and pointed to the double strand of pearls. "Does this look like the jewelry of a girl who is broke?" But in her awkward English, the sentence came out: "Does this look like the jewelry of a girl who is broken?"

In fact, Egon thought she was quite the opposite. She always seemed to have something new: a bottle of nail polish; fanciful barrettes; a smart scarf tied around her neck. Certainly she was not broken in the bedroom, and never tired of pleasing him every way she could. She was an attentive listener, and her own conversation was mostly small talk, except when she spoke of her parents: "I am tearing my hair out with frustration. My father promises he will get papers, but nothing happens. They come for all the wealthy Jews. They will come for him."

Egon didn't know how to comfort her, other than by saying, "You must not give up trying."

In public, Liesl laid claim to Egon by keeping her eyes on him in a way that Meyer said was embarrassingly possessive. Egon didn't tell Meyer that he enjoyed her attention. When they went out in a group, she stayed by his side. On July 4, the seven of them packed up sandwiches, fruit, cake, and thermoses of coffee and took the two-hour subway ride to Brighton Beach. On the train, the men stood over the women and held on to the straps. Liesl wore a pair of shorts and a halter top with a palm tree pattern. When Meyer unabashedly tried to look down Liesl's halter, Egon shot him a glare of angry recognition. Meyer shot back one of defiance, then continued to search for Liesl's breasts.

Meyer hated the beach. The sun made his pale skin itchy and blotchy. He hated his body, which he felt was as thick and squishy as a marzipan pig, and nothing he wanted to parade in front of his friends. Once, when he was a boy, one of his brothers had stuck Meyer's head in the trough long enough for him to think he was going to die. Since then, water terrified him. He thought about the one time he had ventured into a lake. It had been at Helenesee, outside of Frankfurt. He and Carola had been visiting Egon and he took them to the lake. In a burst of bravado, Meyer had dared Carola to stand on his shoulders and jump off. She'd said: "Okay, but I'll kill you if you flip me backwards." He'd promised he wouldn't, then ducked underwater as she took his hands and climbed on. He'd stood up slowly. His arms shook as they both tried to steady themselves. He knew he'd never forgive himself if he let her fall, so he'd fixed his eyes on the tips of her toes, which were painted tomato red. Before then, he'd only waded in the shallow end of the lake up to his waist. But on that day, the thought of his Schneewittchen climbing up his back made the possibility of drowning seem a fair price to pay. Even now, he could feel her slender feet on his naked shoulders.

When they finally got to Brighton Beach, his little group stood shyly around the perimeter of their blankets, none of them willing to be the first to strip down. Finally, Egon sat on the blanket, pulled off his shirt and pants, and stretched out in the sun. *Of course it would be him,* thought Meyer. That body, still a harmony of fine lines and angles. The rest of them wore their winter pallor. Not him. His skin never paled. And now he would tan. The tan would play well against those blue eyes. He'd look exotic and romantic, like a Moroccan sheikh. "Look at him," Meyer said, gesturing to Egon. "The man is fucking Dorian Gray."

Liesl smiled provocatively as she studied Egon's body. The others laughed uneasily, unsure of who this Dorian Gray was. But no matter, it broke the ice, and they all slipped off their clothes and lay in the sun. All except for Carola, who sat shaded by an umbrella.

Meyer took in the sight of her, glimpse by glimpse. During the week, Carola scrubbed floors at a fancy midtown hotel. Her job required her to pull her blond hair back into a bun and wear a net over it, but today it fell softly around her shoulders. Her body, slim and graceful, filled out all the right places in her black knit bathing suit. Meyer poured himself a cup of coffee before allowing himself another look. Without their tomato-red polish, her toes seemed old and discarded, though her legs were pale and young as ever. But wait, what were those blue and purple stains on her knees, like smashed fruit on white linen? Meyer breathed out *"Ach, du lieber,"* and waited until he could make his voice normal before asking, "Did you take a fall?"

"Oh, them." Carola laughed, looking down at her legs. "No, they come with the job."

Max covered her legs with a towel and suggested they all take a swim. Meyer waded waist-deep into the ocean and watched with the Schnabels as Egon and Max dove headfirst into the waves and Liesl swam out until they could barely see her. Carola stayed under the umbrella. After they dried off and ate lunch, Meyer announced it was time to play their favorite game: The Worst Job of the Week.

"Today there is no contest," he said triumphantly. "No one can beat me. Even on normal days, it's exhausting to walk up and down Seventh Avenue wearing a sandwich board, but when the humidity is high and the temperature gets into the nineties like it did this week, I *schvitz* like nobody's business. So, on Monday, my sign says 'Kallen's Shirts: The Best There Are.' The letters are hand-painted in black except for the word *Kallen's,* which is red. At lunchtime, I begin to notice that people are smiling at me. This never happens. Mostly people turn away from me. Then I am aware that some are laughing. One man even nudges his wife and points at me. She puts her hand over her mouth like he's told her a dirty joke. That's when I think I'd better see what this is all about. The next time I pass the store window I stop and look at myself in the glass. Oh brother, what do I notice? I have so much sweat pouring out from me that it's soaked through to the sign. Some letters are smudged and others have dripped away. Now the sign reads 'allen's Shi ts: The Best There Are.' "

Meyer related this with shrugs and raised eyebrows in all the right places, until the others were laughing so hard they were crying. Only Kaethe and Georg were not amused. "So, now that we are in America, are we to become vulgar?" asked Kaethe.

When Georg nodded in agreement, Meyer leaned in to them until their faces were almost touching. "But of course," he said with exaggerated formality. "I forgot I was talking to the first family of Frankfurt."

That's when Egon stood up and put his hand on Meyer's shoulder and said, "Come, walk with me on the beach."

"Gladly," said Meyer. He stood up, still staring at Georg. "Don't tell any dirty stories while we're gone."

Egon nudged Meyer along. "Those people," said Meyer as they walked. "Why did they bother to come here? They're not even trying."

Egon shook his head. "They cannot help it. They have to cling to who they were; otherwise it is unbearable for them. He folds and irons shirts at a dry cleaner's, and she mends other people's clothes in their living room, for God's sake. Their little apartment on Dongan Place is a far cry from his law office and their mansion in Frankfurt. They are older. They do not have everything ahead of them. Surely you can be a little compassionate, yes?"

Meyer stopped walking and used his hands to shade his eyes. "I don't give a shit if they're ninety-seven. They're deluded fools. Carola's on her hands and knees all day. You sell salami and cheese. I walk around with a sandwich board on my shoulders. We do what we have to do and don't act so high and mighty. We don't kid ourselves."

"You are wrong," said Egon, turning to look at a young girl in a low-cut suit. "We all kid ourselves, but about different things. This is how we go on."

"God, I'm sick of us," said Meyer, staring at the same girl. "We've become exactly what they wanted: insular, separate, our own little ghetto. We kiss everyone's ass all week, and by the weekend we hate ourselves so much that we turn on each other because we're all we've got."

Egon used the back of his hand to wipe sweat from his brow. "Meyer, you are the one always telling me to look on the bright side, remember? 'We are in America. We have our lives ahead of us.' Blah blah blah. Have you forgotten your own spiel?"

Meyer studied his friend's silhouette backlit by the sun. "The less you wear, the more cocky you get. I suppose if I looked like you do in a bathing suit and I had a sexy young girlfriend, I'd be cocky too. So okay, we will look on the bright side. Did you see the way Carola threw back her head and laughed at my story? How do you know that she isn't fed up with that dough-faced husband of hers and is finally ready to take up with a real man?" Meyer sucked in his gut and flexed his muscles like the he-men on matchbook covers.

Egon laughed. "I know because you tell me everything."

"I tell you everything I think you should know. And you, do you tell me everything?"

Egon hesitated. "Sure I do."

That was another lie. He still hadn't told Meyer about Catrina, but really — what was there to tell?

15.

Of all of them, Meyer battled most ferociously to learn the language and customs of America. Each night he would copy a story from *Life* magazine until he covered three pages of writing tablet. He would read the comic pages aloud, assuming the voice of Buck Rogers or Popeye. Often, at the Saturday gatherings, he'd entertain the group by acting out one of the strips. After one of these readings, Egon asked him when he thought he might start writing again. Meyer puffed out one cheek, then the other, as if swishing water between them, and answered, "I suppose when I have something to say."

"Do you ever not have something to say?"

"You can make fun as much as you like," said Meyer. "But one of us gets paid for our opinions, and it isn't you."

Egon understood what Meyer meant when he picked up the September 22, 1939, issue of the *Aufbau,* the five-year-old German Jewish weekly newspaper. There, under the byline Meyer Leavitt, was a column called In the Free Country.

In Germany, we lived as Germans first, assimilating easily with our neighbors. Until the unpleasantness began several years ago, our Jewishness was mostly not the point. Here, in the free country, we have ghettoized ourselves. Where we were once citizens of a continent, we now live within a fifty-block neighborhood that we might as well call "Frankfurt on the Hudson." Because we have neither the money nor the time, few of us have strayed from our territory. Nobody I know has been to the Statue of Liberty, for example, but we all look to the stately George Washington Bridge, with its steel cables and painted aluminum beams, as our Reichstag. There is almost no place in Washington Heights where the reverse arches of this mighty bridge can't be seen floating like clouds over the Hudson River. So central is it in our lives that I recently heard one person, when talking about the first president of the United States, refer to him as President George Washington Bridge.

Right now ours are small lives. We are mired in our work and our survival, and it is on these things we must focus. But let us never lose sight of the fact that someday, we will have children, and our legacy and duty to them is to break out of our mental and physical ghettos, let in fresh air, and once again become citizens of the world.

Egon shook his head, remembering how, weeks earlier, at Carola and Max's house, Kaethe had let slip something about how she and Georg walked over the President George Washington Bridge. She'd said it softly enough that Egon hoped Meyer hadn't heard, but here it lay, coiled in the one newspaper he knew all of them read.

That night, he phoned Meyer. "So, the

Aufbau? When were you going to tell me this?"

"You mean to say, how dare I keep a secret from you, or is this your backhanded way of congratulating me?"

"A little of both, I suppose."

"Yes, well, we each have our little secrets, don't we?"

"Maybe. And we each have our small betrayals, do we not?"

"I don't know how you mean that," said Meyer.

"The President George Washington Bridge. Kaethe said that."

"She did," said Meyer. "I wasn't sure you heard her."

"Are you so ambitious that you will make fun of your friends in public?"

"Egon, I'm a writer. I use everything, and make fun of whomever I have to. This conversation, for example. Perhaps it too is a good column."

"And do you not think there is something wrong with that?"

"I think there's something wrong with so many things: that you sleep with Liesl, for starters; that Carola works on her hands and knees . . . Shall I go on?"

"You have made your point."

"Good. Now that we've finished with my

shortcomings, let's discuss yours. Who is 'this woman,' whose name you never give?"

"I am not sure I know what you mean."

"Pfft, this is so much bullshit, I smell it from here. For the past two months, you keep mentioning 'this woman' who comes into the store. You talk with her. She has a dog. Who is she? You betrayed me to get Liesl. Are you now betraying Liesl too?"

Egon put Johnny on his lap and took a deep breath. "Okay, her name is Catrina Harty. The truth is, there is nothing going on other than she comes into the store now and then. We talk. Once we went for coffee and cake."

"Where's she from?"

"If you mean is she from Frankfurt, the answer is no."

"What do you see in this Catrina Harty?"

"She is very pretty, a different type from the women we know, very American in her manner. And she cares about animals the way I do. All of this hardly matters, as I only see her in the store. I am afraid to ask her for a real date because . . . well, Liesl. But also, if she says no, she might not come back, and I like talking to her. It is different than talking with Liesl. We have real conversations."

Meyer had the habit of cleaning his teeth

with a toothpick while he talked on the phone. If he went silent during one of their conversations, as he did now, Egon guessed that was why. Finally, Meyer responded, "She has to see you as someone other than the man behind the delicatessen counter. Maybe she could help you with the animals on some weekend."

Egon said, "This is not your worst idea."

"Of course it's not," said Meyer. "I save my worst ideas for my really good friends."

"Meyer, you must promise me you won't say anything of this to Liesl."

He went silent again. "No, I'll leave that to you. But I'll be ready to catch her when you throw her off."

"That is a terrible thing to say."

"Yes, but an even worse thing to do. When will I meet this Catrina?"

"When I have a good reason to introduce you. And how about you? Will I be reading more of Meyer Leavitt in the *Aufbau*?"

He cleared his throat. "On October 2, I hang up my sandwich board and say shits to Kallen's, and become the fourth member of the *Aufbau* staff. They're giving me a column, In the Free Country, something to write every week."

"That is wonderful, it really is. When were you going to tell me this news?"

"When I was sure it was going to happen."

It was one of the few times Egon heard his friend sound sheepish. He knew what this job meant for Meyer. Only in America were these kinds of things possible. That thought gave him the courage to ask Catrina if she would care to help out with the animals some weekend. He was surprised and a bit terrified when she said yes.

Catrina came to his apartment at nine on a chilly morning in October. Liesl had left at eight, as Egon said he had to start work early that day. He hadn't lied, exactly. He was working; he simply did not mention a coworker. A cloud of her new Shalimar perfume hung over the bathroom. Before Catrina arrived, Egon opened the window, then remembered to hide Liesl's toothbrush and various lipsticks. It amused him how she had a way of inhabiting a place as if she owned it.

Their first patient was a spaniel who had a gash in his hind leg. The woman who brought him said he'd been hit by a car. Egon tried to calm the dog, who kicked and thrashed. He scratched the spaniel's chest and talked to him in a soothing voice until finally the dog relaxed and allowed him to examine the leg. "Nothing to be scared about," Egon said to the dog. "We will fix you up to be better than ever."

He'd turned part of his living room into a treatment room and kept all of his supplies in his oak desk. "Can you please hand me the thread from the third drawer from the bottom?" he asked Catrina. "And the scissors, please, in the middle drawer. The tape should be next to them."

After the spaniel and his owner left, Catrina asked him, "What did you say to that dog? I couldn't hear, but it sounded almost as if you were humming."

Egon laughed. "No, we were talking. Nothing special."

"Whatever you said, you calmed him down."

"Yes, we seemed to understand one another. So it went well, no?"

"Mmm." Catrina studied her nails, then looked up. "You did everything. I thought you wanted me to help."

"You did help."

"I brought you things. That's not the kind of help I had in mind."

"What kind of help did you have in mind?"

"The kind where I actually get to do work, not watch you do it all. I know something about animals too."

"I see. I did not understand."

Later that morning, a man from Nagle Avenue brought in a boxer named Boris who'd split his tail from thumping it too hard against the wall.

Egon tried wrapping the tail with gauze pads, but Boris kept wagging the pads away. "This one has complications, don't you, sweet dog?" said Egon. "We stop the bleeding, but then what? He bangs his tail against something else and the wound stays open."

"Maybe this will work," said Catrina. She reached into her pocketbook and pulled out a Kotex sanitary napkin.

"I cannot imagine how," said Egon, his face reddening.

"Let me try." She folded the pad in half, wrapped it around Boris's tail, and taped it up.

They watched Boris twist around and try, unsuccessfully, to bite the tail and its bandage. Egon laughed. "I have to say, this would not have occurred to me. You are a natural."

For the next two Saturdays, he told Liesl he had to start work early, and Catrina showed up promptly at nine. Together, they freed a chicken whose head had gotten wedged between the bars of its cage, sewed up a cat with a half-chewed-off ear, and fixed a parakeet's claw so he could grab onto his perch again. They worked easily as a team, agreeing on most treatments and that they should only charge people what they could afford, or nothing at all. Rarely did they talk about anything other than the animals.

One fall afternoon, after Catrina had extracted a rotting tooth from an old cat, someone dropped off a baby bird that had fallen from its nest. It was muted brown with spotting on its breast, long legs, and a straight, thin beak. Egon identified it as a wood thrush and said they must keep it warm. He emptied out a shoe box, rolled up his sleeves, and filled a hot water bottle. He put the hot water bottle on the bottom of the box, covered the bottle with tissues, and gently placed the wood thrush on top of it.

He'd always worn long sleeves. Now Catrina saw that his arms were strong and just hairy enough. "You seem to know your birds," she said. "I've noticed you have pictures of them all over the house."

"Yes, I know my birds." Egon stared up at one of his mother's drawings. "One minute. I have something to show you."

He went to his desk and picked up a cloth pouch, which he turned over until the glass eye fell into his hand. "It was my mother's," he said, holding it out for her to see. Catrina recoiled.

"Not her actual eye. A gift from her father when she first began to draw birds. Hers are the birds that hang here."

He showed her his mother's drawings and told her about their time together in the Stadtwald. "She could sit silently for hours and watch them. As close as she got to them, they rarely flew away, as if they knew a friend. My parents were famous naturalists in Europe. He wrote books and she illustrated them."

Catrina asked to see the books, and admired the beauty and precision of the work. "Did you ever think you wanted to do the same thing?"

"I offered once, but I do not have the talent either of them had. Like them, I seem to have a sympathy with the animals. And some people." He stared into Catrina's eyes. She looked away.

"My father didn't write anything, but he was a good storyteller," she said. She described the rides on his shoulders, and their Sundays at the duck pond. "He made up funny poems about the people we saw. I can still hear him." She made her voice growly with an Irish accent: " 'That man's so fat, his wife's a skinny marink. He eats her dinner, that's what I think.' His poems were more than funny. He watched people and noticed things about them. I loved him, but he walked out on us and we never heard from him again. I consider him dead. And you? Do you miss your father?"

Egon rubbed his eyes with his thumb and forefinger. "He is not the kind of man one misses. He was very attached to my mother and sometimes I felt I was in his way. I admired him, though ours was not the kind of relationship you describe with your father. But not a day goes by that I do not miss my mother. I wonder what she would think of me, treating animals?" He shook his head, then asked about her mother.

"She still works in the same hospital she worked in when I was younger. She raised me, and my brother, Kiefer. I'd say she's very stubborn, strong, and practical. She doesn't suffer fools. You'd like her. Maybe, if you're not already busy, you'd like to come to our Thanksgiving dinner next week. It's nothing fancy, us and some friends."

"I am flattered to be asked," said Egon, who knew little of Thanksgiving.

She wrapped a piece of hair around her finger. "Well then, that's settled."

They talked into the long shadows of afternoon. He told her how his mother had died; she told him about James. "That's the kind of love you never stop grieving," she said. "But you and I are lucky. At least we were both once adored. Some people never have that."

Egon remembered his talk with Meyer months earlier and his voice sharpened. "I'm tired of people telling me I am lucky."

"You *are* lucky," she said.

"Not so much anymore."

"Do you think you deserve better than what you have?"

"As a matter of fact, I do." He told her about his practice in Germany, his office, the operas and theater performances he attended.

"I was fancy once too," said Catrina. She told him about Walter, the brownstone on 185th Street, the silver fox and the people she'd met at the Blue Moon. "Famous people knew my name." When she got to the part about Walter's inglorious end, she shrugged. "I don't know, maybe we get what we deserve."

"This is not what I deserve," said Egon, reaching for the cardigan on the chair behind his desk and pulling it over his shoulders. "Do you not think you deserve better?"

The sun was setting. The wood thrush was

making sad warbly sounds, and the smell of old Johnny hung in the air. The room that had seemed bright and bustling in the river light now felt small and chilly.

Catrina folded her arms across her chest. "I feel lucky to have what I have. Seems to me you're damn lucky to have a place to sleep, food to eat, and a job that pays a salary."

"You mean because I am a refugee that I am lucky to have these things?"

"That's exactly what I mean."

His voice rose. "I happen not to share your point of view. I worked hard for what I had; nobody gave me anything."

"A lot of people worked hard. Not all of them got to come to this country."

"Is this what you Americans do when you celebrate your Thanksgiving, you tell each other how lucky you are?" Barely had the words spilled from his mouth before Egon regretted that he'd said them and how he'd pronounced Thanksgiving, *Sanksgiving.*

Catrina gathered her purse. "That's right," she said, jamming her arms into her jacket. "We start by giving thanks for our blessings, those of us who think we have any."

"Will there be prayers or that kind of thing?" He meant to continue the conversation so she wouldn't leave, but he could hear how condescending his words must have sounded.

Catrina opened the door. "If you mean Jesus and crosses, you've got the wrong holiday, come back at Christmas. On second thought, don't come at all. I don't think you'd enjoy it."

Egon heard the crispness in her voice. He walked over to where she was standing and put his hand on her elbow. "I did not mean it that way. I would love to come to your Thanksgiving. Please, do not go."

"I have to feed Sasha."

After she left, he sat at his desk staring at the glass eye. It drew him to another time and place: the morning his mother died. The smell of coffee coming from the kitchen. Her joy as she told him she'd collaborate with his father on the flower book. The table littered with her sketch pad and pencils. "I'm glad you're so happy," he'd said. "You deserve it."

"*Ach,* nobody deserves anything. It's not about that," she'd answered.

He thought about the possibility of Catrina and about the animals and how after so short a time, he was making his way in America.

Maybe she was right. Maybe he was a little lucky.

16.

By eleven thirty on Thanksgiving morning, Catrina had peeled five potatoes; sautéed the bread, onions, and celery for stuffing; stuck the turkey in the oven; snapped the ends off a pound and a half of green beans; and set the table. She'd taken the old pilgrim candles from the closet and propped them up at either end of the table. Rose had always helped with these chores, but Catrina insisted she rest. Lately, her mother had felt weak and tired. Her breathing was slow and her skin the color of old newspapers. Rose was certain that whatever it was, it had come from all her years of breathing in the rot from the laundry. Catrina missed her mother's stern voice warning her that she was going to burn the turkey. The quiet in the kitchen and the empty chairs gathered around the table underscored her loneliness. She needed to get out of here.

She took Sasha and headed to the river. She stared at the water, the choppy currents and stabs of reflected sun never failing to excite something in her. She remembered how she and Kiefer would jump into the cold water and swim halfway to New Jersey, or so it seemed. Kiefer's long black hair would fan out around his head like the halo of an angel. She smiled to think about her brother's hair: still black, but now a bald spot the size of a fifty-cent piece capped his head. She wondered if her father had gone bald, and it started her thinking about the ones who'd disappeared from her life. She commanded herself to stop the sad thoughts and count her blessings. So she began. Sasha. The animals. This flawless day. The briny smell of the river. Egon? He'd seemed like a blessing. She'd miss him today, but at least now she felt she could get through the day.

She came home, took the apple pie she'd baked the day before from the refrigerator, and got dressed. Rose helped her set out the hors d'oeuvres. At four thirty, the doorbell rang. Martha and Lou Delaney, the upstairs tenants, were there. When they moved in, two years after Walter died, Martha and Catrina had become friends. Lou had worked nights then, and Martha would

253

often bring down lemonade and listen patiently as Catrina poured out her heart. Martha never talked much about Lou, though Catrina had her own opinion of him. She had often heard him screaming at Martha, his brutal words seeping through the walls.

Lou stepped in first and bent over to Sasha. "You know me, don't you, you pretty girl?" He held out his hand for her to sniff, but Sasha backed away and growled. Catrina grabbed the dog by the collar. "Now, now, Sasha, be nice." She led Sasha into the bedroom and helped her onto the bed. *Dogs,* she thought, *they always know.* "We're off to a swell start, aren't we, sweetie?" she said, chucking Sasha under the chin.

She walked back into the living room, where Rose was offering Martha and Lou toast bits with mushrooms. Martha sat on a wooden chair by the telephone table with her purse on her lap while Lou settled into the armchair and rested his hands on his ample stomach. "I forgot, what happened to the dog's back legs?"

"She was hit by a car," said Catrina.

"Does she ever topple over?" He smirked as if he'd said something clever.

"No, she's smart. She's figured out how to compensate. If you'll excuse me, I need to go and check on our dinner."

Catrina closed the door and leaned against the icebox. How differently she'd envisioned this day. Egon would have made these people bearable. He'd have appreciated how Sasha growled at Lou Delaney. Kiefer would have been impressed by how down-to-earth Egon was, particularly compared with Walter.

The bell rang again. "I'll get it," shouted Catrina. It was Kiefer. She threw her arms around him. "Thank God you're here." When he smiled, Catrina thought, he looked younger than his thirty-one years; although she was two years younger than he, today she felt she looked ten years older. She seated him on the couch, across from Lou, then retreated to the kitchen. She could hear Kiefer tell Martha how pretty her dress was and ask Lou about his job as an accountant. Kiefer spoke little, and when he did, he used as few words as possible, but he asked questions and listened well. He even got shy Martha to talk about her favorite stores on Dyckman Street.

When it was finally time for dinner, the group gathered at the table. Rose asked Kiefer to lead them in grace.

Dear Heavenly Father, thank you for this special day . . .

Catrina lifted her eyes and noticed how, for the first time, Lou and Martha were dressed up: he in a striped suit and blue silk cravat, she with a fox stole around her neck.

Thank you for the family you have given us . . .

Rose sat straight as if to show, at least outwardly, that her body had not betrayed her. Even now, in her fifties, her hair was thick, with only smudges of gray at her hairline.

. . . for family and friends who have gathered together to eat this Thanksgiving Day meal . . .

Kiefer was short. When she hugged him, she could rest her head on his. Egon was tall. If he hugged her, she could probably rest her head on his chest. It was probably a hairy chest. She imagined his chest hair, ticklish against her cheek, and the way it might run like a funnel down his stomach, and the odor, sweet and musky . . .

. . . Amen. Praise God, from whom all blessings flow.

"Amen," said Catrina. She jumped from the table and ran to the kitchen, where she began slicing the turkey and spooning stuffing into a dish.

After a while, Kiefer came up behind her. "Did you invite someone else to Thanksgiving?"

"No," she said.

"Well, there's a man here, says he's a friend of yours, that you'd invited him to come, an older fella with an accent. Sound like someone you know?"

Catrina turned around and looked at Kiefer. "I know who it is."

"An Eeekon something-or-other. Odd name."

"Yeah, something like that. I don't even know how he got my address."

"Telephone book," said Kiefer. "Ever heard of it?"

"Very funny."

"Want me to get rid of him?"

"No, I'll handle it."

"Who is he?" asked Kiefer.

"A friend, sort of. I invited him. Then we had a fight and I uninvited him. I don't think he should sail in here like everything's okay."

Catrina wiped her hands on a dishrag, took off her apron, and ran her fingers through her hair.

"You look nice," said Kiefer.

"I smell of onions, and I look a mess."

Conversation stopped when Catrina walked into the living room. Egon stood by the table and smiled at her. She didn't smile back. "What are you doing here?"

"I came to bring you something. Your brother, Kiefer, was kind enough to let me in."

"I know my brother's name."

Everyone stared at Egon. "On this holiday, I thought you should have . . ." He pulled a white box from the brown bag he carried. "This."

Catrina took the box and saw that it was from Nash's. "Chocolate peach cake?" she asked, not meeting his eyes. "How lovely."

Rose started to get up. "We need another place setting."

"I'll get it, Ma," said Catrina, retreating into the kitchen.

Egon followed. "Was this a bad idea?"

"Only if you think barging into someone's house after you've been uninvited is a bad idea."

"I go then." Egon started for the door.

"For God's sake, you're here now. You've charmed them, you might as well stay."

When everyone was settled, Kiefer said to Egon, "We've already said grace, but feel free to say whatever it is you say."

Egon scanned the table. "Thanks to you for letting me be here."

Catrina ignored Lou's slight grin when Egon's "thanks" came out as *sanks*. They all raised their glasses.

At dinner Kiefer talked about the recent assassination attempt on Hitler. "Better luck next time," he said.

Egon said that an assassination was too easy a death for him. "Something slower, more painful perhaps."

Lou Delaney asked Egon what line of work he was in. Egon told him about the grocery store, and said it was only temporary. "I am interested in becoming an animal doctor. I already treat animals on weekends." He started to explain how similar veterinary medicine was to ophthalmology. Then Catrina brought out the apple pie and began to cut it.

Martha commented, "That's a nice pie server, Catrina, where did you get it?"

"It's nothing special," said Catrina. "I picked it up at the five-and-ten."

Although Egon was sure no one noticed, the words *five-and-ten* bolted through him. Only days before, Carola and Max had decided they would do their version of Thanksgiving at their apartment. "Sauerbraten instead of turkey," Max had said, "with spaetzle stuffing." Meyer had promised to bring wine; Liesl had said, "Leave the decorations to me." Even the Schnabels seemed excited and offered to bring the apple strudel from Nash's. Egon had remained quiet, trying to decide how much truth to tell and how much to leave out. "It will be a complication for me," he finally said. "I already have an invitation for this day, a friend from the store. No one special." He avoided Liesl's gaze but couldn't ignore the seesaw pitch of Meyer's voice when he said, "How lovely for you, Egon. We'll all be sure to give thanks for your friendship."

Egon wondered what they were all doing now. Were they speaking in English or German? Did anyone play the piano? Was Liesl suspicious? He imagined Meyer seated between her and Carola, making them laugh with one of his stories. He envied them, how at ease they must be. At their table, he would be free to say whatever came to mind, while at this one he measured every thought and word. Here he was a foreigner, and even worse, an uninvited guest. Every time he spoke, that pugnacious neighbor, Lou Delaney, asked him to repeat what he'd said, as if his accent were impenetrable. Catrina wouldn't meet his eye, and Kiefer kept watching him as if he suspected that Egon might slip the silverware into his pocket. Coming here had been a terrible mistake.

Martha slid a piece of apple pie onto his plate. It was sloppy, with yellow fruit and syrup oozing from its sides. This was why

German Jews didn't eat pie. The scoop of ice cream that Rose plopped on top only added to the mess. He waited to see how everyone ate this. Fork? Spoon? People made *mmm* noises as they shoved the mush into their mouths. Egon found the fruit too sweet, the crust tasteless. He wished Catrina would offer him some of the chocolate peach cake, but she'd kept it in the kitchen. A part of him thought she'd done that out of spite. He managed to finish the pie, and at the first lull in conversation pushed back his chair. "Thank you very much for this delicious meal and the company, but I am afraid I must go and take care of a sick dog that stays in my house. Happy Thanksgiving to you."

Even though he'd pronounced all of his *S*'s with the proper sibilance, Lou Delaney cupped his ear with his hand and said, "I'm sorry, could you repeat what you just said?"

Kiefer reached across the table and shook Egon's hand, Martha smiled, and Rose said how nice it was to meet him. Catrina was watching him, but when he turned toward her, she stood up and started to clear the table.

As he headed uptown, he thought about how he'd lied to Liesl, and he could hear the mocking tone in Meyer's voice when he'd said, "We'll all be sure to give thanks for your friendship." Maybe this humiliating afternoon was what he deserved.

Meyer and Egon met for coffee and cake that Sunday, then went back to Meyer's apartment. They sat at his metal card table facing each other in the meager light that leaked through his window. Egon asked his friend the question that had been running through his mind: "Do you believe we get what we deserve?"

"I believe we do what we can to set the score straight," said Meyer.

Egon looked puzzled. "What do you mean by that?"

Meyer rummaged through some papers on the table until he found a copy of the story he'd written for the following day's *Aufbau.* "Here," he said, pushing the paper in front of Egon and pointing out a paragraph. "See if this makes sense."

Egon read:

When our leaders betrayed us, we ran from our country. When our beliefs betrayed us, we ran from our country. When our religion betrayed us, we ran from our country. Now, in the free country, we try to set the record straight. We swipe rolls from restaurants and shove them into our pockets, we lie to our friends. These are only small betrayals, but they add up. We may never get even, but at least we are trying.

Egon put the paper in his lap and held out his hands like a magician who'd made a rabbit disappear. "Are we to play out our whole lives in the pages of your column?"

"Not entirely," said Meyer, "only the parts I find interesting."

"Be serious. I feel as if we are all being held prisoners 'In the Free Country.' "

"That's good, Egon, criticism from a man who lies to his friends and his girlfriend. So tell me, do you now count among your blessings the beautiful Catrina?"

"Quite the opposite. We had what you might call a disagreement right before Thanksgiving. She told me not to come, but I decided to go anyway. I think it was not the wise choice on my part. She seemed very annoyed. Now I am not sure what to do."

Meyer pulled his chair closer to Egon and propped his elbows up on the table. "What do you want to do?"

"I like her. I want to see her again."

"And what about Liesl?"

Egon ran his fingers through his hair. "This will sound unkind, but I know Liesl like the front — or is it the back? — of my hand. This one is different: an American, a mystery. She is also a natural with the animals. Like no one I have ever met."

Meyer started blinking hard. He rubbed his eye until the fleshy part around his socket was red and his eye was tearing. He blew his nose and rubbed his eye again.

"Are you having an asthma attack?" asked Egon.

Meyer shook his head. "No, no, there's something in my eye, a sharp pain like a sting." He rubbed it some more.

Egon got up. "Let me have a look. Come by the window."

Meyer stood up next to him. Always a study in contrasts, they were never more so than at this moment. Meyer's shirt was untucked and wrinkled; a pink part of his belly poked through the bottom two buttons. His thinning hair sprawled across his head like weeds. Egon towered over him in a pale blue sweater and crisp navy pants. He bent down to look in Meyer's eye. "I see nothing." Meyer squinted and Egon leaned in closer until their noses almost touched. "There is nothing —" But before he could finish his sentence, Meyer grabbed him around the neck and jammed his mouth up against Egon's. It was a kiss of sorts, but more put-upon than most kisses are. Teeth mashed against teeth, and for a moment, Egon could feel the wetness of Meyer's tongue and taste the coffee and *apfelkuchen* he had eaten earlier. Then, with equal intensity, Meyer pushed Egon away and wiped his mouth with the back of his hand.

Egon backed himself against the kitchen wall. "I do not know what to say."

"You can ask me how is my eye."

"Okay. How is your eye?"

"My eye is fine." Meyer's voice rose and fell. "There was nothing wrong with my eye to begin with, as any doctor who claims to know anything about the eye would have noticed right away."

"I am not understanding," said Egon.

"What's to understand? I wanted to see what it was like to kiss the great Casanova, Egon Schneider."

"That was not funny, I am not amused."

"I'm not amused either," said Meyer. "Frankly, you're a terrible kisser."

■ ■ ■ ■

Part III
In the Free
Country

■ ■ ■ ■

17.

Friendships are of a different nature here. Where we used to behave with decorum and formality, now we break all the rules. We cling to each other when we are frightened, and turn on each other when we feel threatened. We are spinning in our freedom, excited about possibilities and terrified of where they might lead.
— Meyer Leavitt, *Aufbau,*
December 29, 1939

The *Aufbau* office was a single room with four wooden desks, two telephones, and two typewriters. "My desk even comes with a lamp," Meyer bragged to Egon. "I sit in the lap of luxury."

The lap of luxury had two windows that never shut or opened properly, so the four men who worked in it kept their coats on during winter and rolled up their shirt-sleeves in summer. There was hardly room on the desks for any photographs or memo-rabilia. Meyer kept *The Pale Princess of Prussia* on his. Next to him, Norman Blum, round as a sausage and equally hairless, had a photograph of his young daughter posing with a clown at the circus. Grace was solid, with the same round, pasty face as her father.

On a freezing Friday in December, Nor-man came into the office looking paler than usual. There had been a mishap at his home that morning: "I accidentally stepped on Grace's turtle," he said. "Part of his shell is cracked, and Grace is heartbroken. She loves that turtle, and I'm beside myself." Meyer could only imagine the effect of Norman's footfall on the poor turtle and reached for something reassuring to say. He told him about Egon and how good he was with animals. Then he had another thought. "He works with a woman, her name is Ca-trina, and she is especially handy with the smaller animals. You should ask for her. Surely she should be able to fix a turtle. I'll give you his address, and you can go there on Saturday morning."

Meyer couldn't wait to phone Egon that evening. "I am going to tell you something that might change your life," he began. "Your friend, Meyer, ignoring the voice of reason in his head, listened instead to the goodness in his heart. And please, feel no obligation to thank me. I did what I did because you are my friend and I want you to be happy."

"Mein Gott," said Egon. "This scares me. What did you do?"

Meyer told him everything. "Don't you see, now you have a reason to call Catrina that has nothing to do with your lascivious desires and everything to do with how much you respect her. She'll be happy to help an animal in need, and what happened on Thanksgiving will be beside the point. It's a brilliant scheme, if I do say so myself."

Egon sighed. "This makes me uncomfortable."

"Nothing to be uncomfortable about," said Meyer. "She'll be flattered."

"That is not what makes me uncomfortable. You do. This is so unlike you." In his own way, Egon thought, Meyer was trying to make up with him about the kiss.

"You mean it's so unlike me to do a favor for my dear friend? If we don't help each other, who will? So call her. I told Norman that you'd see the turtle tomorrow morning."

Egon hung up and checked his watch. It was 9:12, still early enough to call Catrina.

They hadn't spoken since Thanksgiving. He had never called her at home. What if she hung up when she heard his voice? What if her mother answered and said Catrina never wanted to speak to him again? What if no one answered; how often would he call back? His doubts piled up into a convincing blockade. When he next looked at his watch it was 9:23. He would never call a woman past 9:30. He dialed her number.

Catrina picked up on the second ring. Her voice, once she learned who was calling, wasn't steely, but it wasn't silky either. Efficient was more like it, with no obvious pleasure at being asked to the task. All she said was "I can be there at nine thirty," and, "Do you have a large sewing needle?"

Saturday morning, Catrina showed up at Egon's apartment. They were cordial, but exchanged little small talk. Grace and her mother came fifteen minutes later. Grace was carrying the wounded animal in a shoe box. When Catrina knelt down, she saw that Grace was crying. "What's his name?" she asked.

"Dribble."

"How old is he?"

"I don't know."

"Turtles can live until nearly one hundred. Dribble's got a long life ahead of him." Catrina reached into her pocket and handed Grace three lemon sour balls. "Suck on these while I fix him. Turtles find the smell of lemon soothing."

To close up a shell, Catrina figured she'd need something stronger than the usual suture thread. She'd dug out the spool of thinly spun wire she and Egon had used to cobble together a hamster cage a few weeks back. After cleaning Dribble's shell with hydrogen peroxide, she dabbed on some ether. For the next twenty minutes, she could feel Grace's lemony breath on the back of her neck as she stitched the shell back together. When she finished, she handed Dribble back to her. "Good as new."

Mrs. Blum stroked her daughter's hair as she turned to Catrina. "I don't know how to thank you. How much?"

For the first time, Egon spoke up: "For mending a cracked turtle shell, two dollars."

After they left, Catrina went to the kitchen sink, washed her hands, and poured herself some water. "My first turtle. How did you come up with two dollars?"

"It seemed reasonable. And you? Do turtles really find the scent of lemon to be soothing?"

"I have no idea, but I thought that Grace would find it soothing."

Egon shook his head and smiled. "Can I make you some tea?"

"That would be nice."

Egon's back was toward her as he placed the kettle on the stove. His black hair curled above his collar, and his lanky frame, slightly bowed, gave him the posture of someone playing the cello. She touched him on the shoulder. "Thank you for letting me handle this one."

He turned and faced her. They stood so close that a scalpel could barely have fit between them. He saw how the whorls of her auburn hair played against her pale skin. And those eyes. She was beautiful in such an unpredictable way. He took her chin in his hand with the intention of telling her so but instead kissed her mouth and then the faint blue vein that ran beside her throat. He felt her body yield and unbuttoned her cardigan. She wore a rayon chemise beneath her blouse, and the fabric was smooth in his hands as her body swayed against his. When she unfastened the snaps on her skirt, lemon sour balls spilled from her pockets and skittered across the floor. "You certainly come equipped," he said.

"It's not every day you get to fix a turtle."

Her smile was shy. The way she moved her body was not. She put her arms around him, and he could feel her strength. There was something urgent about the way she unbuttoned his shirt and undid his trousers. The two of them fell into the velvet chair and might have stayed there the rest of the afternoon had the teakettle not started to whistle. At first they disregarded it, but a persistent teakettle is not a thing to be ignored, and eventually Egon made his way to the stove and turned off the water. They moved to his bedroom, and for the rest of that afternoon, Egon and Catrina made love, slept in each other's arms, drank lukewarm tea, and then started all over again. Somehow, Johnny knew to stay under the bed.

"I thought this was over for me," she said as she stroked his bare shoulder. It was thin and smooth like a young boy's. "That I had used up all I had in this department."

"I have missed this too."

"I don't think you've missed it very much."

"How do you mean that?"

She sat up. "The lipstick, the nail polish, the second toothbrush. I've seen your medicine cabinet."

"You opened my medicine cabinet?"

"Of course I did. Haven't you ever looked into anyone's medicine cabinet?"

"No, of course not."

Catrina moved away from him. "Well, before you get on your high horse, let's talk about this. Who is she?"

Egon took a deep breath. "There is a woman. She is also from Germany. It is nothing serious, not like you." He reached down to kiss her. "It has been a lonely time until you. You are a surprise in every way." He didn't tell Catrina the nature of his surprise: how her breasts were too big to fit into his hand; how, when he rested his head on her belly, it was cushiony, not bony like Liesl's; how her frankness upended him; how nothing about her was familiar, yet everything about her seemed necessary.

Both of them had to laugh at their hunger, despite all the hours of lovemaking. Afterward, Catrina lay back. Her face was drenched with sweat. Hair stuck to her forehead like streaks of mud. "So what are we going to do?" she asked.

"You are bored already?" he asked.

"No, about Miss Lipstick and Nail Polish? What are we going to do about her? Rather, what are *you* going to do about her?"

Liesl had become such a fact of Egon's life, he hadn't given much thought to what it would be like without her. Her struggle to get her parents out of Germany had become his struggle. He'd written imploring letters to them and even engaged Meyer's help in trying to find someone in Frankfurt who could go talk to them in person. By now, his apartment was filled with the little presents she continued to bring him: a ceramic owl, sheets, a photo album. Her company was easy; their lovemaking pleasant, though nothing like what he'd felt with Catrina. He tucked Catrina's hair behind her ear. "Perhaps this is a conversation for another time," he said. "Let us not ruin what we have today."

"What we have today will never go away," she said. "But it can't happen again if there is someone else."

"I understand."

"Good," said Catrina. She told him that after Walter died, she'd found out that he had been unfaithful through most of their marriage. "I'd rather be alone than always looking over my shoulder."

Egon was quiet. Catrina got out of bed and walked into the living room. He could hear the rustle of her chemise and the snap of her skirt fastener. "You think about it and let me know what you decide," she said as she walked into the bedroom, combing her hair.

"I wish you would not go," said Egon. He

lay naked under the sheet, feeling miserable and vulnerable.

"Thank you for a lovely afternoon." She headed toward the bedroom door. "And for the turtle."

Egon got up, draped the sheet around him, and came up behind her. "This was not merely something to fill an afternoon," he said, kissing her neck. "Since I met you, you are in my mind all the time. I want to see you again. Give me some time to sort out my complications."

"I'll give you all the time you need. I'd like to see you again as well. Call me when you have something to tell me."

He wanted to change the mood back to what it had been before. He almost said, "I love you," but he knew what promise those words held. Instead, he tried to think what Meyer might say — something that would make her smile. "Do you really look into other people's medicine cabinets?"

"Of course," she said. "Everyone does."

18.

Here is a sanctuary and freedom from persecution. These are not small gifts, and they come with a price. Some of us put our heads down and carry on with the humility and gratitude this country expects of its immigrants. Others take what they can from anywhere they can get it, then cross their fingers, hoping no one will notice.

— Meyer Leavitt, *Aufbau,*
January 5, 1940

In Germany, Liesl had believed the letters from America and the promise of riches. No one had told her she'd have to work with people who couldn't pronounce her name, or that she'd be on her feet for nine or ten hours a day in a place that smelled of insect killer, or that her paycheck would barely cover her rent and food. It was humiliating enough that when she couldn't afford a hairdresser, Carola had to cut her hair, but to have her boss — a woman, no less — order her to dust last year's Christmas cards for this year's Christmas, or tie ribbons around stacks of dishtowels so they'd look more expensive — this was unbearable. She knew that the candles and the underwear and the balls of twine and everything else sold here was worth one-tenth of what was charged, and that customers were seduced by aisle after aisle of choices. Why not a pair of socks, a new broom, some potholders? Item by item, they seemed cheap enough, but add them up at the checkout counter and customers were likely to stretch a dollar to two and tap the limit of their weekly budget. As her father's daughter, Liesl understood money. She knew the difference between a good and a bad investment and had no doubt that this crummy five-and-ten-cent store owed her more than she owed it.

She started with little objects: lipstick, a compact, Dr. Scholl's foot plaster. It was easy. Her job was to keep the inventory stocked and clean, which meant her fingers were all over these items anyway. Tucking one or the other into the sleeves of a baggy sweater was simple. With time, she got bolder, rolling dresses and blouses into balls and shoving them into one of the store's brown bags. It was amazing what one woman with a quick hand and a large bag could accomplish. Linens, dishes, pens, playing cards, ceramic animals. She didn't take only for herself; Egon and his friends were so appreciative of the gifts she gave. Slippers, soap, hairbrushes. She told herself these were things her parents would need when they came to America, but mostly she stole because she could. It was her way of getting even with her boss, with her coworkers who never included her in their conversations, with the people who shoved her on the subway, with her father for being so intransigent. The gamesmanship of it made coming to work almost pleasant, and her secret victories reinstated the feelings of being indulged that she'd left at home.

She certainly wasn't going to let Egon Schneider burst her little bubble.

It was laughable, really, that he was the one who told her they had to break it off. He was an old man almost, no money, no future. He smelled garlicky, like the salami he sliced all day. His idea of a good time was a walk through the park looking at birds. The birds, everywhere the birds. And the sick animals. The way he pretended he was an animal doctor. The old furniture in his apartment. He snored. Even his dog was old and smelly.

No, this man was a bad investment.

She told herself that she was glad he was the one who broke it off, because sooner or later she would have had to tell him these things. This way, it was less cruel. She wanted a man with a future, with ambition. She didn't think Egon was such a man.

They were on one of their Sunday walks through the park when he told her. He'd been talking about the new year and had become unusually animated. "Nineteen forty! I cannot believe it. When I was a young boy, I went with my father to an automobile exposition in Berlin. They had a picture of the 'Car of the Future,' the car of 1940. It would be powered by gasoline and go as fast as sixty miles an hour. I remember thinking that 1940 was so far away and I would be an old man by the time it happened." He'd laughed. "Now here I am, in America, in a new life. I could have never imagined . . ." He turned and looked at her. "Liesl, I have been thinking about us and how we are both starting out in a new country. Of course we shall always be available to help one another, but now we deserve the chance to find our own America."

She'd nodded.

"Do you understand what I am saying?" he'd asked.

"Yes, you want to be free to do what you want to do," she'd said, conscious of keeping her voice steady. She didn't ask him why, or whether there was another woman; it would sound too much like pleading. No man had ever called it quits with her, but she knew that to make a fuss would be unseemly, so she hid her feelings behind the polite rhetoric that came so easily: "The time with you has been delightful, thank you. I hope your work with the animals goes well."

"You are a wonderful girl," he said with relief. "We shall always be friends."

"Of course," she said. "But for now, I'd like to take some of the things I left at your apartment."

They walked back in silence. She gathered up her toiletries, then went home to do the thing she knew would vex him more than anything. She would call Meyer.

Meyer. There was a man with ambition. He'd already written a book, and now he had a column in a newspaper. Egon and Meyer argued all the time, and Egon mocked Meyer behind his back. Liesl knew how competitive the two of them were, despite how they confided everything to each other. Meyer liked her, she could tell from the way he watched her and how he addressed her as "Lovely Liesl." Surely Egon and Meyer had talked about her.

How would she begin the call? She'd tell him about Egon, that he'd ended it. Egon had probably talked to him already. She'd sound wistful but not brokenhearted. She'd suggest maybe they go for a walk, or get some coffee at Nash's. Then what? What if he said no? What if he said yes? Would she be smart enough to keep up with him? What if they had nothing to talk about? How hard would it be to seduce him?

She needn't have worried about any of it.

"Lovely Liesl. What a cheerful surprise on such a dreary day," said Meyer when he heard her voice. "To what do I owe the honor of this call? I hope this is nothing serious about your parents."

"No."

"Then you are calling about the *Aufbau*? Perhaps a story about the fine work you are doing at the five-and-ten-cent store?"

Liesl could never tell if Meyer was making fun of her, but she had to laugh. "No, not that."

"Then it is a personal matter, a matter of the heart perhaps?"

"Yes, I suppose."

"Aha, Egon. He has broken your heart."

"Oh no," said Liesl, a lift in her voice. "But it's what you call a breakup. We have made a breakup."

He became silent.

"Meyer, are you still there?"

"I'm here," he said. "I'm cleaning my teeth with a toothpick. It helps me to think."

She laughed. "So that's your secret. I was thinking too. I thought maybe you'd like to have some coffee with me on the weekend."

Meyer picked some more. "Instead of coffee, I could cook us dinner at my place. It isn't fancy, but I am a decent cook."

"Only if you let me bring something."

"I'll tell you what, I'll make the meal and you bring dessert."

"That sounds wonderful."

He gave her his address, and she promised to show up Friday at seven.

He made spaghetti with cheese, minute steak, and niblet corn. She brought a box of Oreo Sandwiches, two Baby Ruth bars, and a bunch of toothpicks (all easy grabs). Together they drank nearly half a can of pineapple juice and a bottle of Chablis. They talked about old times, new friends, and how Liesl wanted to learn to jitterbug. When Glenn Miller's "In the Mood" came on the radio, Meyer said he knew how to jitterbug and would teach her. He took her hands ("Such smooth skin, Lovely Liesl") and rocked back and forth — heel-toe-heel-toe. Liesl knew that what he did bore no resemblance to the jitterbug but followed his steps nonetheless. He spun her around. She put her hands on her knees and kicked out her legs. He unbuttoned his shirt and waved his arms in the air like a man drowning. She picked up a dishrag and twirled it above her head. He clutched her around the waist and tried to dip her. She threw back her head the way she'd seen Marlene Dietrich do it. After all the wine, his hold was tenuous and her balance tippy. She might have fallen had he not grabbed her by the double strand of pearls and pulled her to standing, but not before one of the strands burst. The clopping sound of pearls hitting the linoleum was the closest to music they heard for the rest of the night.

Liesl dropped to her hands and knees, and Meyer dropped down beside her. She crawled under the table and around the chairs, snatching up the wayward pearls and stuffing them into her pocket. "I'm so sorry," said Meyer. "What an oaf I am."

She wanted to say it was nothing, that it was only a stupid necklace. But if she talked, she would cry, and if she cried, he might tell Egon, and Egon would know she was not crying about the pearls. Meyer crawled up beside her and put his hand on her shoulder. "Let me have the pearls. I will get them restrung, I promise." He rubbed her back and she sidled up to him. *Now or never,* she thought, and nuzzled her head against his shoulder.

He got on his haunches; she got on hers. When he wrapped his arms around her neck and kissed her, she didn't pull away. ("You smell like vanilla.") He kissed her again. What happened next was even more awkward than she had imagined it would be. She tried to slow him down, but Meyer pushed her to the floor, straddled her, pulled open the top of her dress, squeezed her breasts, then undid his pants and, with a lot of grunting and heaving, pushed himself inside of her. Just as quickly, he pulled out and rolled over. He lay beside her and closed his eyes. Maybe he'd passed out. Liesl was practiced at keeping the mood, no matter whether she'd been satisfied. But this was nothing close to sex. She sat up and checked her neck to make sure the other strand had not come undone. She waited as long as she could before she said, "I think I must go now. Please tell me when you get the necklace restrung."

Meyer grabbed her arm. "This is not what I intended," he said. "It was the wine, then the pearls . . . I wanted to make love to you, real love; I hope you know that."

Liesl looked at him lying on the floor. What a miserable sight. His body was thick. With his shirt open, she could see his nearly hairless chest. There were orange spaghetti stains on his mouth, and his eyes were red. She thought about Egon: his thick chest hair, his elegant physique. Meyer was the brilliant one; he would succeed. But in the looks and bedroom department, Egon was master. She'd done what she came here to do, and hoped Meyer would tell Egon his version of this night. Wasn't that the point?

She mustered her tact. "Thank you for a wonderful night," she said. "The food, the dancing, it was all so much fun. You can tell your friend that you swept me off my feet, and I won't disagree."

Snow was falling when she left Meyer's, tiny pricks of it that burned her eyes and made them tear. The icy wind blew through her thin coat, and her lips were chattering by the time she reached the subway. A few men said things to her under their breath; women looked her up and down. She knew what they saw: a young girl with lipstick smeared, hair disheveled, wine on her breath. Had she even remembered to button the top of her dress? In Frankfurt, had she seen a woman who looked like this, she'd have thought *whore* and turned away. She let herself imagine coming home and sitting in front of a warm fire. The maid would bring her hot tea and ask if perhaps on such a cold night she'd like some schnapps. Yes, that would be lovely; she'd like that very much. Soon, she'd change into her flannel nightclothes and get into bed under the thick goose-down covers. She would have a warm and trouble-free sleep.

Tonight, this fantasy felt more poignant than it usually did. She couldn't go home, not alone to her dreadful apartment, one room, not enough heat, the fire escape that looked like a cage. She'd go to Carola's and sleep on the couch. She checked her watch: 10:12. Too late. Carola worked early on Saturdays. Maybe better that way. She wouldn't have to say where she'd been or why she looked the way she did.

The subway was empty. Old newspapers curled around her feet and empty coffee cups rolled back and forth. As she neared her stop, Liesl took out her keys and turned up the collar of her coat. She walked quickly down the dark street, staring ahead in the way New Yorkers did to make themselves feel invisible.

That same evening, Egon phoned Catrina. "Can you come here tomorrow morning and help me with the animals?"

"And your complications?" she asked after a brief silence. "Will they be there too?"

"Come and find out," he said.

When Catrina got to Egon's apartment that Saturday morning, he took her coat and asked if she'd like to use his bathroom. "I'm fine, thank you," she said.

"But perhaps you would like to wash your hands," he insisted.

"My hands are fine."

"Then maybe you would like to look inside my medicine cabinet."

Catrina went into the bathroom and opened the cabinet. Egon followed. The shelves were empty save for a bottle of Kreml, some shaving equipment, one tooth-brush, and a tube of toothpaste.

She looked around the rest of the bath-room. "What happened to the lipstick and nail polish?"

"That is finished," said Egon.

"Finished? Just like that?" Catrina snapped her fingers.

"No. Just finished."

19.

America is a land of refugees and immigrants. Everyone was once a stranger here.

— Meyer Leavitt, *Aufbau,*
February 9, 1940

Meyer had never learned to ride a bicycle. He'd tried. There had been an old one at the farm that had rusty spokes and one handlebar that bent skyward. He'd roll a few feet, shift his hips to the left or lean his shoulders to the right, and *hoppla,* he'd be on the ground. His father had said that a boy with his head in the clouds should keep his feet on the ground, and his brothers had taunted him, saying that he was too fat for the bike's rickety frame. Neither was true. Balance was Meyer's problem, all kinds of balance. He'd say too much, laugh too loud, go too far. Look at what happened with Liesl Kessler.

So typical, he thought.

Despite his arrogance, Meyer paid dearly for his insecurities. One self-doubt would beget another, until he'd nearly suffocate in a loop of *what if*s and *how could I*'s. *How could I have started with Liesl? She's beautiful and young, and Egon was right, so far out of my league. Why would she want an old fatty like me? How could I have served that disgusting gummy spaghetti? What if I had roasted a chicken or boiled some bratwurst instead? What if I hadn't drunk all that wine? I'm clumsy enough to begin with; how could I have dreamed that I could dance with her? I can barely walk like a decent person. I shuffle. I have an uneven gait. I'm sloppy. I can't even keep my shirt tucked in. What if I hadn't kissed her? How could I have attacked her like an animal?*

Meyer buried his face in his hands. *As if I'm not humiliated enough, she'll no doubt tell Carola. Egon will figure out that the real reason I sent Norman's turtle to Catrina was so he'd get involved with her and Liesl would be fair game for me. Fair game, ha. That was no game; that was a horror show. Did I get what I deserved? Yes sirree bob, as they say, I certainly did.*

Meyer let his head fall onto the kitchen table. When he was young, his father had beaten him. A few times, he'd cried, but that had only incited his father to hit him harder. Tears would be as pointless now as they were then. He'd call Egon and tell him everything, and Egon would most likely say, "You make everything into a drama. Save it for your column," and they'd go on as always.

When Egon picked up the phone, Meyer blurted, "I have a confession to make."

"I too have a confession," said Egon.

"Mine is probably more important."

"I don't think so." Egon sounded excited. "I'm going to invite Catrina to our next gathering at the Schnabels'. What do you think?"

Meyer sat up. "What I think is this may be the dumbest idea you've ever had."

"I can't keep her hidden forever."

"This isn't forever. You've only been friends with her for a few months."

"Yes, but she did invite me to meet her family at Thanksgiving."

"And may I remind you, she then uninvited you."

"That was for a different reason."

"Can you honestly imagine how it will be to say, 'Kaethe and Georg, I'd like you to meet the woman who shares my bed, Catrina Harty. Her people are from County

Mayo, Ireland?' "

"I grant you that, it could be awkward. Well, Carola and Max will be kind."

"I wouldn't count on that. Do you forget that Carola is Liesl's best friend? Max will be silent. That leaves me and Liesl. Naturally, I will be my usual charming self, but Liesl will not warm to the next Mrs. Cheese Man. So you see what I mean, it will be more than awkward. It will be awful."

"You were the one who wrote that we were ghettoizing ourselves and we should let in fresh air. Now it is time for the fresh air."

"I applaud your optimism, but don't say I didn't warn you."

Meyer hung up, relieved that Egon had not asked about his confession and excited about entering into a new drama that didn't involve him.

Kaethe and Georg's table was set as it usually was for coffee and cake, only this time there was a lace doily under the platter and a smaller one under the cream pitcher. Meyer noticed that Kaethe had put on lipstick and pinned back her hair instead of knotting it in her usual bun, and that Georg had doused himself with an aftershave that smelled like fermented fruit. Max wore a brown tie with yellow squares, and Carola had powdered her face and rubbed two dots of rouge into her cheeks. He realized that they'd all gotten dolled up for Catrina, their first American.

The only one who had not arrived yet was Liesl. Meyer ran his hands through his hair and jiggled his foot. Would she snub him? Make some pointed remark about their shabby evening together? Liesl's manners were proper, yet she was the least predictable of all of them. Egon was so taken with Catrina that the thought of seeing Liesl didn't seem to unsettle him. Meyer envied his detachment.

The first thing he noticed when Liesl arrived was that she was wearing one strand of pearls. *Idiot,* he thought, remembering his promise to restring the other. She had on a pale blue suit that complemented her gray eyes and showed off her small waist and swimmer's shoulders. She kissed Carola and Max on the cheek and handed Kaethe a package. "A little something I picked up," she said. "Thank you for having me."

Kaethe unwrapped the two bars of Lindt chocolate and said, "It is so thoughtful of you to remember us." Meyer realized that she stressed the word *thoughtful* because none of the others had brought a gift. After Kaethe introduced the two women, Liesl nodded to Catrina and ignored Egon. She hugged Meyer and gave him a provocative smile that he knew was for Egon's benefit.

Georg offered Catrina the seat of honor, a curvy wooden armchair, while the others arranged themselves around her. Liesl sat on the couch, close enough to Meyer that her thigh was touching his. When he crossed his legs, she moved even closer, until their shoulders were pressed together. He wondered if anyone noticed and hoped they did. They all stared at Catrina in silence until Egon announced that she lived in a nearby brownstone on 185th Street. Max speculated it had most likely been built around the turn of the century in the Renaissance style. His lips were red and chapped, and Meyer became distracted, imagining Max kissing Carola's tender skin. Georg asked him a question, and Meyer asked him to repeat it.

"I am asking how you like your job at the *Aufbau.*"

It annoyed Meyer that Georg's questions always sounded like commands, but in deference to Catrina, he held his tongue.

"I enjoy writing about our experience in America."

"It's obvious that you do," said Georg, who had been cool to him ever since he'd referred to President George Washington Bridge in his column.

Egon clenched his jaw, expecting Meyer to respond, but Liesl intervened. "Meyer's column is the most entertaining feature in the *Aufbau,* don't you think?" She turned to Catrina, who had not yet said a word.

Catrina smiled and said, "Unfortunately, I can't read the *Aufbau,* but I have no doubt that Meyer is very amusing."

"Foolish me," said Liesl, "of course, it's not in your language."

"Speaking of amusing," Meyer said to Carola, "are you finding time to play the clarinet?" He'd been searching her face for signs of what she might know about him and Liesl, but Carola gave away nothing. "You used to love it so."

Carola glanced at Max. "I haven't in a long while, but soon I may have more time."

Kaethe called everyone to the table and served coffee and crumb cake. Max complimented her on the cake. Georg struck his coffee cup with a spoon. He stood up and addressed the table as if he were delivering an argument in court. "I want to welcome you to our little gathering. Kaethe and I are delighted to have old friends to our home and to welcome new ones." He nodded at Catrina. "So please, enjoy our modest repast

297

and let us share many happy memories and good times together."

Meyer caught the bewildered look on Catrina's face and realized that Georg's accent was so thick she hadn't understood a word he'd said. Liesl scraped her chair closer to Meyer's and whispered in his ear, "I drink to the good times." No one heard what she said, but everyone noticed how Meyer, for a rare moment, was at a loss for words.

Egon asked if anyone had seen the new movie *Gone with the Wind*. No one had.

Meyer recovered enough to say, "I did see *Modern Times*."

Max allowed as how that Chaplin fellow was a genius, and Meyer countered that apparently he was a genius in the bedroom too. "After all, he swept Paulette Goddard off her feet, and she's half his age."

"That's what older men will do to you," said Catrina, smiling at Egon.

Egon looked surprised, and Liesl looked straight at Meyer. "Some of them," she said in a flirty voice.

Meyer could see how Liesl's little game was beginning to bother Egon, and it gave him a prick of spiteful pleasure. He'd keep the game going: "So Catrina, Egon says you have a position at the ASPCA. What is the nature of your work?" He knew full well the nature of her work but couldn't resist raising a subject that would make the Schnabels squirm.

"I can't think of how to say this in a polite way. I help prepare dogs who will be killed."

Kaethe waved her hand in front of her face as if she were slapping at a mosquito. *"Phooy,"* she said. "This is not a subject for the dining table."

They fell into small talk about Fort Tryon Park. Egon said how much he enjoyed the tapestries at the Cloisters, and Max explained how the Cloisters, built on a bluff overlooking the Hudson, was a re-creation of a twelfth-century castle. Conversation bumped along like that until everyone finished eating. Catrina helped Kaethe clear the table. She wiped the crumbs off the plates and stacked them in the sink, putting all the forks in one glass and the spoons in another, exactly as they'd done at the Blue Moon, then rejoined the rest of them in the living room, where things had grown tense again.

Meyer was leaning across the table, shouting at Egon. "Roosevelt might as well have issued them all a death sentence right then and there!"

Catrina raised an eyebrow as if to ask what all the fuss was about. "They're talking

299

about the *St. Louis*," Carola said in a low voice. "You must have read how America turned away a shipload of Jewish refugees after Cuba rejected them. God knows what will happen to them now." Catrina shook her head, even though she knew nothing about the *St. Louis*.

"Perhaps the people on the ship didn't have their papers in order," said Georg.

Meyer jerked around so fast, he knocked over the cream pitcher. "I swear, Georg, if you weren't a Jew you'd be one of them, and you'd be a very good one."

Georg wagged his finger at Meyer. "With you it is impossible to have a civil conversation."

Catrina wiped up the cream with her napkin. Meyer nearly flew out of his skin. "With you, it is impossible to be in the same room."

Uncomfortable with the tension, Catrina retreated to the kitchen, where she washed and dried the dishes and wiped down the counters. When she returned, they had fallen back to discussing old Frankfurt friends and the café in Berlin that Meyer and Egon used to frequent. No one paid her attention except Egon, who caught her eye and tapped his watch as if to say *We'll get out of here soon.*

The sun had set by the time they all left. Liesl held out her coat for Meyer to help her with it. Together they walked out without saying good-bye to Egon or Catrina.

In the street, Egon took Catrina's arm, helping her around the mounds of dirt-capped snow. "This was not so bad," he said.

"Are you asking me or reassuring yourself?"

"I guess a little of both. You charmed them, as I knew you would."

Catrina stopped walking. "Egon, they barely spoke to me. Little Miss Lipstick was horrible. She and your friend, Meyer, seemed very cozy. I don't know why he had to ask what I did at work, and I must say, you weren't much of a help either."

"Yes, I noticed what you are saying about Liesl and Meyer. Whatever that was is news to me. But they all tried, Catrina. We all tried. You know, you are the first guest they've had here who is not one of us. I think they accepted you."

"What you're saying is I'm the first gentile they've had, and a Catholic no less."

"I suppose I am."

"Well, thank you very much, but my tiny world is quite enough, I don't need to be accepted into yours."

After the guests left, Kaethe walked into her kitchen expecting to find a sink full of dishes. Georg was already sitting in his chair tuning in the radio when he heard her cry out, "Georg, you must see this." He came in and looked around. "What is it?"

"The dishes. They have been washed and dried and put away."

Georg stared at the cupboard. "So they have."

"Well, I didn't do it," said Kaethe. "Egon's girl must have cleaned up while we were all talking." She let a smile stretch across her lips. "Georg, do you think she really is his girl and not his girlfriend?"

In Germany, they'd all had maids who served their food and washed their floors. In America, they called them "girls," and none of their circle could afford to have one.

"They're good housekeepers, the Irish." Georg smirked. "Maybe so."

20.

We move awkwardly into the new country. We wear bow ties and Stetson hats and, you betcha, we talk the American slang whenever we can. In Frankfurt, my friend was a respected doctor. Here, he works in a grocery store and is known as the Cheese Man. To his surprise, he doesn't mind this title. He says it gives him definition and an identity. We take our place in America anywhere we can get it. This newspaper, like the Cheese Man, is all about reconstructing oneself in a new country. In that spirit, we will add a subtitle to our logo and from here on we shall be known as *Aufbau: Serving the Interests and the Americanization of the Immigrants.*
— Meyer Leavitt, *Aufbau,*
June 14, 1940

"I never said I liked being called the Cheese Man!" Egon shouted into the phone when

Meyer picked it up. "I believe I said that it has given me some recognition and that *Art* is the one who likes it."

"*Ach,* Egon, who cares? So I took liberties. I'm an American journalist now, that's what we do. Put your petty grievance aside for a moment, and I will tell you something that you will like. The *Aufbau* is looking to help its readers assimilate into America. Remember our old game, 'The Worst Job of the Week'? Well, I had the idea that we make it a regular column and call it 'Job of the Week.' The editor loved it. He scheduled our first one for Labor Day in September, and guess who it's going to feature?" He didn't pause long enough for Egon to respond. "Never mind, you'll never guess. You and Catrina! Your old friend, Norman Blum, has never gotten over how you both saved his daughter's miserable turtle. He was the one who suggested the two of you. Everyone thought you'd be perfect. You'll meet with Norman and a photographer — yours truly — at your apartment sometime over the summer. I'll give you a date as soon as I know. We'd like it if you could also have one of the animals you've treated to pose with you in the photograph. So you'll arrange that and tell Catrina, yes?"

"Interesting," said Egon. "But one thing.

Is this a good idea, to make public us treating the animals?"

"I don't see why not," said Meyer. "It's a good advertisement for you."

"But do I want to advertise about the animals?"

"Sure, why not? The authorities won't care, if that's what you're worried about. They don't come after people like you."

"And what if Catrina says no?"

"Why would she say no?"

"She has her own opinion about things and may not want to be in your *Aufbau*."

"Fine then, I'll ask her. Though, honestly, must I do everything?"

"Never mind, I will do it."

Lately, Egon had been feeling on the side of luck, but he knew how luck could play a person both ways, and he wasn't willing to tip the balance. He still worried about Catrina's comment about his tiny world, and had taken care not to drag her into it too often, though she was not at all self-conscious about bringing him into hers. He had become a regular at the Hartys' Friday-night dinners and would always bring a chocolate peach cake.

Egon was Rose's first Jew. She'd met some at the hospital but never talked to them or shared a meal with them. She told Catrina that he wasn't what she'd imagined a Jew to be. He wasn't pushy or loud or fat. God knows he wasn't rich. His fingers were slim, like a woman's, and his nose was long but straight and flat, as if it had been pressed between the pages of a book. Because of his accent, she had to strain to understand what he was saying, but at least he wasn't fawning in the way that Walter had been, always kissing her hand and calling her sweetie. Egon's manners were curiously formal. He used his knife to push food onto his fork and always took her arm when they walked. Sometimes he brought fresh fruit or slices of rare roast beef for her, claiming they would make her stronger.

"When he asks about my health, he seems genuinely interested in my answers," Rose told Kiefer. "Most men won't give you the time of day." She felt a kinship with anyone who'd suffered, and this man had suffered, she could see that. She told herself it didn't matter that he was Jewish. In God's eyes, a good man was a good man. Most of the time, she believed it, particularly when she saw how he was with Catrina, but each week she prayed for forgiveness for her daughter, who was living in sin with this very good man. Walter had had a way of grabbing at

Catrina that made Rose uncomfortable. His touch had been rough and greedy, whereas Egon would stroke her hair as if she were a child, or slip his hand into hers as they sat on the couch. He called her *liebchen* and followed her everywhere with his eyes.

Kiefer called Egon Buddy, sometimes Bud, mostly because he didn't like the foreignness of *Egon.* Conversations were easiest when Kiefer asked him questions about politics. Kiefer figured he was an old guy from the old country, so he probably knew stuff about Mussolini and Russia. Egon would answer as best he could — more often than not, he admitted to Catrina, by quoting Meyer. Sometimes Bud asked Kiefer about his work, and Kiefer would tell him about his precinct or some tough who'd been brought in on robbery charges. Kiefer told Catrina that Buddy was an okay guy, a whole lot better than that lowlife she'd married. He didn't tell Catrina how it gave him the creeps the way Bud always found a way to touch her. Even if she walked by, he'd stroke her shoulder and smile in a hungry kind of way. Guys were like that, but this one was old and a foreigner. No, it wasn't that, really. What really made him uncomfortable was the thought of Bud's Jew fingers all over his sister. Kiefer hated himself for thinking that, because it brought him back to who he was: his father's son, exactly who he didn't want to be.

Egon waited until the time felt right before asking Catrina about the column in the *Aufbau*. It came late on a Saturday afternoon in June as they left the Cloisters. A light wind blew off the river. Egon stopped walking. He took in a deep breath. "Mmm, smell that. What do you think is in that air that makes it smell so inviting?"

Catrina sniffed several times. "Water. Probably freshly cut grass, early summer." She turned to him and smiled. "You ask funny questions."

"If you think that is a funny question, will you believe this one?" He spelled out the facts of the Job of the Week column as quickly and monosyllabically as a child in a school play. "They also want to take our picture. Can you imagine?"

"I don't know anyone who reads that paper." She shrugged. "We can do it if you like."

"Everyone I know reads that paper," he said. "It would be a good way for us to let the word out that we care for the animals."

Catrina and Egon rose early to prepare for

the *Aufbau* interview. A typical August day, it was muggy and already eighty degrees. Catrina opened all the windows. She swept the dog hair from the floor, and, though he felt foolish doing so, Egon polished the brass plaque with *Doktor Egon Schneider* engraved on it and propped it up on his desk. They scrubbed Johnny, then washed and dressed themselves. He put on his only suit, a clean white shirt, and his father's cuff links. "Very handsome," said Catrina, stroking his cheek.

"I feel ridiculous to be dressing for Meyer."

"You're not dressing for Meyer, you're dressing for the readers of that newspaper who are about to be introduced to Dr. Schneider."

Egon stepped back to get a good look at Catrina. She wore a green dress with a belted waist and black pumps. "You look very, um, respectable. So respectable, I would like to relieve you of your respectability."

He leaned down to kiss her, but she pushed him away. "Not now," she said, laughing. "Boris will be here any moment."

Minutes later, the doorbell rang. It was Gerald Elmlinger, the man from Nagle Avenue with Boris the boxer, whose tail had

309

split after he'd thumped it too hard against a wall. Catrina had chosen Boris to pose in the picture with them because, she said, he had the most regal bearing of all the animals they'd treated. Soon after, Norman Blum arrived. Norman took Egon's hand into his own pillowy one. "Thank you so much for fixing my daughter's turtle. I don't know what we would have done without you."

Egon withdrew his hand and said, "Catrina is the one you should thank."

Norman reached out to Catrina, but before he could touch her, she stepped back and said, "How is Dribble doing these days?"

He smiled. "He ambles around as if nothing happened. A remarkable turtle, I must say."

Just then, Meyer came in with a Rollei slung around his neck. He circled Egon's apartment as though he'd never been there before, thumbing through a book at his bedside and picking through papers on his desk. He studied the brass plaque, then put it down when he spied the cloth pouch containing the glass eye. He dug out the eye and held it up. "Perfect."

Norman asked a lot of questions, mainly of Egon. Meyer had Catrina sit behind the desk holding Boris's tail, straight as a pencil, and he had Egon stand beside her listening to the dog's heart with a stethoscope. The glass eye was centered on the desk in front of Boris. "Say 'Cheese Man,' " Meyer cajoled as he snapped the shutter.

Two weeks later, Catrina and Egon sat at Nash's eating chocolate peach cake and waiting for Meyer. He rushed in as if he were being chased. "I have the article," he said, slapping the paper on the table. "First, I order, then we read. I think you'll be pleased."

Under the headline THE CHEESE MAN OF WASHINGTON HEIGHTS was a photograph, two columns wide and three inches high. Catrina picked up the paper and stared closely. "My face is enormous, like the man in the moon."

"Your face is beautiful," said Egon. "But I am slightly stooped, like a stern professor."

"No, more like a worried doctor," said Catrina.

"The only one who looks like himself is Boris," said Egon.

"What does the article say?" asked Catrina.

"I will interpret," said Egon. "It is a quote from me saying how ophthalmology is one of the few medicines that translates to veterinary medicine as well. 'I feel fortunate,' I say, 'that I am able to apply my skills to the animals of Washington Heights.' " Egon paused to take a bite of his cake. "Here I talk about the glass eye. 'My mother, Elisabeth Schneider, was a world-famous nature illustrator. She gave me this as a reminder that I should always look at the world with fresh eyes. My parents were known as the Audubons of Europe.' "

The article went on about Egon's walks through Fort Tryon Park; his beloved dog, Johnny; and how he'd become a favorite with the customers at Art's. All that was missing was Catrina, who was only mentioned once in a caption as "Mr. Schneider's assistant."

Egon put down the story and turned to Meyer. "This you think will please me?"

Meyer raised one eyebrow. "You're famous, what more do you want?"

"This whole thing makes me uncomfortable. The Cheese Man of Washington Heights is not how I wish to be famous. The picture is horrible. And what about Catrina?"

"So, now you're not only an animal doctor, but also a critic? Norman Blum worked hard on this piece, and I happen to think the photograph is very distinguished."

"Well, I happen to disagree." He chose not to bring up his disappointment about not being called Dr. Schneider. "I am sorry, there must have been an oversight," he said to Catrina.

She twirled a piece of hair around her finger. "There was no oversight. If the *Irish Echo* ever does a story about us, believe me, they won't write much about you." She excused herself and went to the ladies' room.

Egon pulled his chair closer to Meyer's. "What are you doing? Again, you put me in a bad situation in your newspaper. Then there was that business with Liesl. You claimed the song and dance with the two of you at the Schnabels was nothing, but I have not seen her in a long while, have you? I should not have to ask you a question like that. We are supposed to be friends, or have you forgotten? And we have never mentioned what happened at your apartment, or have you forgotten that too?"

The article. Liesl. The kiss. Meyer hadn't forgotten any of it. It was so typical of Egon to stay quiet all these months, then spit out his complaints in one chocolaty huff. But Meyer could justify his behavior.

"Being known as the Cheese Man is a good thing. You've made a name for yourself in a

very short time. Feel proud of that."

"Believe it or not, Liesl chose me." (Egon would never believe that.) "You threw her over, what do you care who she picked next? But no, I haven't seen her since then."

The kiss was a joke on both of them. "Surely, Egon, even you see the humor in that."

Meyer started to enumerate his answers but saw Catrina heading back from the ladies' room. "Shall we conduct this confession in front of your Virgin Mary, or would you rather flog me in private?"

Egon looked down at Meyer as he stood to pull out Catrina's chair. "Georg Schnabel is right about one thing. With you, it is impossible to hold a civil conversation."

For the next two months, there was an uncomfortable stalemate between them. No more phone calls, and they rarely saw each other. Conversations with Meyer used to be Egon's reward for a long day at Art's. Now he had to stop himself from calling. With Meyer, he had never held back. It had been a relief not to have to be polite, to speak in German when he felt like it, to ask Meyer's advice and to banter with him. Meyer was maddening, often inappropriate, and embarrassingly vulgar. He'd hurt Egon's feelings in so many ways, yet Egon depended upon his raw interpretation of life.

On a rainy fall night, Egon was awakened by a ferocious pounding at his door. He was accustomed to midnight emergencies. Animals don't get sick or injured on anyone's schedule. He pulled his housecoat over his pajamas and stepped into his slippers, calling, "Yes, yes, one moment, please." He opened the door expecting to see a cat or dog cradled in someone's arms. There was no animal, only a person whose face was red and contorted, as if someone had punched it. The body was slumped and sounds were coming from a place deep within it. It took him a moment to recognize the arched eyebrows and the unmistakable gray eyes.

"Liesl, what is it?"

She stared past him and reached into her pocket. A telegram. She shoved a yellow piece of paper in front of him. Strips of words were pasted onto it, and the letters were capitalized and evenly spaced. Egon held his breath. It was from the Red Cross. YOUR PARENTS HAVE BEEN LOCATED IN BERLIN. They both knew the language of these telegrams: *Your son has been located at Mannheim. Your sister . . . in Frankfurt.* The

315

people who had been "located" most likely had been taken; alive or not was a whole other question. The page held little room for hope. Egon opened his bathrobe, wrapped it around Liesl, and drew her to him. Her body was drenched and shaking.

"You are freezing," he said. "Come inside." She stood in his foyer while he ran to the bathroom to get a towel. She sat as passively as a child while he pulled off her soaked jacket and wet shoes and dried her feet and arms. She continued to shiver. He took her by the hand and led her to the bedroom, where his sheets were still warm with his sleep. "Get in," he said. He tucked his quilt around her and rocked her back and forth. She let herself be rocked until she finally stopped shaking. Her eyes were closed and her body was quiet. Egon got up and started to tiptoe into the kitchen.

"Don't go," she said in a hoarse voice.

He sat down next to her. "I was going to make you something warm to drink."

"I don't want anything to drink." She reached her arms from under the blanket and grabbed him around the neck, yanking his face close to hers. She kissed his neck, his face; hard kisses, more like bites. She pulled his hair and dug her fingers into his back. She gripped his thighs so that he would straddle her, and pushed him inside of her. She needed somebody, anybody, to fill her loss. Egon knew he was that anybody, yet he found the sex exciting and her grief moving. He watched her through the night, and under his gaze, she slept fitfully until a begrudging sun announced another rainy morning. In the grim light she looked beautiful.

He left his housecoat on her side of the bed, got washed and dressed, and quickly took Johnny across the street. Liesl was still sleeping when he came back. Quietly, he prepared coffee. It was early, and he hoped she would wake up soon so he could leave. When she finally did appear, he had to smile. Her eyes were red and her voice nasal. Her hair, still limp from the night before, fell into her face, and his bathrobe flowed around her so the only visible parts of her were her bare feet. "You are a sight," he said.

She ignored his teasing. "Can I use that pink toothbrush in your bathroom?" she asked. Though Egon was sure she emphasized the word *pink,* he answered as nonchalantly as possible, "Sure, use whatever is there."

At breakfast, they didn't talk about the night before. Egon told her not to give up on her parents. "For all you know, they were detained for a day or two and are home in Frankfurt."

Liesl put down her butter knife. "Do you really suppose the Red Cross has time to notify all the families whose loved ones are detained for a day or two?"

"We will ask Meyer to see what he can find out," said Egon.

"Hmmph, Meyer. What does he know?"

"A lot. Meyer knows a lot."

Egon had betrayed Catrina. Catrina must never find out about this. It was awful, he knew. Even worse, he resented Liesl for bringing him back to the world of Herr and Frau Kessler. He wished she would leave. He thought about his dinners with Catrina, Rose, and Kiefer; the stories Catrina told about her father; the way Kiefer talked about his cases. He loved saying their names. Ryan Walsh. Rose Walsh. Kiefer Walsh. Catrina Harty. So much more melodic than Egon Schneider, Kaethe Schnabel, Liesl Kessler. He regretted last night. Then again, what choice had he had? Liesl had been hysterical. Anyone with an ounce of compassion would have done the same thing. Never mind that he enjoyed it, he couldn't blame himself for that. But it wasn't the kind of sex that meant something, the kind of sex he had with Catrina. That was love sex; this had been desperate sex. There was a difference, was there not? He wished he could ask Meyer.

Egon cleared the table. He deliberately took time closing his overcoat and tying his scarf, hoping the right words would come to him. He didn't want to be dismissive, but he didn't want to encourage Liesl to stay or come back. "Of course you will call the store and tell them why you are late," he said. "I am sure they will understand. And take whatever you need, more food or coffee. We will get to the bottom of this, I promise." He considered kissing her on the cheek, but the gesture seemed oddly intimate. "Are you okay?"

Liesl took the remainder of her coffee and got back into bed. "I'll be okay."

"You get some rest, yes?"

If she answered, he didn't hear her.

Egon headed to the park. He was so rushed, he forgot the bag of bread crumbs for the birds. Fatigue weighted his steps. The Cloisters was shrouded in a squeamish light. No one was out on this morning. It was hard to find hope in a day like this. How would he make it through all those hours at Art's? The insides of his eyelids burned, and he felt nauseated. He sat on a bench and closed his eyes. Sleep didn't come, but thoughts, unbidden, did. What would he do if Liesl was still there when he came home? Had he been kind or cowardly with her? He should tell Meyer about Leopold Kessler.

Meyer, could he be a homosexual? This was not the first time he'd had that thought. The way Meyer carried on about women, Carola, Liesl, sex in general, was that all bravado? Egon had never known a homosexual, not that he was aware of. He'd seen them on the streets of Berlin, their lips puckered in a certain way, their hips swaying provocatively. Meyer was physically awkward, but not in that way. Even if Meyer was one, Egon would still be his friend, though he would have to tell him to never kiss him again.

Egon must have dozed, because when he lurched forward, spittle trickled down his chin and the sun was shining on the arched windows of the Cloisters. He looked at his watch. He had enough time to run down the hill and get to Art's.

He got to his place behind the counter just in time, tied his apron around his back, and touched his fingers to his button to make sure it was fastened. When he looked up, a man in a blue overcoat and a gray fedora was waiting for him. It took him a moment to register that it was Kiefer. Most of the times he'd seen Catrina's brother, they'd been sitting around a table, and Egon hadn't realized how short he was.

"I am surprised to see you here," said Egon. "Is everything okay?"

Kiefer kept one hand in his pocket. "Ah, not really. Catrina tried to call you last night but there wasn't any answer. She asked me to drop by. It's about Rose. She collapsed last night. She's in Bellevue now with Catrina. She wanted me to tell you."

After so much news about people from home disappearing or getting beaten up in the streets, Egon's first thought was that a hospital was a luxury. His second thought was to send a comforting message to Catrina and Rose, but before he could figure out what it might be, he saw Art walking through the produce section in his direction. Later he would blame what he said to Kiefer on fatigue, guilt, and nervousness about Art. "Thank you for your business. Please give your family my kindest regards."

Kiefer nodded as if those words made perfect sense. Egon could hear him jiggling the change in his pocket as he turned around and walked out of the store.

21.

We remember the wounded and the man-
gled from the last war. Do we really want
to rush into another?

— Meyer Leavitt, *Aufbau,*
January 31, 1941

By early 1941, everyone was tracking the
maps of Europe in the *New York Times.* The
areas that Hitler occupied were saturated
with black ink; the others remained white.
Denmark, Norway, Belgium, Luxembourg,
Czechoslovakia, the Netherlands now left
smudges on everyone's fingers, a daily
reminder that any day, America could be
sucked into this war. The only question was
when. Surely the president would answer
that in his third inaugural address. When
Inauguration Day arrived, the country virtually shut down as the speech was piped into
every home, school, and business that had a
radio.

Meyer had asked everyone to come and listen to the speech together at Nash's. "That's an uncharacteristically gracious gesture on your part," Egon had said when Meyer phoned him.

"Not as much as you think," answered Meyer. "I'm doing a story about the reaction to the president's speech, and I need to be with a group of landsmen."

This was true. It was also true that Meyer wanted an excuse to be with his old friends. He'd barely spoken to Egon in the past months and hadn't shown up for any of the *kaffeeklatsche.* Egon was his best friend, his only friend, really, and while he joked and argued with his colleagues at the *Aufbau,* he revealed himself to no one except Egon. Other than at that gathering at the Schnabels', he hadn't seen Liesl since that awful evening they'd had together either, though he'd called several times. He'd use any excuse to gaze upon the beautiful Carola and even felt some perverse nostalgia for the Schnabels. Max he could do without.

Nash's was packed that morning. The Schnabels and the Cohens came early. Meyer kept his eye on the door, worried that Egon might not show up. Just as Henry Wallace was being sworn in as vice president, Egon ran in with Catrina behind him.

Meyer tried not to show his relief when Egon took the seat beside him. The two men nodded at each other as Chief Justice Charles Evans Hughes administered the oath of office to President Roosevelt. Only Liesl was missing. There was silence as a January wind whooshed through the microphone. Roosevelt began: "On each national day of inauguration since 1789, the people have renewed their sense of dedication to the United States . . . In this day the task of the people is to save that nation and its institutions from disruption from without."

Egon put down his coffee and leaned in toward the radio, which sat next to an apple tart on the counter. Meyer kept his eyes on the few tendrils of Carola's hair that had come loose. In less than thirteen minutes, Roosevelt made his intentions clear:

In the face of great perils never before encountered, our strong purpose is to protect and to perpetuate the integrity of democracy. For this we muster the spirit of America, and the faith of America. We do not retreat. We are not content to stand still. As Americans, we go forward, in the service of our country, by the will of God.

"Bravo," said Egon, once the muffled applause of a gloved Washington crowd subsided. He rose to his feet, as did the woman at the next table holding a Pekingese under her arm.

"Bravo," shouted a waiter, who put down his tray of cups and saucers to applaud.

Two men in the first banquette stood up, as did Max and Carola.

Only Meyer and the Schnabels remained seated. "This is it," announced Meyer. He scribbled in his notebook, then turned to Catrina. "Your boyfriend won't be shouting bravo when your brother is wallowing around in the trenches over there."

"Kiefer doesn't wallow," she answered, pushing back her chair.

"Does this mean you're in favor of the war?"

"The war's inevitable. It's the only way to defeat Hitler," she said, rising to her feet.

Georg leaned in to Meyer. "Hitler won't last. The German people will overthrow him. It's not necessary for the Americans to get involved."

"They show no sign of wanting to overthrow him," said Meyer.

"America should take care of itself; we deal with our own problems."

"We are not them anymore, thank God," said Meyer, continuing to write. "And I'd

325

prefer to leave Germany's future, such as it is, in the hands of Mr. Roosevelt."

Georg's face reddened. "Your Mr. Roosevelt doesn't seem to worry so much about the Germans, particularly the Jews, does he?"

"He's hardly mine, but right now he's all we've got."

"Please," said Egon, who sat down in time to hear their exchange. "We see each other so infrequently these days, can we be civil?"

Max waited until the room quieted before he raised his finger and said, "Carola and I have a little news of our own." He took her hand. "We are expecting a child in June."

Meyer glanced at Carola's stomach, willing himself not to imagine the moment of conception. "Wonderful," he said in his singsong voice. "May I be the first to congratulate you on hatching a Jew at such a propitious time."

Max's smile froze. Carola placed her hands on her stomach. Georg held his fork midair and said, "Meyer, why must you always be so vulgar?" In a gentler tone, he said to Carola, "On behalf of Kaethe and myself, I congratulate you. Having a child is not something we all can do. Even those of us with fancy jobs."

"At least I know where to find my balls,"

snapped Meyer, "which is more than I can say for some people here." He kept writing.

Egon touched his arm. "Look at us. We are in America for three years now, some of us more. First when we came, we slept on each other's couches and shared our food. Now we bicker like children when we have much to be grateful for. The Cohens will have a child. We all have jobs. America will go into this war and get rid of Hitler. We are here, not there."

Meyer slammed his notebook shut and called for the check. "Heartwarming speech, Egon, but I'm afraid this little celebration is over. Some of us have work to do." He threw three dollar bills on the table and walked out.

Egon caught up with him before he reached the subway. "Hey, Meyer, we're the lucky ones. Remember?"

In the frigid air, Meyer's mouth twisted as if it couldn't keep up with his words. "Some of us are more lucky than others," he said, holding up his notebook. "I got my story, I'll tell you that. And I'll tell you something else. If that self-righteous prick Georg says another word to me, I will cram his precious little dinner bell up his ass."

"Why can you not let him be? He is jealous of you. You have a future. He and

Kaethe do not; they are counting the days until the Führer welcomes them home."

When Meyer laughed, cold-weather tears ran down his face. He grabbed Egon by the shoulders, happy to be sparring with him. "You're beginning to sound like me."

Egon jerked away. "Uh-oh, you are not going to kiss me again, are you?"

"No, no, that was a once-in-a-lifetime piece of luck, my friend."

Meyer couldn't wait to get back to his typewriter. He wrote his story exactly as it happened:

The Cheese Man shouted, "Bravo!" and rose to his feet. A Pekingese and his plump owner followed. Waiters put down their trays, customers pushed aside their sachertortes and eclairs to stand up and clap. Even the Non-Jew stood up, applauding the man who she hoped would someday defeat Hitler. Only the Loyal Germans stayed seated.

Meyer dubbed himself Struwwelpeter, after the unkempt character in a series of gruesome fairy tales for children, and detailed his argument with the Loyal German. He ended his piece with Herr Blobbo announcing that he and the lovely Schneewittchen were going to have a child:

Only in America do people greet the news of war and the conception of a child with equal optimism and celebration. Struwwelpeter felt neither. He was swamped with desperation and sadness. The world he'd left behind was destroying itself, and his new world was about to enter into a horrific war. He hated Hitler as much as the next man, but he was not a warrior. He was not a lover or a father either, and the prospect of ever becoming any of these things seemed, at that moment, impossible. An isolated angry man surrounded by revelers, Struwwelpeter left Nash's abruptly and headed for the subway. His friend, the Cheese Man, ran after him and told him not to be such a sourpuss. "We are the lucky ones," he said. "We have jobs. We are here, in America;

we are not there." His friend's
words did not lift the weight
from Struwwelpeter's heart, but
his gesture was a stab at friendship and made Struwwelpeter
think that if one is to cultivate
an optimistic outlook these
days, having a friend is a place
to start.

Of all the columns Meyer wrote, this was
the one that got the biggest response. People
wrote letters to the *Aufbau* saying they
agreed with the Loyal German, asking when
Schneewittchen's child was due, or rooting
for Struwwelpeter. Meyer's editor insisted
that he continue to write about these characters because they humanized the immigrant experience.

Meyer tried to explain to the Schnabels
and Cohens and Egon and Catrina that the
Loyal Germans, Herr Blobbo, Schneewittchen, the Cheese Man, and the Non-Jew
were fictional, characters out of his imagination, very loosely based on some of them.
"Am I such a masochist that I would call
myself Struwwelpeter, the most unappeal-
ing of them all?"

The Schnabels had no problem with
Meyer's characterization of them. "That my

point of view is public is not a bad thing," said Georg. Carola and Max were so preoccupied with her pregnancy they barely paid attention, and Catrina, of course, never read the *Aufbau.* Even Egon, moved by Meyer's naked display of sentimentality, resigned himself to being the Cheese Man.

22.

Secrets. By now, we all have them.
— Meyer Leavitt, *Aufbau,*
February 7, 1941

Catrina slept with her lips pursed, as if she were about to blow a bubble. Her limbs were splayed, and her hair flowed around her like the current in a river. Watching her sleep on this Sunday morning was Egon's first pleasure of the day. Johnny was curled at his feet, and the sun was striping through the Venetian blinds. Catrina had completely abandoned herself to her sleep. Sleeping in front of another person was the ultimate act of trust. He hoped he was worthy of hers. Maybe she had secrets too. He leaned over and kissed her hair.

There was a noise — nothing startling, the rustle of a curtain perhaps.

Again. This time, an insistent tapping. Careful not to disturb Catrina, Egon got up, walked to the window, and peeked through the blinds. A bird with a red-brown breast and a pattern of mustache-shaped stripes had alighted on the rail of the fire escape. He recognized the head, with its watchful black eyes and short hooked bill: a peregrine falcon. They'd been known to nest on bridges or on the ledges of apartment buildings. The falcon stood stone still. Then a new sound: *rehk rehk rehk.* A larger falcon alighted next to him. The female. It was winter and they were house hunting. The longer he watched them, the more the falcons, with their eager eyes and imposing statures, made him think of his parents.

Foolish thoughts, he told himself, waving his hand in front of his face. *Stare at anyone long enough and they look familiar.* The gesture sent the falcons flying.

"*Scheisse.*"

"What is it?" said Catrina, sitting up. "Come back, I'm cold."

Egon got into bed and explained what he'd seen: "I know I sound crazy, but they reminded me of my parents."

"Ah, you're having a visitation, aren't you?"

"What do you mean, 'visitation'?"

"Some part of you believes they *were* your parents."

"Nonsense. I know what happens when people die, and I can tell you that they do not come back as birds. What an odd notion."

Catrina got out of bed and walked over to the window. "Suppose those birds were a sign that your parents were watching over you. Would you find that such an odd notion?"

"Yes, I would. There was nothing affectionate about these birds. They had hard eyes and made a harsh sound. I would like to think my parents were more kindly than that. Now, please, can we stop this foolish conversation? Come back to bed."

Catrina sat next to him, wrapping her arms around her knees. "I wish I'd seen them."

"Next time," he said, stroking her foot. "You are cold. Now we concentrate on fixing that." He kissed her toes, her ankles, and the backs of her legs, working his way up to the flesh of her inner thighs. After all this time, the smell of her and the way her skin pressed against his lips still stirred and welcomed him.

Meyer called the following morning. He resumed his usual banter with Egon, as if nothing had ever come between them:

"Hello, Mr. Big Shot, how does it feel to have your name in the paper? What other secrets do you keep from me? Ah, you're sleeping with Eleanor Roosevelt. That's it, isn't it?"

"What are you talking about?"

"There's an item in this morning's *Herald Tribune* about you being the favorite animal doctor in Washington Heights. That picture I took of you and Catrina with the boxer, it's there too. Someone must have read the piece in the *Aufbau* and given it to the *Trib*. Did you know about this?"

"Not at all. What does it say?"

"Nice things, although — you're not going to like this part — they call you a recent immigrant from Germany."

"In the picture, do they identify Catrina?"

"No, she's still your assistant, as she was in the *Aufbau*. But they call you a Good Samaritan."

"This makes me nervous."

"You haven't killed any animals yet, have you?"

"No, but what does that have to do with anything? I still have no license."

"Everything. The *Tribune* readers don't care about your license or if you're German. All they know is that you're a good doctor. If things had gone badly, on the

335

other hand, you'd be the Quack Kraut. Worse, you'd be the Quack Kike. So be happy for what you have."

"Meyer, you are giving me a headache. I have to take Johnny out. We will keep this between us, okay? I am not even going to tell Catrina."

"It's not up to us. Have a good walk."

Egon hung up. He bent down and snapped Johnny's leash onto his collar. "I do not like this at all," he said to the dog. They walked to the drugstore on 187th Street, where Egon bought a copy of the *Herald Tribune*. Thumbing the pages, he stood with his back to the street. There it was, on the bottom of page 8: the picture, the headline, ALL EYES ON WASHINGTON HEIGHTS ANIMAL DOC:

Dr. Egon Schneider, a recent immigrant from Germany and former
ophthalmologist, has been treating sick animals for free, or
for whatever people can afford,
in his cozy Washington Heights
apartment since he arrived in
this country three years ago.
Says one grateful spaniel owner:
"I took Nellie to the doc's office at ten one night. No fuss,
no muss, and no bucks either. I

came home at midnight with Nellie and three new pups." When
he's not tending to ailing critters, Good Samaritan Schneider
is slicing up cheese and cold
cuts at Art's Grocery Store on
Overlook Terrace, where he goes
by the name of the Cheese Man.

No one will see this, Egon reassured himself. Such a little picture, so far back in the
paper. As he headed into Fort Tryon Park,
he allowed himself a moment of private
satisfaction: *At least they called me Dr.
Schneider.*

Egon shoved the *Tribune* into his coat
pocket and had nearly forgotten about it
until he arrived at the store, where Art was
waiting for him with a copy of the paper
rolled up in his hand. Art watched Egon
take off his hat and coat, slip his apron over
his head, and tie it around his waist.

"You're a graceful man," said Art.

"Thank you," said Egon.

"I'll bet you were a lady-killer in Germany,
with those big blue eyes and all."

"I had some fun."

"And a doctor no less, that couldn't have
hurt."

Egon stared at Art, whose narrow eyes

seemed barely open this morning. "To what do I owe these kind words?"

"What a comedown it must be to work here. I mean, from doctor to a delicatessen counter, you must hate that."

"I am grateful for the work."

"I run a tight ship, you've probably noticed."

"Yes, I admire your efficiency."

"I keep my nose clean and expect the people who work for me to do the same."

"Of course." Egon noticed Art's liverwurst complexion growing rosier.

"What my employees do in their own time is their business."

"I appreciate that."

"But what I cannot tolerate is having my good nature taken for granted, which every now and again happens. What I'm saying is . . ." He opened the *Tribune* to page 8. "This kind of thing."

Puzzled at what Art was getting at, Egon picked up the paper and looked at it again. "So, you are not pleased about this article?"

"I would be more pleased if you didn't make it sound as if working at this place was what you did in your spare time. I mean, I pay you good wages. Do these 'ailing critters' of yours bring you in a single penny? Could you afford your 'cozy Washington Heights apartment' without your salary? Would you have food on your table or clothes on your back without Art to sign your checks? I think not."

Egon could see that Art was enjoying his discomfort, but this was no time to be proud. "I am at a loss for words. It is true I treat the animals, but only after work or on my days off. I would do nothing to jeopardize my job here. I know you to be a fair and kind man and I will continue to try to be the best Cheese Man in New York City." His smile was faint.

"The truth is, even though this place comes off as a second thought, we could turn this article into something useful for us." Art smiled as if he had suddenly tapped into his own genius. "I'm going to put a copy of it, along with the picture, in the window. I'll write in big letters, 'Come In and Meet the *Herald Tribune*'s Good Samaritan: Our Very Own Cheese Man.' Good idea, eh? We'll give it time and see how it works. But listen, no more publicity unless it comes from right here, do you understand?"

"I do. Thank you for your kindness."

Egon's stomach gurgled like water draining from a tub. For the first time in months, his insides burned, and a familiar acidic taste filled his mouth. He'd phone Catrina on his break. No, he'd call Meyer.

Meyer answered on the first ring. "Are you busy?" asked Egon.

"No, not at all. I've been combing my hair all morning hoping you'd call. What is it?"

Egon told him about Art's plans. "The last thing I want is to draw attention to myself."

"Too late, that's already been done for you."

"And Catrina, she certainly will not want her picture in Art's window."

"Catrina will be fine. So you'll be a little famous. Women like famous men. You'll see, they'll line up to take a little nibble out of you."

"Thank you, Meyer, you've been a great help, as always. I am hanging up now."

Egon took two Tums and went back to work.

Before his next break, a woman with a Polish accent wished him luck. Later, an older man leaned across the delicatessen counter. "Saw the paper today," he whispered. "We don't need folks like you being our Good Samaritans, we got our own."

Egon handed him a piece of cheese. "Thank you," he said in a loud voice. "I appreciate your business."

It wasn't until lunchtime that he finally got around to calling Catrina at the ASPCA. "Hello, Mr. Good Samaritan," she greeted him. She sounded cheerful.

"Then you have seen the article."

"I have, and so has everyone else you know. Why do you sound so glum? It's nice."

He told her about Art's plan. "I am sorry to drag you into it."

"I don't care. My name isn't even in there. And my picture's so small, who will see me?" She laughed. "But Boris the boxer will be pleased."

"Well, I am glad you are so good-natured about it, but it makes me uncomfortable."

"You're a funny one. You miss being a doctor and how you were regarded in Germany. Then you get praised here for being a doctor, and a Good Samaritan, and now you're upset about that? Sometimes I don't understand you."

Egon whispered down the phone, "This is a conversation for another time."

23.

The Cheese Man was the first among us to get mentioned in an American newspaper. His fame, such as it was, came at a price.

— Meyer Leavitt, *Aufbau,*
February 14, 1941

The cellophane packet of ball and jacks was an easy swipe. Liesl had never played jacks; she'd never even heard of it. But there they were, alone in the toy department, the dull metal jacks and tiny pink ball. They'd been sitting on a back shelf gathering dust for more than a week before she swept them into her smock pocket. Ten jacks and a rubber ball would fit in perfectly with the others: five address books, a set of measuring spoons, six coasters, two ashtrays, and a stuffed toy duck. They had all been rejected by the customers and would have fallen into the trash bin or been taken down to the basement and stashed away with last year's Christmas ornaments if it hadn't been for her. In her apartment, they lived together on the nightstand next to her bed. Orphans, that's what they were. They needed a home, and she had given them one. She wished someone would do the same for her. She knew this would probably sound nutty to most people, but most people didn't understand the corrupting logic of loneliness the way she did.

She wasn't the only one. Egon thought that pretending to be a doctor made him one. Because Meyer wrote a stupid column for a newspaper that nobody read, he called himself a journalist. The Schnabels were certain they would return to Germany any day, and the Cohens took for granted that they would be embraced by America as soon as they had their baby. Compared with their delusions, Liesl figured that treating inanimate objects like orphans who were grateful to be rescued was a minor personality quirk.

Her grief about her parents — that was more than a quirk. It etched her face and stole whatever it was that had made her a beauty. Attracting men had never been a problem for her, but these days she couldn't remember the last time a man had flirted with her or caught her eye in the subway. Even when she'd had no money and couldn't speak the language, her arrogant beauty had kept her aloft. She'd enjoyed slowing down in front of store windows and studying her reflection. In those moments, being Liesl Kessler had been enough to drive away the worries that pecked at her. But these days, she walked quickly past those windows, avoiding a glimpse of that woman with the downturned mouth and hooded eyes. She turned inward. At work, the girls would take their lunch outside if it was nice, or to the basement if it wasn't. She never joined them, because she figured there was nothing to talk about except this crummy job, and that was hardly something to discuss.

Except for Carola, she had stopped seeing the Frankfurt group. She was still infuriated with Egon. After their last night together, she had stayed at his apartment. Even in the state she was in, she'd made the bed, tidied the kitchen, and bought groceries with the intention of cooking dinner for him. He never even phoned to see how she was. Only when it came to be early evening did she realize he would not be hurrying home. The pink toothbrush. She knew about Catrina. So what? Liesl never fought with other women over a man and wasn't about to start now. Sex with Egon had happened on her terms, and he had more than willingly gone along with it. She wondered if he had told Meyer about their night together, or if Meyer had told Egon about their dismal encounter. Of course, Liesl had told Carola about both of them. Carola, in her sweet way, had tried not to act shocked. "You've always been an active girl," she'd said. "You know that Egon is not someone to take seriously as a potential husband. He's already thirty-nine and has never been married. He adored his mother and she adored him back. He's always had plenty of girlfriends — why not, he's a good-looking fellow — but he'll never find anyone to replace his mother. And Meyer?" She shook her head. "Beneath that bluster he's soft — a sentimental man. He's one who could really get his feelings hurt."

Carola and Max's apartment was the only place Liesl felt at home. She and Carola could spend hours sitting on the lumpy couch and talking. Lately, Carola would bring the conversation around to Liesl's past, as if force-feeding her ego would restore her to life. There was Liesl playing in a tennis tournament, winning a freestyle race, or picking strawberries with some handsome boy. In Carola's telling, the boys were always handsome and hungering after Liesl. Liesl dissolved into these tableaus, retrieving the crisp pleats of her tennis dress, the power in her shoulders as she cut through the water, the smell of ripe strawberries. The boys. Their names were interchangeable. She remembered pink lips and pampered hands. So young and strong; none of them could have dreamed how their strength would be tested. Where were they now? Who among them was still alive?

One evening, while Carola was in the kitchen preparing dinner, Liesl stood in front of the china cabinet the Cohens had brought with them from Germany. The shelves were loaded with souvenirs that friends had brought them from their travels. The tiny silver spoon from Baden-Baden and the cowbell from Lucerne were probably cheap knickknacks, but in this magnificent mahogany cabinet with its curved glass and double doors, they took on the grandeur of museum treasures. Liesl never got tired of looking at them. For the first time, an object on the top shelf caught her eye: a porcelain man sitting cross-legged, no larger than an egg. The chubby figurine wore a black cap and what appeared to be a green cape slung over his shoulders. Simple dots and lines defined his features. He wasn't smiling, exactly: There was a slight bend in his mouth that suggested a private joke. *Mein Gott,* he looked like Meyer. He looked so much like Meyer that it made Liesl laugh out loud.

The china cabinet had four shelves and two big drawers on the bottom, making it nearly as tall as the ceiling. Often, Carola would take out this item or that and explain to Liesl where it had come from. The stories were her way of visiting her past, and Liesl would listen as if it were the first time she was hearing about the snow globe from Berlin or the teacup from Cologne. Not once had Carola ever mentioned the little man on the top shelf, and though Max prized the cabinet, he was indifferent to its contents. The two of them would have had to stand on tiptoes to even see the figurine, which they probably never did. He was abandoned, reasoned Liesl, who felt no qualms about wrapping the little man in a page from the newspaper lying on the coffee table and stuffing him into her purse. The potbellied man with his smirking face would preside over her orphans.

She sat on the couch waiting for Carola to finish with dinner. Absentmindedly she flipped through the pages of the newspaper.

It was a little picture, but the tall elegant bearing of the man in it caught her eye: Egon! Catrina! He looked old, slightly stooped. She had dark circles under her eyes. Liesl felt immediately more cheerful.

The Saturday-afternoon *kaffeeklatsche* had changed since Liesl stopped coming and Catrina joined the group. Egon and Meyer came intermittently while Kaethe and Georg barely came at all and made it clear that they found Catrina an intrusion. The last time she had come, the conversation had turned to the subject of rent. Each had told how much they were paying. When it came to Georg, he had glanced at Catrina and said, "This we'll discuss at another time." Not only did the Schnabels consider Catrina a foreigner, but with the way she chewed with her mouth open and put her elbows on the table, they thought her manners not up to par, that she was of a lower class. Meyer reminded an infuriated Egon that in America, German Jewish immigrants were nearly at the bottom of the class heap. "The Schnabels enjoy having someone they can feel superior to. They haven't felt able to turn their noses up at anyone since they came here. Now they can. Hooray for them."

On the Sunday after the article appeared, Catrina and Egon were late to Nash's. The *Herald Tribune* article plus Art's sign had been in the shop window for two days. As they neared the table, they saw that most of the group was there. Max, of all people, raised his coffee cup. "Here he is now, our Good Samaritan."

The others, except for the Schnabels, raised their cups as well: "Hear, hear."

"Such a modest fellow," said Meyer. "He blushes all the while he's in the limelight."

"Perhaps the limelight is not the best place for him to be," said Georg. "Should we be calling attention to ourselves in this way, particularly when we are doing things for which we are not qualified?"

Catrina squeezed Egon's knee under the table and looked at Meyer, who put down his cup and said to Georg, "Who's qualified to do anything? Is Carola qualified to scrub floors? Am I qualified to write for a newspaper? Are you qualified to press trousers? No, but we do it anyway. That's the wonderful thing about America."

Carola tried to change the subject. "You look very handsome in that picture, though your posture could be better," she said to Egon. "And Catrina, you photograph very well."

"I thought I was frowning," said Egon.

"My hair was a mess," said Catrina.

"*Ach,* nonsense," said Meyer. "Egon, you look like Clark Gable, and Catrina, such a dead ringer you are for Rita Hayworth. Even the dog, for heaven's sakes, as handsome as Fala." He kissed his fingers the way French people did in movies and said, "The crème de la crème."

Kaethe shook her head. "At home, such a notice would never appear." She turned to Egon. "You are a doctor, not a man who sells cheese. The way they talked about you, it was very coarse."

"It's okay, Kaethe," said Egon. "I appreciate your concern, but Catrina and I are not ashamed —"

Georg cut him off. "Excuse me, but I think this is a discussion we should save for another time."

Egon put his arm around Catrina. "This is that time. I do not think there's anything left to discuss."

By now Egon had lived through three Thanksgivings. He was still trying to understand all the fuss over apple pie and pilgrim candles when along came another befuddling American holiday. "Someone decides that there is a day in February when I am

350

supposed to give Catrina a present and a card with hearts on it? Does this make sense?" he asked Meyer on February 13.

"Not at all," said Meyer, "but Americans use any excuse to eat, drink, and give presents. You've seen what happens at Thanksgiving and Christmas. On the Fourth of July they drink beer and eat a lot of meat because the country is free. And now this. Men give women candy or flowers and cards with hearts that say 'Will you be my valentine?' The women get their trophies, the men get laid, and everyone is happy."

"Catrina won't care about any of that," said Egon.

"You are so wrong, my friend," said Meyer.

"How do you know so much about this?"

"I'm a newspaperman. America is my beat. Have you forgotten that?"

Egon took no chances when he went to Catrina's house for dinner on Friday night, which happened to be Valentine's Day. He brought the biggest heart-shaped box of candy he could find. When he came into the living room, Rose stood up from the couch to greet him. Spying the box of candy in his hands, she smiled broadly, clearly thinking it was for her. Egon didn't want to disappoint her so he made a grand gesture out of placing it in her arms and saying, "Will you be my Valentine?"

She took the box from him. "You are so kind to think of me." She leaned in to kiss him and nearly lost her balance. He hadn't seen her since she came out of the hospital. She was smaller now, her movements more tentative. Even walking across a room made her winded. He helped her back to the couch and could hear her labored breathing. The doctor had said it was her lungs. He'd told her to get plenty of rest and eat as much red meat as she could. Also, to drink red wine. It would give her strength, he said. So that night, they sat down for a roast beef dinner that bled into the boiled potatoes and string beans. Their moods loosened as they drank the red wine that Kiefer had brought. They talked about Rose's health. "It's nothing," she said. "The doctors really don't know what to say, but I'm pretty sure after all those years in that basement, I've got a bad case of pleurisy."

"Ma doesn't listen to what the doctors say," said Catrina. "They want to remove the sick part of her lung, but she says no. What's the point of going to a doctor if you ignore what he says?"

"Egon, would you let them cut open your

body and take out a piece of your lung?" asked Rose, not waiting for an answer. "God put me on this earth with two lungs, and I'm leaving this earth with two lungs. That's how it will be."

"It is a difficult operation, but maybe it would help," said Egon.

"Bah," said Rose. "I'm fine the way I am. Now let's open this box of candy."

Egon apologized for not having visited in a while. "They keep me very busy at the store," he explained.

Kiefer said he hadn't meant to startle Egon when he showed up at Art's to tell him about Rose. "Must be odd for you, that place," he said. "Day and night from Germany, huh?"

Kiefer's words, so abrupt and certain, unsettled Egon. He remembered how he had practically dismissed Kiefer that morning because Art was close by, and how Kiefer had walked out as if he'd understood. Catrina's brother could take the measure of a man in an instant, and it pained Egon to think how Kiefer must have recognized him as a frightened man.

"Art runs a tight ship," he said.

"Yup. I see that," said Kiefer.

"Ma, you know the story I showed you about Egon in the *Herald Tribune*?" asked

Catrina, eager to reroute the conversation. "Well, now the story and the picture are in the window of Art's."

"I don't like that paper," said Rose. "And it wasn't a good picture of either of you."

Kiefer scratched his bald spot and asked Egon, "The article in the window? You think that's a good idea?"

"No, I do not want such attention, I would like them to take it out."

Catrina laughed. "Oh, he's being a fuddy-duddy."

Kiefer nodded at Egon. "Stick to your guns, Buddy."

Rose touched the crucifix around her neck. Egon shoved his hand in his pocket to make sure he'd brought his Tums.

There weren't enough rolls of Tums or tablets of Alka-Seltzer to put out the fire in Egon's stomach when he saw the headline in the *Journal-American:* VALENTINE'S DAY VANDALS: NO LOVE FOR WASHINGTON HEIGHTS SYNAGOGUE.

Someone had painted red hearts with the words *Jews + Death* on the walls of the Fort Washington Synagogue. They'd also ripped pages from the synagogue's prayer books and flushed them down toilets. A member of the synagogue's board found the toilets overflowing and waterlogged pages strewn across the floor. *The desecration of the Ft. Washington Synagogue is the latest in an increasing number of attacks, anti-Semitic in nature, over the past few months,* read the article. These things weren't supposed to happen in America. Book burnings, *Juden Doktor* scrawled across the door. Water-logged pages of prayer books. Red hearts with hateful words painted on a wall. What was the difference? The Fort Washington Synagogue was two blocks from Egon's apartment.

The following Saturday morning, he left Catrina tending to the animals and walked to the synagogue. He noted that a police car was parked outside it. There were red smears on the walls where someone had tried to wash away the graffiti, but the words were still legible. Inside, the Sabbath service was going on as usual. Egon stood by the window and listened. The rabbi and congregation read responsively, and their voices were loud enough to convince him that the sanctuary was full. No one seemed to have been deterred by what had happened. He told himself that this was why he had come to America, that this vandalism was a rare incident, the work of teenagers. His head and heart agreed; his stomach did not. By the time he got back to the apartment, he lay down on his bed doubled over with pain. Catrina sat beside him and stroked his head. "You're the sickest animal I've seen all day. Should we fix you up with some castor oil? A little sugar water maybe?"

Egon sighed. "I wish it was that easy."

"I know. It's ugly and awful. But this is a big city, and there are crazy people in big cities. It doesn't mean anything."

"You do not understand what it feels like to be me, to see what I have seen."

"It's true," she said. "But I do know what it's like to be me and to have seen the words 'Irish need not apply.' Please, let's not have this misery contest now."

They'd had this argument before, and it usually ended badly. This time, he didn't feel up to fighting. "You are right, sometimes I allow my imagination to do the best with me."

Catrina laughed and curled up next to him. "How about I do the best with you and we give your imagination a rest?"

When their fights didn't end badly, they ended like this.

Egon's real trouble began nearly two weeks after Art had put up the article and picture.

Late one night, someone scribbled on the store window *The Jew Man Works Here.* But by the time the store opened the following morning, Art and Egon had already washed the words away. A little after three that afternoon, a boy of about fifteen wearing an oversize coat and a stocking cap walked up to the delicatessen counter. When Egon asked if he could help him, the boy stared at him. Egon later remembered the boy's pale, narrow eyes and how they made fear, like a cold mist, rise inside him. The third time he asked the boy if he could help him, the boy said, "Yeah, you can help me. Get your Jew blood the hell out of here." He opened his coat, pulled out a milk bottle filled with red liquid, and threw the liquid into Egon's face. It dripped from his hair. It stung his eyes. A metallic taste filled his mouth. It seeped through the apron to his shirt and trousers. Some spilled onto his socks and into his shoes. It smelled like iron and felt warm and sticky against his skin. The boy ran from the store before anyone could catch him.

Customers gathered. Egon used the unspattered part of his apron to dab his face as Art hurried over with a wet mop. "Don't worry, folks, it's one of those stupid neighborhood kids. We'll get this tomato juice cleaned up in a jiffy. Please, tend to your business."

Egon whispered to Art, "It is not tomato juice."

Art whispered back, "I know." He poured ammonia onto the floor, and as he began mopping, he said to Egon in a soft voice, "This isn't working, you're attracting the wrong kind of attention here."

"Please, can we discuss this at another time? I must go home." Egon's voice was shivery.

Art looked at his watch. "Wash your face and put a coat over you. You can't be in the street that way. Go home, take a hot shower, change your clothes, and be back here in an hour and a half. We'll forget about this for now."

Egon walked home slowly, careful not to attract attention. When he finally got into his apartment, Johnny was at the door, as if he'd been waiting there all day. Egon got down on his knees. "Look at me." Johnny licked his face. Egon leaned his head against the dog's muzzle. They stayed like that until Egon's leg fell asleep. "I am a mess. I go clean myself now."

He stood up, stripped off his clothes, and dumped them in the garbage. Johnny followed him into the bathroom. Egon stood under the shower. He made the water as hot as he could stand it and still could not get warm. He got out, wrapped himself in his bathrobe, and brushed his teeth. He gargled with salt water, then brushed again. The rusty taste lingered. He'd tasted his own blood plenty of times. This was different. Probably not human blood. Of course, the kid had killed an animal and poured its blood into the bottle. A cat? Oh God, a dog? What if he'd been covered in dog blood? He stroked Johnny's head.

He began to sweat and had trouble taking in a breath. His heart beat so fast he could hear it. His face and neck turned red. Anxiety, when it spiked, could feel like a heart attack. He knew this from medical school yet was unable to calm himself. He held his hands to his head and tried humming, but the thoughts kept looping. *I am humiliated. Catrina will leave me. The authorities will find out. I will be sent back to Germany.* If this were a record, he'd smash it. He opened his mouth as if to yawn, then bit down on his tongue as hard as he could. Blood filled his mouth and coated his teeth. His own blood tasted sweeter. Finally, the thoughts stopped coming, all but the shadow of a premonition that this was only the beginning.

■ ■ ■

The letter arrived on a Tuesday night. The postmark said Washington, D.C., and the return address contained words that were as much of a shock to Egon as blood thrown in his face: *Immigration and Naturalization Service.* He told himself it was a routine notice, maybe something about his forthcoming citizenship or a form letter that all immigrants received, yet his stomach tightened as he read.

February 21, 1941

Mr. Egon Schneider,
This is to inform you that your presence is requested for a meeting with Immigration and Naturalization Service (INS) on Monday, March 24, at 9 a.m. at 29 Church Street, fourth floor, room 407. To confirm that you received this notice to appear (NTA), phone our office at LO7-7085. Your case number is 3619. We require that you bring your passport and this notice with you when you report to INS.

Dean Dowling
Immigration and Naturalization Service

Egon read the letter four times, searching for a grace note, a *please* or *would you be so kind as to* . . . To him, the message was as stark and menacing as the dictates in Germany informing Jews not to enter this park or eat at that restaurant.

24.

Someone left the dog on the Cheese Man's doorstep. The dog was mangy and had one chewed-up ear. The Cheese Man took him in and fixed him up. Eventually, they trusted one another. The dog and the Cheese Man loved each other like nobody's business.

— Meyer Leavitt, *Aufbau*,
March 24, 1941

Old and blind, Johnny must have smelled his way around the contours of the apartment, because he never bumped into walls. When Egon took him out, he kept him on a short leash, yanking it gently when he was about to step off the curb: a seeing-eye man leading a blind dog. After Johnny's back legs became wobbly, Egon cooked him chicken and minute steak, hoping to strengthen him, but Johnny kept getting thinner until his ribs poked out, much as they had when

362

Egon first found him. Sometimes Egon had to carry him back from their walks.

A year earlier, Johnny had stopped barking. Whether the effort was too much for him or his voice was gone, Egon couldn't tell, but conversely, the more he diminished, the stronger his odor became, as if it were the only way he could mark his presence. Not even a weekly bath could wash it away. Egon had been treating sick animals long enough to know when they were close to the end, and he always tried to prepare their owners. But now all his knowledge and experience added up to nothing.

On the evening that he got the letter from the INS, Egon sat on the couch with Johnny on his lap and scratched the ridge on the top of his head. "Spring is coming," he said. "That means long walks in the park, you and me. We stick together, eh?" Johnny closed his eyes and rested his chin on Egon's knees.

Johnny must have recognized the new fear in Egon's voice, because in the month since the Good Samaritan article had come out, he'd stayed as close to his master as possible. These days, when every call seemed to be a threatening one, the ringing of the phone was enough to set them both on edge. Often, Johnny seemed to know before

Egon when the calls were coming and would lean against his leg as he answered the phone. At night, he slept snuggled under Egon's arm. Now Egon bent over the dog as if to shield him from his darkest thoughts: The INS knew he was practicing veterinary medicine without a license. There was a case number. He was a case. Had they figured it out from the newspaper, or had someone reported him? If so, who? They could deport him. The State Department had put a squeeze on visas for Jews trying to leave Germany, claiming that Nazi spies might be hiding among them. Given how suspicious Americans were of the German Jews already here, they could deport a German who had broken the rules with the snap of a finger.

He called Catrina. In a voice that sounded as if he were asking her to the movies, he said, "I would love to come over now, is that okay?"

She heard the false ease and asked, "More trouble?"

"You might say so."

"Sure, come now."

Egon hung up and sat back down on the couch. Johnny settled into his lap and licked Egon's cheek. "I am fine," said Egon. "It will be okay." He kissed the dog's head and stood up. "Going for a walk. I will be home soon."

Catrina and Rose were in their night-clothes when Egon arrived. Rose was lying on the couch half-asleep, and Catrina whispered that she'd had a bad day.

"Maybe this is not a good time," Egon whispered.

Rose pulled herself up to a seated position. "What's going on? I'm fine. Just a little nap."

Egon held out the letter. Catrina read it to herself and shook her head. "I don't understand. Why would Immigration Services want to see you?"

Rose asked if she would read it aloud. Catrina narrowed her eyes as she read. When she finished, Rose shook her head. "I don't like the sound of this."

"I am afraid this has something to do with the article that talks about me being a Good Samaritan," said Egon. "I was worried someone would find out that I have no veterinary license."

Catrina asked if he had told Meyer about this. "Not yet, but I know what he will say. He will start yelling that we need to find out who told the INS. He will make all sorts of accusations. He will write a column, 'The Adventures of the Cheese Man,

Continued . . .' "

Catrina interrupted him. "This is serious. You've been getting threatening phone calls, and now this. We need to figure out a plan or something, I don't know."

Rose tried to speak but began to cough: dry explosions that seemed to come from deep inside her.

"That doesn't sound good," said Egon.

She waved her hand. "It's nothing," she started to say, but the cough came again. "Kiefer," she finally managed. "He understands all this legal malarkey. Call him. I'm going to bed. I'll pray for you, Egon."

He saw the effort it took for Rose to get off the couch, and how Catrina had to put her arm around her waist and nearly carry her up the stairs. When Catrina returned, Egon pulled her onto his lap. He wrapped his arms around her waist and rested his head on her back. Her pale yellow housecoat smelled of her, of him, and he breathed them in. "I am a burden to you," he whispered. "All my problems; all my worries. Can you imagine ever marrying a man like me?" He closed his eyes and waited for her to reassure him.

Catrina sat up so quickly she nearly toppled from his lap. "You've got to fight back. Nothing's going to happen if you sit around feeling sorry for yourself. You're a strong man. You got yourself out of Germany to America and made a go of it. You can get through this."

"What is it that you think I should be doing?"

"For one, you should talk to Meyer. He writes for a newspaper and has access to many people. I don't know what he can do, but I'll bet there's something. And Ma is right about Kiefer. He can at least show you the ropes."

"I am scared," he said quietly.

"I'm sure you are."

Egon heard the annoyance in her voice. He wanted her to commiserate with him, not get angry. He raised his hands as if to ward her off. "Please, this is bad enough without you being impatient with me. Okay, I'll call Kiefer. Then can we stop talking about this?"

"Sure," she said, reaching for the phone. "I'll dial his number."

Egon explained everything to Kiefer. He read him the letter, pronouncing INS as *ins* and NTA as *enta,* and asked him if he knew this Dean Dowling.

"Dean Dowling isn't a real person," said Kiefer. "They make up names so the letter can't be traced to anyone." He explained that there would probably be a preliminary interview. "If they do an investigation, you'll need a lawyer. It could go on for months. The Feds take their time."

"Months," said Egon, shaking his head at Catrina. "Months seems like a long time."

Catrina spoke loud enough for Kiefer to hear: "Is there anything he should do now?"

"Yup," said Kiefer. "Do everything you can to build support for your case."

When they hung up, Egon shook his head. "This is getting worse."

"Call Meyer right now."

He shook his head. "You can be a real bully sometimes," he said as he dialed. "Never mind. Talk to Meyer."

Meyer picked up on the first ring, and in a rush of words, Egon told him about the letter and *enta* and *ins* and a man named Dean Dowling, though that wasn't his real name, and how Kiefer said he needed to build support for his case.

"Slow down," said Meyer. "What letter? *Enta* isn't a real word in any language. Who's Dean Dowling? What case? Now, we start over."

Egon read Meyer the letter.

"March twenty-fourth? That's less than a month away. Not a lot of time at all."

"Time for what?"

Meyer was clearly picking his teeth because he had stopped talking. "Somebody must have snitched on you. Who do you suppose it was? It sounds like something our law-abiding friends might do."

"No," said Egon. "The Schnabels would never do that to me. Anyway, this is not the point. It was there in your article."

"Don't be silly," said Meyer. "The authorities would never even see that article. Besides, they would only come after someone for bigger reasons than treating neighborhood animals. Could it be the owner of one of the pets you treat?"

"Why would they?"

"Do you think it really could be one of ours?" asked Meyer. "Max. Carola. Liesl. Liesl?"

The conversation came to a halt. Both men had their secrets with Liesl.

"This is a discussion we should save for another time," said Meyer. "To the matter at hand, I will write something in the *Aufbau*, and you need to start gathering letters."

"What kind of letters?"

"Letters from anyone you can think of who will say what a good doctor you are, what a fine American citizen you would make, how you are a man of your word, of good character, blah blah blah. We write to newspapers. I write in the *Aufbau.* All of us. Kiefer. Rose. Art. The people you work with in the grocery store. The man whose boxer we photographed. We write to President Roosevelt. We get everyone and anyone to write on your behalf."

Egon rolled his eyes at Catrina. "That's ambitious, Meyer. But what if all that writing does not work?"

"Then," said Meyer, "we write some more."

When he hung up, Egon repeated Meyer's suggestion to Catrina. She grabbed a pencil and paper. "Okay, I'll start making the list."

"Must we do this tonight?" he asked.

"Yes," she said. "You heard what Meyer said. That way you can start asking people tomorrow. And no, I never have second thoughts about marrying you."

He called the INS first thing the following morning, as if punctuality might work in his favor. The man on the other end was as chilly as the letter itself. Egon wondered if it was Dean Dowling.

"What is your case number?" he asked.

This was worse than he thought.

He read the numbers, then asked in the calmest voice he could summon, "Is there a problem? Is there something I should know? Maybe there is something I can do to fix this?"

"Nothing that I know of, sir," the man said. "We'd like the opportunity to talk with you. I have you on the calendar for Monday, March twenty-fourth at nine a.m." The man repeated the address. "Got that?"

Egon said he did.

"Good, so we'll see you then."

The man hung up.

On Thursday night nearly two weeks after he received the letter from the INS, Egon came home to a dark and still apartment. He called Johnny's name, but the dog didn't come. In the past few days, he had been retreating to a spot in the back of the hall closet. Egon turned on the light in the closet and noticed his mother's old satchel, where he kept her dishes, silverware, and a few linen tablecloths. That's when he remembered that it was his turn to host Saturday afternoon's *kaffeeklatsch*.

Distracted by Johnny and the meeting on Monday, he couldn't imagine entertaining those people. He'd have to get the cake, make the coffee, and set the table with the fusty silver forks and fragile cream and sugar bowls. All that phony elegance and pretend formality seemed ridiculous to him. No one, with the exception of Kaethe and Georg, even wanted that life anymore. Look at them: a grocer, a tailor, a cleaning woman, a journalist, a store clerk, and a dry cleaner. Had they not known each other in Germany, would they have even become friends in America? Not likely. The more Egon thought about it, the more impossible Saturday seemed to him. Thank God Catrina was coming. She promised to bring Kiefer and Rose — if Rose was up to it. They would make it more bearable.

On Friday night, Egon began pulling the folding chairs and his mother's old table settings from the closet. Johnny must have felt the commotion, or sensed Egon's nervousness. Whatever it was, he wanted no part of it. He refused his food. He wouldn't be budged from the corner of the closet, and slept there all Friday night and Saturday morning. At a little before two in the afternoon, Egon tried to coax him out for a walk, but Johnny didn't move. Egon crouched among the forgotten shoes and placed his hand on the dog's rump. Johnny didn't stir the way he usually did when touched. Egon saw that his eyes were closed. He put his arms around the dog, hoping to feel his heart beating. He held his hand to his nose to feel his breath. Egon told himself the dog was resting. He kept his eyes on Johnny, willing him to move, to breathe. He stared at him long enough for his brain to register what his heart could not accept. Johnny was gone. No, that couldn't be. Johnny would never leave him. He took one of his paws in his hand and gently shook it. The paw was as warm and bony as it always was and it gave Egon a surge of hope. "Okay, you sleep now," he said, letting go. The paw dropped to the floor.

Egon picked Johnny up. He was heavy and inert, like the slabs of meat Egon handled every day. He laid him back onto the floor and curled up next to him. Death was Johnny's only betrayal, and he had done that so quietly and uncomplainingly that Egon allowed himself the thought that he might come back.

The tears that had never come when his mother died; when he found the awful writing on his office door; when he had to leave Germany; when he was humiliated at the store; when the boy threw blood on him; when he got the threatening phone calls; when he got the letter from Immigration Services, came now. He heard himself make gulping noises. He cried until his eyes swelled and he could not catch his breath.

When he looked at his watch, it was 2:52, eight minutes before eight friends were to show up at his door expecting him to serve them coffee and cake.

There were dust balls on his trousers, and he knew he smelled as putrid as poor Johnny. He figured he'd ignore the bell when it rang and they'd all go away. But with all that was going on, Meyer, in particular, might assume him dead or injured and call the police. The police would break down his door and find him lying in the closet with a dead dog. That wouldn't look so good. No, he'd have to let them in and explain about Johnny. But where would he put Johnny? It would be unseemly to leave him in the closet. The bathtub? What if one of them had to use the toilet and found Johnny in the tub? No. The oven? Crazy. Best to come out with it. Wrap him up in a blanket and keep him on the floor.

Like the punctual Germans they were, Meyer, Carola, Max, Kaethe, and Georg arrived promptly at three. Egon stood before them in his stocking feet and rumpled clothes. He was covered with dust and gave off the unfortunate smell. His eyes were red. A trail of snot ran from his nose. Johnny lay by the closet door wrapped in a beige blanket.

Carola leaned in to kiss Egon's cheek, then pulled back. "Are you all right?" she asked, then noticed Johnny. "Is he all right?"

Egon blew his nose. "Neither of us is all right. Johnny has passed away. I decided to keep him here until I had time to bury him."

Carola stepped back into the doorway and looked at Max. He took her arm. "Carole" — he emphasized the American pronunciation — "and I are sorry about the dog, but it's not healthy for the unborn child to be around certain kinds of pets."

"You mean dead pets?" asked Meyer.

"It's best not to take any chances," said Max.

"I'm so sorry for you, Egon," said Carola. "But I'm sure you understand." She and Max headed down the hall.

Meyer leaned against the doorframe. He looked at Johnny, then at Georg.

"What do you think, Georg, maybe you should call Immigration Services to tell them that the animal doctor couldn't even keep his own dog alive."

"Why would you say something like this to me?" asked Georg.

"Why shouldn't I?" asked Meyer.

Kaethe stepped over Johnny and took her place next to Georg. "You make fun, but it's unnatural," she said to Meyer. "This attachment to the animals. And now . . . this."

Georg turned to Egon. "In Germany, your specialty was the eye; you had a respectable practice. Then you come to America and suddenly you are another kind of doctor? I would never report you to anybody, but do you understand how your duplicity makes the rest of us seem suspicious?"

Egon started to answer, but Meyer cut him off. "Won't it be a relief to go back to Frankfurt, where all the Jews are being treated so cordially?"

"I can assure you, it will be more civil there than it is right here," said Georg. "Come Kaethe, I've had enough." The two of them hurried down the hall as Catrina, Rose, and Kiefer came out of the elevator. They all looked startled when Meyer shouted, "Give my regards to the gracious Mr. Hitler!"

"Good heavens, are we late?" asked Rose. Catrina and Kiefer were on either side of her, holding her arms.

Meyer was taken aback by Rose's labored breathing and weakened state. "Come, sit," he said, pointing her to the couch. He propped a pillow behind her back and sat next to her.

She spoke slowly. "What's going on here?"

"It's Egon's dog, Johnny. He died."

Catrina took in the sorry sight of Egon, who looked worse than Johnny. "What a terrible thing." When she put her arm around Egon, she could feel how he was shivering. "You poor man," she whispered, rubbing his back. She crouched down to kiss Johnny's head. "We'll give you a proper burial, I promise." Then she led Egon into the bedroom. "Come, let's get you cleaned up.'

Meyer gestured everyone toward the kitchen, where the table was half set and an unopened box from Nash's sat on the counter. "We'll start without them."

They drank and ate without speaking. Occasionally, one of them glanced at Johnny. Rose broke the silence. "He was an old dog. He had a good life. Now was his time to go. There's nothing wrong with that. We should all pray that God grants us that kind of death."

Her words weren't lost on Kiefer or Meyer. They exchanged quick glances before Kiefer moved to another subject: "What did you mean when you told those people to give your regards to Hitler?"

"I was teasing, but not really," said Meyer, biting into his napoleon. "The Schnabels are very loyal Germans, even now. They follow the rules to a T. I know they're upset about Egon treating animals without a license, and it wouldn't surprise me if they were the ones who reported him to the INS. Does that sound plausible to you?"

Kiefer ran his thumb and forefinger over his mustache. "It usually is a friend or relative."

Catrina sat down and helped herself to a piece of *Linzertorte.* "He's showering," she whispered.

"We've got to get this foul-smelling dog out of here," said Meyer, dunking his napoleon into his coffee. "Kiefer, you'll help me, won't you? We'll take the dog to Fort Tryon Park, dig a hole, and in he goes."

"Burying animals in public parks is illegal."

"So we should hide him under the bed? I'm sure the superintendent has a shovel in the basement."

"You could carry Johnny out in a laundry bag," suggested Rose, fingering the cross around her neck.

"I'll go hurry Egon along," said Catrina.

"Let's get this done quickly," said Kiefer.

While Egon dressed, Meyer stuffed Johnny into a laundry bag that Catrina found in the bedroom. Egon and Catrina walked behind Meyer and Kiefer, who had slung the laundry bag over his shoulder. They went to a corner of the park overlooking the river but obscured by the overhanging oaks. Kiefer dug fast and deep, then gently laid Johnny in the hole.

Rose crossed herself.

Catrina stared at Rose as if rehearsing for her own loss while Kiefer kept his eyes on the ground, not wanting to take in anybody's misery.

Meyer saw the hurt in Egon's eyes. "We're all sorry for the loss of your loyal four-legged friend, but you must remember that you will always have your two-legged ones."

Catrina held Egon's hand as he stared into space. If ever there was a time for prayer, this was it, but no one came forward. Egon bowed his head and hummed to himself. It was *"Hänschen Klein,"* the song about little Johnny, the dog's namesake, who leaves home but eventually comes back to his heartbroken mother.

25.

And then the dog died, and once again the Cheese Man's world was shaken. Now there was a new crisis on the horizon, this one even more immediate and threatening. He was frightened, but he was not alone.

— Meyer Leavitt,
Aufbau, March 31, 1941

Egon awoke earlier than usual on the Monday of his meeting with the INS. The apartment felt unbearably empty without Johnny — his absence seemed larger than his presence. Egon had to get out. He walked through the park up the hill toward the Cloisters and sat on his favorite bench. Scattering stale bread crumbs around him, he waited for the assembly of pigeons to gather at his feet and hoped it would bring him some peace. He studied the bone-white sky for other birds, falcons perhaps, and thought about what Catrina had said that morning he'd seen two of them at his windowsill: His parents were watching over him. He closed his eyes and tried to summon them. His father's voice when he said to the turtledove, "Sweet thing, how far away from home you are." His mother's colored pencils scratching paper as she sketched a warbler in the Stadtwald. The welcoming smell of coffee in their kitchen. The memories swarmed like the pigeons at his feet, yet on this morning, neither brought him the comfort he craved.

He walked back to his apartment and changed into the clothes he'd laid out the night before: his blue suit, a white linen shirt, his father's mother-of-pearl cuff links, and a blue striped tie that Catrina had picked out for him. *I am dressed for a wedding,* he thought, staring at himself in the mirror. *Or a funeral.*

The subway ride downtown took forty-five minutes, though he allotted an hour. Twenty-nine Church Street was a stubby redbrick building that looked as if it had been built at the turn of the century. Room 407 was small and plain, with frosted glass on the top half of the door, a battered oak desk, a filing cabinet, and a window facing a bare tree across the street. Egon had pictured something grander, with a map of the United States and paintings of American landscapes on the wall, maybe even a flag. The person behind the desk was as non-descript as his office. "How do you do," he said, offering Egon a languid handshake. "I'm Roland Broadman, and you must be . . ." He pulled some papers from the folder in front of him. "Eh-gon Schneider. Is that correct?"

"Ee-gon Schneider."

"Please, Mr. Schneider, take a seat."

The seat was straight-backed and small enough that when he sat, his knees nearly rose to his chest. Mr. Broadman swiveled right and left in his oak chair. He tapped the eraser end of a pencil against his forehead and studied the papers before him. What hair he had was custard yellow, and his eyelashes were so light they appeared to be made of cellophane. He was as thin as he was pale, not a Broad Man at all. *Probably not his real name,* thought Egon, remembering what Kiefer had said about how they all used fake ones. Certainly not a Roland. More like a Frank or Harry.

When Mr. Broadman looked up, he said, "So, Mr. Schneider, seems you've gotten yourself in something of a pickle here. No veterinarian license, yet you care for animals. In your home, no less. You know this is illegal in this country, do you not?"

"I do."

"What do you have to say for yourself?" He poised his pencil over the blank sheet of paper in front of him.

Egon explained his background, and how he was studying veterinary books in his spare time. "My plan is to become an American citizen and get the required license for treating animals."

"Wonderful," said Mr. Broadman, leaning back in his chair. "But until then, do you plan to continue treating them?"

"No, sir, not if it is against the laws."

Mr. Broadman asked to see Egon's passport. He asked if he was a member of any social or political organizations. Any Jewish organizations? He asked who he was still in touch with in Germany. Was there any correspondence back and forth? "What about your acquaintances in America? You people tend to stick together, don't you? What do your other friends do?"

"By 'you people,' do you mean German Jews?" asked Egon.

Mr. Broadman nodded.

"We are cleaners, seamstresses, and store clerks. One is a journalist, another mops floors, and another works in a five-and-dime."

Mr. Broadman put his elbows on the desk and folded his hands under his chin. "May I have their names and addresses, please?"

Egon was taken aback. "My friends are not breaking any laws. What I do, I do on my own." No need to bring Catrina into this.

"I understand that," said Mr. Broadman, moving his folded hands in front of his mouth. "I would like their names and addresses, nothing to worry about, it's routine."

Egon felt he was being pushed into a confession. If he objected too much, he'd paint himself a guilty man. Yet giving out names and addresses seemed like a betrayal.

"If you are wondering whether we are affiliated with anti-American, pro-German groups, then I must tell you, Mr. Broadman, that each of us is grateful to be in America. We are all working hard to become the kind of citizens to make this country proud. None of us would do anything whatsoever to bring shame to America."

"Very nice," said Mr. Broadman, getting ready to write, "but I still need their names and addresses."

Egon had no choice but to comply. Roland wrote furiously, and when they finished, he put down his pen and leaned across his desk. "You seem like a decent fellow. I'd like to see you walk out of here and never have to come back. But I can't do that. What you've committed is a serious infraction of our laws, and it's beyond my power to resolve this. I'm going to have to set up a hearing for you with the Immigration Court. It won't be for another few months. We'll contact you with a date. In the meantime, hold off on filing your declaration-of-intent papers for your citizenship, and go about your business. But please, no more practicing medicine on animals, Good Samaritan or not. Understood?"

Egon understood. He wanted to say more. Who he was in Germany; his parents; how deportation would mean certain death. But there was something final about the way Mr. Broadman closed his file and slapped his hand on top of it.

Egon stood up and extended his hand. "Thank you, Mr. Broadman, I appreciate your . . ." He paused, as he didn't appreciate anything about Mr. Broadman. "I appreciate your consideration."

Roland stood up and extended his hand. "Good luck, Eh-gon."

Egon took the stairs two at a time, eager to get as far away from Roland Broadman and the INS as fast as he could. At the first phone booth he found, he stepped inside and slipped a nickel into the machine. Thank God Meyer answered.

Egon told him word for word what had happened. "He asked for everyone's name and address. There is going to be a hearing. This can only be bad."

Meyer pictured Egon, eyes swollen, standing in front of Johnny's grave. "I'm sorry for you, this is a hard time. Tonight, I'll gather everyone in my office. We'll get started with our letters. I'll write in the *Aufbau.*"

"I am scared, Meyer. It is all so fast and official."

"I know," said Meyer. "Remember when we were first roommates and I had that awful asthma attack? You promised me it would be better. You tried the coffee and the cold air and you stayed up with me the whole night. Finally, it was better. Now I stay with you, and we try everything, as long as it takes. It will be okay."

Meyer hung up and called all their friends. It was urgent, he told them. They had to come to his office at six o'clock that night.

To Meyer's surprise, they all showed up: Egon; Carola; Max; the Schnabels; Catrina, of course; even Liesl. When they gathered around his desk, he explained about Egon and the INS. "I don't think this will amount to anything, but they made him give our names and addresses — except for Catrina. There will be an investigation and a hearing in front of the Immigration Court. The consequences of such an investigation?" he asked, as if interviewing himself. "Who knows, but deportation looms as something we can't ignore. It's that serious. I know we've had our differences —" He glanced at Georg, then surreptitiously at Liesl. "I am not blameless, God knows, me and my big mouth." Kaethe and Georg exchanged small smiles. "But we put all that aside now. Our friend may be in trouble, and we must do what we can. I am suggesting we each write a letter to President Roosevelt and say what an honest man and fine American Egon is. I know it sounds grandiose, but I feel certain it will make a difference."

The room fell quiet. After a while, Max raised his hand. "And if there is an investigation, might we all be investigated, now that they have our names and addresses?"

"For this answer, I turn to Georg," said Meyer, with a dramatic sweep of his arm.

"He knows these things better than I."

Georg answered in full voice. "It is not likely that in America, an investigation would extend to friends of the person being investigated or to people who write letters of support, but then again, this is a particular situation."

"But he did break the law," said Liesl. "We all know you can't pretend to be a doctor if you don't have a license."

Meyer raised an eyebrow. "And who among us has not done something that the authorities might consider illegal? I suggest we put aside these judgments for the kind of infractions that can hurt other people. As far as I know, Egon has only helped the animals he's treated and the people who own them. This is not an infraction that deserves deportation."

Kaethe asked if the president would really read their letters.

"Probably not," said Meyer. "But if the name Egon Schneider shows up often enough, he might take notice. I plan to write about Egon as much as I can in the *Aufbau*. We're fortunate to live in a country that takes its citizens seriously. Who knows, maybe I can even sell a story about him to *Life* magazine."

At the mention of *Life* magazine, the

group nodded and some muttered, "Ohh," as if the article had already been published.

"We have no time to waste," urged Meyer. "The hearing could happen sooner than we think. The letters must be written as quickly as possible."

Catrina waited until everyone else had left before she spoke to Meyer. "This probably doesn't mean anything," she said, "but when I worked at that fancy restaurant, the Blue Moon, I knew a lot of well-connected people. I was wondering . . ."

"Yes," said Meyer. "Write them. Any of them. All of them. I'll find their addresses. We turn all the stones . . . however that saying goes."

26.

Egon Schneider was a respected ophthalmologist in Frankfurt. In America, his German medical license is useless, so he's taken his skills and translated them into caring for animals. In America, he works five days a week at a grocery store, slicing bologna, taking out garbage, weighing slabs of meat, and of course handing out free slices of cheese. In his off time — parts of weekends and late evenings — he and his companion, Catrina Harty, treat the animals whose owners can't afford to pay the steep prices charged by veterinarians. Sometimes they treat them for free, other times, for whatever the customer can afford. Egon Schneider has embraced the American work ethic, and, despite his own modest means, has been charitable and generous to those who have even less. Now he is in danger of being persecuted by the United States government for committing one crime, and one crime only: the crime of kindness.

— Meyer Leavitt, *Aufbau,*
March 31, 1941

In a full-page article about Egon, Meyer described his friend's background, his parents' work, and his difficult time in America. *"The tedium . . . the humiliations . . . the small victories that started to pile up . . . a job . . . an apartment of his own . . . a dog . . . a companion . . . new friends. A house of cards maybe, but one that began to resemble a life."* Photographs of two of Elisabeth Schneider's drawings, a bittern and a crossbill, ran with the article, along with quotes from Rudolph Schneider's text. At the bottom of the page, Meyer created a form, which ran the *Aufbau*'s address above the message: *We are not powerless in this witch hunt against Egon Schneider. If you cannot come by the* Aufbau *office in person to sign a petition asking for the government to drop the case against him, please fill in your name and address, indicating that you give me permission to sign on your behalf. Mail it to me at the address at the top of this form.*

Heady with all the talk of President Roosevelt and *Life* magazine, the friends had promised Meyer that they would write their letters as soon as they got home the evening of the meeting. All except for Max and Carola. Carola asked Egon to stop by their apartment after work the following day.

Their baby was due in a little more than three months, she explained as she sat next to him on her living room couch. "Max is concerned that if we write a letter, the government might view us as potential troublemakers, or keep track of us because we are associated with someone they believe has broken the law. He worries our child would be getting off on the wrong foot." Carola squeezed Egon's hand. "Of course, we don't think you're going to get deported, or anything like that. Max is being extra careful. You know how he is."

Egon crossed his arms. "Max is a practical man, and you are a loyal wife. But tell me, Carola — or do I call you Carole now? — do you think your child would be getting off on the wrong foot?"

She waved her hand in front of her face. "Silly, to you I am always Carola. Max calls me Carole because he thinks it's more American. Do I think our child would be getting off on the wrong foot if we are investigated? Let me just say that if there's even a chance of that happening, then I would choose to err on the side of caution."

"You know, they really could deport me for practicing without a license."

"Max says they're only warning you, that's all."

"I hope you are right."

Egon stared out the window and noticed the statue of the Virgin Mary in front of Our Lady Queen of Martyrs. She was exactly as he remembered from when he'd slept in this apartment during his first weeks in America: the shawl draped over her head and body, the row of pigeons squatting on her outstretched arms. In those days, he had been comforted by how Mary shouldered all those birds; today, the memory of his lonely younger self saddened him.

He looked up at Carola's face. Normally it was pale as wax, but now it glowed with the promise of a child. He put his hand on her belly and spoke to it as if Carola weren't there: "So, little one, you will be our first American. To you I will be a foreigner. You will think I am odd, and my accent will embarrass you."

"It won't be like that," said Carola. "You'll always be part of our family." She patted her stomach. "You understand, don't you?"

"Of course I do," said Egon, who didn't really. She was his cousin, the only one of them who had known him as a child, known his parents. He remembered first meeting her, when she came to the house in her too-fancy-for-a-hot-summer-day dress, her pale skin and lace gloves; how she was afraid of his box turtle; how, when he met her again in Berlin, she'd grown into her frail beauty and allowed Meyer to worship her, his Schneewittchen. Then came Max. Max was from a wealthy family. He had ambition and opinions and kept his nose clean. He would do fine in America.

As he left, Egon looked out at the Virgin Mary again and noticed, for the first time, how her shawl, head, and body were crusted with bird droppings. He hoped Meyer wouldn't take the news about Carola and Max too badly.

"That ass-kissing coward," Meyer said when Egon told him. "I'm going to call him right now."

"Please," said Egon. "I have more things to worry about than you alienating the one relative I have left in this world. We can do without them. There will be others."

Catrina called Kiefer and Rose after the meeting with Meyer and asked if they too would write a letter. Kiefer said that as a member of the police force, he felt it wasn't appropriate for him to get involved.

"This isn't about the police force," argued Rose. "It's about your sister. She loves this man. Look, I don't want her marrying a Jew any more than you do. At least this one is honest — for the most part. He's kind to her and makes her happy. I'm not leaving any money or worldly goods behind when I go. God help me, the least I can do is write a letter, and so can you."

That night, they agreed on this compromise:

To Whom It May Concern,
The character of one Egon Schneider seems to be in question over a matter of treating animals without a veterinary license.

I am originally from Ireland. I came here as a young girl. I have worked hard in America and raised two children by myself. I am a Catholic and live according to the teachings of the Bible. I am an old woman now with not much time left. Much of my life belongs to memory. But one thing I have not lost is my ability to recognize the few souls who are pure and decent without motive. Egon Schneider is one of those people. I never knew a Jew before I met Mr. Schneider, but I believe he is a credit to his race. I know this because of the love and generosity he has shown my daughter. She, by the way, is a lapsed Catholic, but a hard worker, and she helps Mr. Schneider with the animals. When customers can't afford to pay, they treat them for free. With all that's going on in the world today, does such a man deserve to be punished?

I hope you will agree with me when I say certainly not. Thank you for your attention.

Rose Walsh

P.S. My son, Kiefer Walsh, is a detective in the New York City Police Department. He has read this letter and agrees with everything I say about Egon Schneider.

When Kiefer walked into the *Aufbau* offices the next day, Meyer was at his typewriter. He typed with two fingers, and moved his lips as he wrote. He pounded the keyboard so hard that often his *D*'s and *O*'s left holes in the paper. Until he finished whatever he was writing, he didn't look up and was oblivious to the noise and people around him. Kiefer stood silently and studied Meyer. His hair shot up at different angles, and his shirt had ink stains on it. Kiefer nearly smiled at the thought that it looked as if someone had been typing on Meyer. He figured Meyer had hit the last period when he lifted his finger from the keyboard with the bravado of a pianist finishing a concert. "Yah," he snapped, without looking at Kiefer.

"I've brought you this," said Kiefer, handing him Rose's letter.

Meyer read it carefully, nodding as he went.

"This is good, excellent," he said with a smile. "Please tell your mother how much we appreciate her effort."

That morning, Egon had explained to Art about the potential hearing and asked if he would write a letter on his behalf.

One of Art's rules of management was to never interfere in an employee's personal life, so his immediate answer was "Absolutely no can do." Art figured that once you meddled in an employee's private affairs, the next thing you knew, he wanted to borrow money. Or even worse, he'd confide something awful about himself, like how he liked to dress up in women's clothes when he was in bed with his wife, and then you were stuck knowing that forever. Also, Art never got involved in politics. Writing a letter to the president wasn't politics per se, but in this day and age, with feelings running so hot and cold about the impending war, he felt it best to keep his nose out of anything but his own business. Though he had to admit, the whole Cheese Man idea had worked out well. Egon had brought customers into the store. He gave them free cheese and often they bought more than they had expected they would. But this whole thing with the newspaper, the blood-throwing and threats, it was getting to be too much.

On the other hand . . . Art had to laugh at himself. To his way of thinking, there was always the other hand. On the other hand, people came into the store and asked how Egon was doing. Egon was the underdog. This neighborhood was crawling with German Jews, all underdogs. They identified with him. Supposing Art did write a letter of support, and then let it be known that he'd written it? Could be good for business. It would make all those immigrants feel as if he understood their problems. Art Able, champion of the underdogs. Big-hearted Art Able. He had to admit, it had a nice ring to it.

"On second thought," he said to Egon, "maybe I'll give it a try. It will be a business letter, of course, strictly professional. I'll keep it short and to the point. You'll have it by the afternoon."

Dear Mr. President,
I run a food establishment in Washington Heights. Egon Schneider is one of my employees and has been for the past three and a half years. He is a hard worker who never complains about long hours or unpleasant duties such as sweeping the floor, throwing out garbage, or handling meat. He has never missed a day on the job.

As a business manager and a native-born American, I know what it takes to be a good employee and a good citizen, and Egon Schneider has all of those things. His treating the animals has never interfered with his work at the store. If anything, it has made him more popular among the customers and drawn more business for the store. As a manager, I can hardly complain about that.

Yours truly,
Arthur Able

Egon brought the letter to Meyer that

evening. Meyer read it and put his hand on Egon's shoulder. "I commend you on your meat handling. That should do the trick. Americans love their meat." He put down the letter. "I have something to tell you that will surprise you."

"This is what I need," said Egon. "More surprises."

"No, this isn't that kind of news," said Meyer. "You'll never guess who called me first thing this morning. I'll give you a hint, it wasn't the president or Mrs. Roosevelt, but it was a couple around the same age. Do you give up? Okay, I'll tell you. Georg Schnabel. Isn't that something?"

"What did he want?"

"He wanted me to help him with his letter about you. He called me four times, read me four different versions. He hand-delivered the final one this afternoon. Do you want to see it?"

"Sure," said Egon.

Meyer pulled a sheet of paper from his desk. Egon noticed that the heavy stock was embossed with the name of Georg's old law firm and that his penmanship was the formal cursive they'd been taught in gymnasium.

Your Excellency,

I am writing on behalf of one Egon Schneider. A recent immigrant from Germany, he has been summoned to appear in front of Immigration Services as it has been called to their attention that he has been practicing medicine for animals without a license.

I have studied and practiced the law, as you have, and am aware of the implications of engaging in a discipline without the proper license. I understand that consequences for an individual having done so can be harsh. In regard to Mr. Schneider's case, I urge you to consider that he was a respected ophthalmologist in Germany and he is working hard to find his place in America. To my knowledge, all of the animals he has treated have prospered. Their owners, many of whom cannot afford the fees of licensed practitioners, have paid what they can to Mr. Schneider, and sometimes nothing at all.

I don't have to tell you that these are difficult times. Perhaps you can see your way to the decision that in an extreme case such as this one, for once altruism can trump the law.

With all due respect,
Georg Schnabel

Egon read the letter several times. "That is very generous of him, considering . . ."

"Considering what?" asked Meyer. "Considering that we've treated them like shit? That I've nearly torn out his throat more than once?"

"Well, yes," said Egon. "All of those things."

After returning home from the meeting at Meyer's, Georg had sat at his desk and Kaethe on the rocking chair they'd brought over from Germany. She was darning a sock as they talked, in German, about the favor Meyer had asked of them.

"After all we did for him in Frankfurt, and then we come to America and he mostly ignores us," said Kaethe. "I don't see why we should now come to his defense."

"But you mustn't forget, Kaethe, he did help us when we came here," said Georg. "We stayed in his apartment. He introduced us to his friends." She stopped darning and raised her eyebrows at Georg. "Whether or not that was a good thing is another matter," said Georg. "Still, he is relatively young and discovering his way. At least he has found something in America he likes to do. We're old, we don't have the energy or interest to start a new life the way he does."

"Yes, but you've said so yourself, to practice medicine without a license is against the law."

"*Ach,* Kaethe, today the law is made of moth wings. Nobody cares like they used to."

"Then you are saying we should write the letter?"

"Yes, I'm saying it would be tragic if Egon was deported. He has a future in America. He has that Irish girl, a job, and something he wants to do. He has a chance."

Georg opened his desk drawer. "I'll try my hand at something and we'll see what we think."

The English was hard for Georg. "I don't want to sound like a dumb immigrant in front of the president," he said to Kaethe. "I'm going to call Meyer and get his help."

"Don't call him, he's crazy," she said.

"If he acts crazy, then we stop."

Kaethe stood next to Georg each time he read Meyer the letters over the phone. Georg held the earpiece so Kaethe could hear what Meyer was saying. They argued over how to address the president. Meyer said he was being too formal; Georg insisted it was proper. Meyer suggested he take out longer references to Georg's old law firm; Georg agreed. "You don't need the paragraph about your World War I experience." Georg finally agreed to that. On each phone call Meyer was respectful and never said an unkind word. In the end, he thanked Georg for his efforts. "Your letter is very distinguished. I'm sure it will make a difference."

Georg said, "I couldn't have done it without your help."

Kaethe made a *tsk* sound. "I still think he's crazy."

Twenty-four hours after the meeting in his office, Meyer had heard from everyone except Liesl. The thought of phoning her made him anxious. He would be the last person she'd want to hear from. And he *still* hadn't restrung her pearls as he'd promised. But time was running out; he had no choice.

"I'm thinking about it," Liesl said when Meyer asked about her letter.

"What's to think about? I can help you if you'd like."

"It's not that. I'm thinking about whether or not to write one."

"Of course you'll write one, we all have to do that."

404

But she was not so sure. "I'll let you know what I decide."

Liesl liked to keep score. She tallied the rights and wrongs in her life the way other people kept a budget. She deserved to steal from the store. She was right to go to Egon's after the news came about her parents. He was wrong to leave her alone after their night of sex. She was wrong to seduce Meyer in an effort to get back at Egon. Egon was wrong to practice medicine without a license. She was wrong to consider turning him in to the authorities in order to get back at him for breaking it off with her. Only when she figured out that writing a letter would allow her to subtract one of the wrongs from her list did she put her pen to paper.

Dear President Roosevelt,
You do not know me, but perhaps you have heard of my father, Leopold Kessler. He was president of the National Bank of Frankfurt before the German government removed him for being a Jew. Now my parents are missing in Germany.
But I am writing you about another matter. A man named Egon Schneider

has been called before the Immigration authorities for treating animals without a veterinary license. Like me, Mr. Schneider comes from a prominent family in Germany. He was a successful doctor before he came to America. In fact, he treated me and my friends for many years. Mr. Schneider does not deserve to be punished for treating animals. Like many of us who came here, he works hard to become who he was. Thank you for your attention,

Liesl Kessler

Liesl must have slipped the letter under Meyer's door in the middle of the night, because it was there when he awoke the next morning. He smelled the paper before he read it. Vanilla. Her smell.

Now it was time for him to write his. He wrote letters to President and Mrs. Roosevelt, long letters similar to what he'd written in the *Aufbau*. He enclosed a copy of his book, *The Pale Princess of Prussia*, and, knowing that the president was a birdwatcher, a rare copy of *European Ornithology*.

There was only one letter left to be written. The man from Nagle Avenue who'd brought in Boris, the boxer with the broken tail.

"I don't write letters," he said when Egon asked him.

"A short one will be fine," said Egon.

Dear President Roosevelt,
Egon Schneider is a swell man. He and his girlfriend fixed Boris's tail. Boris is a boxer. They only charged me $1.00. Pretty square deal. I hope he gets one too.

Gerald Elmlinger

27.

Two thousand and fourteen and counting. That's how many have, so far, signed the petition urging the government to drop its case against Egon Schneider.
> — Meyer Leavitt, *Aufbau,*
> April 7, 1941

The waiting was excruciating. Every routine was fraught.

At Art's, Egon worried: Would there be another attack? Would someone approach him with an envelope from the government?

When he came home, he stared at the wall of mailboxes in his lobby as if facing a firing squad. Slowly, he would turn the key and survey what was inside. Postcards: a relief. Envelopes: threatening. Thin envelopes: better than thick ones. White: ominous. Any other color: safe. New York City postmarks: okay. Washington, D.C., postmarks: not so good.

Upstairs, the apartment still smelled of Johnny. Egon never unlocked his door without hoping the dog would come bounding out to greet him, and never failed to be heartbroken when he didn't. His stomach seized up when the phone rang. Now that he'd stopped taking in animals, there were almost no visitors, so every knock on the door felt catastrophic.

It had been a few weeks since he'd been to the INS. He missed the animals. Even more, he missed taking care of creatures who couldn't take care of themselves. He missed Rose, who'd passed away days after the INS meeting. He'd hoped she would live long enough to see he and Catrina not living in sin. Meyer came to her funeral, as did Iris and Susanna from the ASPCA and all the surviving women Rose had worked with at the laundry. Each of the laundresses in turn took Catrina's hands into hers — scarred as Rose's had been — and told her things about her mother that she'd never known.

"She kept a photograph of you in your wedding dress taped up in her locker."

"She wrote us funny poems on our birthdays."

"On her break, she'd go behind the hospital and feed the pigeons. Scraps from her lunch."

This time, Egon held Catrina graveside.

After that, they took turns trying to bolster each other. "Come, *liebchen,* let's walk in the park and look at the new buds."

"I bought you a sketch pad so you could draw me a nice fat robin."

"Today I have a treat for you, a chocolate peach cake from Nash's."

Talking about marriage turned them toward the future. Egon started looking into schools that offered degrees in veterinary medicine.

Every few nights, Meyer called to say how many people had signed the petition. Two thousand and fourteen after eight days.

The group reached for any good news they could find, but the newspapers rebutted their boldest attempts.

There's not a Jew left in Mendel or Danzig.

There was little food in Paris this winter. The Germans collected it before it reached the markets. A turnip was a gourmet meal.

The population of Jews in Germany has dropped by one-third to 250,000.

Jews have been completely eliminated from the economic life of Germany. There are no business enterprises, no Jewish lawyers, craftsmen, actors, or doctors. Those who are left perform manual labor upon a virtually slave basis.

No country is willing to take in European Jews at a sizable number anymore.

For so long Egon had distanced himself from the ones left behind. He was one of the lucky ones, but maybe now his luck had run out. He couldn't stop his mind swinging between the apocalyptic and the mundane. What if he was deported? Would Catrina come with him? *Could* she come with him? What would he do in Germany? What if he was arrested? Would he even be capable of manual labor? Did they have Tums in Germany? If the spirit died, how long would it take for the body to follow?

At least twice a week, Art took him aside and whispered, "Any word from Immigration?" When Egon answered, "Not yet," Art would shake his head and blink his buttonhole eyes. Egon knew this was meant to make him feel as if they were in this together, but all it did was make him more anxious.

Before work on most days, he still took his bag of crumbs up to the Cloisters and sat on a bench, where he fed the birds. His heart wasn't in it, but it was the one part of his day that was his own, and afterward, he always felt as if he'd regained a bit of himself. On one of those mornings, Egon walked into Art's humming "When You Wish upon a Star." It happened that Art walked in behind him and Egon could hear him laugh. Art pointed at Egon's shoulder and said, "Looks like while you were wishing upon a star, a pigeon was shitting upon your jacket."

Egon twisted his head around and saw the white stain, like a blob of paint with black ink in its center. If anyone but Art had pointed it out, Egon would have shared in the joke, but the nasty way Art's lips twisted when he said it made Egon feel ashamed.

"It will come right off. A little warm water is all," said Egon, heading to the bathroom.

Art was waiting for Egon when he came back. Art watched Egon slip his apron over his head and tie it in the back. "Aren't you missing something?" Art asked.

Egon looked around. "The meats and cheeses are in place. The signs with today's specials are tacked up behind the slicer. No, I think everything is where it should be."

"And what about the button? Where is that?" asked Art.

Egon patted the place on his chest where it was usually affixed. "Oh, I must have left it at home."

Twice this month, he had lost his Cheese

Man button, and each time, Art had replaced it. Now, Art looked doubtful. "If it's lost again, this one's on you. Eighty-five cents. I want to see it by tomorrow."

Egon looked around to see if anyone was nearby. It was still early, and no one else appeared to be in the store. "I've been meaning to talk to you about that." He bent down and spoke in a conspiratorial voice: "I think people might be getting tired of the Cheese Man. It has been a long time."

Art laughed. "Okay then, would you rather be known as the Bologna Man?"

Egon thought Art was joking, yet he could picture it: the button, the customers smirking as they called him Mr. Bologna, how Meyer would congratulate him for moving up in the food chain from dairy to meat.

The following morning, Egon showed up with the button pinned on his apron. Art shot him a sailor's salute. "Nice to have you back," he said.

That Sunday, as Egon sat with Meyer at Nash's, Meyer pointed to Egon's pants and said, "You know you have a bloodstain on your thigh, don't you?"

Egon looked down. "Probably from the roast beef."

"It's not attractive."

413

"Who cares?"

"You're the neat one, I'm the slob. Shouldn't you care?"

"Meyer, you are the one who always complains how wedded to form we are. So I ask you, does anyone really care if I have blood or bird shit on my pants, or that your hair stands up like a cactus, or that Catrina sometimes chews with her mouth open? The world is going to hell. We are not going to fix it by wearing clean clothes or bettering our table manners. I have played by these rules my whole life, and for what? So I can be put on a ship and sent back to Germany? Yes, there is blood on my pants and I am wearing the same socks I wore yesterday. So what?"

Meyer ran his hands through his hair. "Does it really stand up like a cactus?"

"That is not the point."

"I know, but this is: You have to take hold of yourself. While we have some semblance of human dignity, we owe it to the people around us to be civil and not surrender. May I remind you that at this moment you are a free man in a free country? That's not nothing. Giving up now is pointless. Besides, defeat stinks like cow shit. People can smell it from ten miles away. Even the kind ones will hate you for it."

"Thank you for that," mumbled Egon. "This is good to know."

Later, they met Catrina and walked through the park. Egon told them how, on Friday, they'd received a shipment of matzoh at Art's. "The new clerk was carrying at least twenty-five boxes of them when he tripped on something in the middle of the store." Egon threw his hands in the air. "The boxes went flying and landed so you could hear every matzoh crumble. They are like eggshells, you know." He raised his eyebrows. Attempting to be lighthearted and use the flourishes that had always worked for Meyer, Egon failed on both counts.

"That's awful," said Catrina. "Art must have given that poor clerk hell."

"Matzoh," said Meyer, as if he hadn't even heard the story. "Of course. It's almost Passover." He raised his finger. "I have a thought. Maybe we should have a Seder this year. It's a good excuse for all of us to get together and take stock of where we are and where we've been."

"That's a nice idea," said Catrina. "I could have it at my place."

They both turned to Egon. "What do you think?" asked Meyer.

"Suddenly we are religious? I thought we were supposed to be Americans. That was after we were Germans. Meyer, when did you become a Jew?"

"The same time you did. When they nearly killed us for it."

"And when was the last time you celebrated Passover?"

"Never."

"So now you are feeling holy?"

"Listen, I'm not suggesting we wrap ourselves in *tallisim* and grow *peyes*. I thought it would be a way to celebrate spring. We've made it through another winter and we're all still here. Frankly, Egon, I thought it might be a nice thing for you to have us all together and talk about things that aren't morbid or frightening for a change."

Egon stopped walking. He closed his eyes and rubbed his temples. "Passover. That is when we celebrate that we are no longer slaves. Oh yes, the holiday with the plagues: locusts, frogs, boils, Immigration Services, Art's Grocery Store. Then there are the bitter herbs to remind us of what our lives have become. And of course the singing of 'Dayenu,' a celebration of all the wonderful things God has done for us: Johnny's death, Rose's death, starvation, war. *Dayenu.* But there is always next year in Jerusalem. For me, it could be next year in Frankfurt." He opened his eyes. "Honestly, I would rather skip Passover this year."

Meyer and Catrina exchanged looks. Both started to speak. "You're not the only one in the world having a hard time right now," said Catrina. "Can you really not see how much people are trying to help you? Honestly, Egon." She marched ahead of both of them.

Meyer clapped his friend on the shoulder. "As I believe I mentioned earlier, no one likes the stink of defeat." He ran to catch up with Catrina.

Egon watched them walk away, the two people he loved most. He looked down and noticed the nubs of hyacinths and daffodils poking through the earth and remembered how, when he first arrived, Meyer had told him that New York springs were like miracles. God's atonement for winter, he'd said.

Egon turned around and headed out of the park. He would go home and change his pants.

28.

Only in the free country can one even conceive of having the president's ear.
— Meyer Leavitt,
Aufbau, May 5, 1941

Daisy Suckley couldn't stop thinking about the letter she'd received weeks earlier. It was as direct and plainspoken as she remembered the hostess from the Blue Moon to be. In it, the woman had described her impoverished Irish childhood and her early days at the restaurant. *It was a time spent living in other people's dreams.* She wrote about the deaths of both of her husbands: *I thought that was the end of my story, and it might have been had not a foreigner entered my life. His name is Egon Schneider. He is an older man, a Jew, a recent immigrant from Germany. While he is a most unlikely companion for me, we plan to marry.* She described Egon's childhood, and his late parents,

418

Elisabeth and Rudolph Schneider: *They are best known for their book on the birds of Europe,* European Ornithology.

The letter said that Egon had chosen his own path and become an ophthalmologist. Because of the situation in Germany, he'd fled to America in 1938 and had to start all over again. Despite working long hours in a grocery store in New York City, she wrote, *he has found time to help his neighbors and the people who couldn't afford to take their pets to veterinarians. In fact, he restored many of the animals, who might have otherwise perished, back to health. Now he is thinking that someday, he might like to become a veterinarian. I am telling you these details so that you will come to know the fine character of the man I am writing to you about.* She described the circumstances that had prompted this letter, and said how she feared the results of the upcoming hearing. *He meant no harm working without a license. It would be beyond my wildest dreams if you would show this letter to your cousin. Perhaps he could convince Immigration Services to put a stop to this unbearable situation and allow Egon Schneider to get on with his life in America. I know this is a desperate measure, and I am sorry to trouble you, but for me and Egon Schneider this is a desperate time.*

Daisy had kept the letter in her purse for weeks, unsure of what to do with it, not knowing when she would next see her cousin Franklin. Should she even bother him with it? Franklin Roosevelt was, to say the least, a harried man; one foreigner's destiny was a trifle compared with what he had to handle every day. Besides, what if he got angry with her for meddling? For all the time they'd spent together, they'd never even had a spat.

On the second weekend in May, Franklin came home to Hyde Park for an overnight visit and invited Daisy to join him for a predawn drive to Thompson Pond in nearby Pine Plains. As they'd done many times before, Daisy, Franklin, and his Scottish terrier, Fala, slipped away in Franklin's Ford roadster and escaped the Secret Service agents, who didn't know those woods as intimately as he did. On this morning, they had the pond to themselves. It was where Franklin had gone as a boy to hear the swamp birds sing at dawn. In spring, the pond was a popular stopover for migratory birds, and Franklin's face lit up as he nudged Daisy and identified the clipped notes of a blackbird and the warble of a marsh wren. As the sun rose, Franklin counted up how many songs they'd heard that morning. Twenty-two. "Good number," he said. "Let's make it an even thirty."

This was one of his favorite pastimes. He'd told her that when he was eleven, his father had given him a shotgun, which he used to collect and then stuff the birds of the Hudson River. Although his mother allowed him to kill only one male and one female of each species, and none during the mating season, he'd collected more than three hundred species by the time he was fourteen. Daisy had seen some of those birds, dusty and faded now, perched on the mantelpiece in Hyde Park next to his vast collection of books about birds. He liked to say that being one of the leading authorities on the birds of Dutchess County was his greatest accomplishment.

Franklin pointed to a stump sticking out of the water. Seated erectly on top of it was a slender white creature with a gentle curve in its long neck. "Egret," he whispered to Daisy. They sat frozen in place, waiting for the bird to spread its broad wings. "They nest on a platform of sticks or reeds, so this one may be looking for a house." When nothing happened, they drove a bit closer and realized that what they'd been staring at was a quart bottle on a stump. "Quart bottles also like to nest on platforms of "sticks or reeds," said Franklin, laughing.

"But what a graceful quart bottle it is," she answered.

Franklin took off his pince-nez glasses and cleaned them with his scarf. "I didn't used to have trouble distinguishing bottles from birds," he said. "Maybe it's time to get my eyes checked."

Daisy squinted at the pond. "I still can't make out that it's not an egret."

Franklin scratched the dog's head. "Well, at least one of us has perfect eyesight, don't you, Fala."

Clearly, Franklin was relaxed and in no rush to return to Hyde Park, where the Secret Service would be waiting to whisk him back to Washington. These were the moments Daisy cherished the most, and she willed time to stand still. She remembered the letter in her purse and thought this was a good time to mention it. "I'm curious, have you ever heard of these people, Elisabeth and Rudolph Schneider? They were German Jews. They wrote about birds."

Franklin squinted and looked as if he was trying to retrieve information. "Have I ever met them?"

"No, I don't believe you ever did. They wrote a book that was apparently famous, *European Ornithology.*"

"Yes, that one's a classic. I have it in my collection, and I own one of the illustrator's original drawings. How on earth do you know about them?"

Daisy pulled the envelope from her purse and opened Catrina's letter. "I don't mean to be a bother or take up much of your time. It's just that this letter about these people, this situation, it's fallen in my lap."

She read it to him. He shook his head. "You mean to tell me that Elisabeth and Rudolph Schneider's son is working in a grocery store in New York City?"

"That seems to be the case."

"When did he come here?"

"It says 1938."

Franklin shook his head. "Lucky he got out. Are the parents still over there?"

She scanned the letter. "No, she mentions his 'late parents.' "

"Why did she write to you?"

"I knew her from the Blue Moon. Remember that place? She's hoping I can have some influence with you." Daisy looked away. "That maybe you can somehow intervene with the INS before the hearing. Possibly get them to call it off. Mr. Schneider may want to study veterinary medicine here. They plan to be married."

Franklin breathed in and exhaled a sigh.

"What do you think, Daisy?"

"He sounds like an honorable man."

"And you, Fala, what do you think?"

Fala licked Franklin's chin.

"Okay, everyone. Concentrate," said Franklin. "We have eight more songs to listen for."

29.

For so long we have lived as if on a ship mid-ocean. Germans in America, we wait the requisite five years until we can apply for citizenship. German is our native tongue, but the taste is bitter, and we struggle to learn English. We work as scrubwomen and grocers and walk back and forth with sandwich boards on our shoulders, jobs that lead us nowhere but pay for our food and board. We are foreigners who take the subway every day and celebrate Thanksgiving and the Fourth of July. Then, overnight, it seems, the ship glides into harbor and we step ashore.

— Meyer Leavitt, *Aufbau,*
July 7, 1941

The notice came in a thin yellow envelope that carried a New York City postmark and was dated June 16, 1941. It looked so inconsequential that Egon nearly discarded it before the word *Immigration* caught his eye. He would wait until he got upstairs to open it. By the time he unlocked the door, his stomach had turned sour.

Inside his apartment, he placed the envelope on his desk and sat down. He felt foolish doing what he did next, but he took the glass eye from its case, cupped it in his hands, and called up the image of his mother. Then he put it down and tore open the envelope. The letter was short. He scanned the page for initials, room numbers, dates, and times, but this was all there was:

Dear Mr. Schneider,
The Immigration and Naturalization Service has examined your case and concluded that there is not enough evidence to warrant a hearing. There will be no further investigation or communication on this matter. You may proceed with your application for citizenship.
Thank you for your cooperation.
Dwight Shoreham,
Immigration and Naturalization Service

At first Egon laughed, wondering where they'd come up with the name Dwight Shoreham. Then he read the message again and again and again, until each letter became its own structure, each word its own city. He studied the sentences, waiting for them to come apart. Maybe he'd read it wrong or missed something subtle. What if this was a hoax?

He spoke each word aloud until they all fit together and made sense. The stiff stationery with the embossed letterhead was no hoax; the letter was official. When the absoluteness sank in, Egon felt dizzy. Time and place were shifting at once, as if he'd crossed a divide. All the clothes he was wearing were from *before*. The food in his refrigerator was from *before*. Right now, Meyer, the Cohens, the Schnabels, Liesl were all from *before*. Even Catrina and Johnny were from *before*.

He called Meyer.

"Listen to this," he said without saying hello. He read him the letter. Meyer was silent. "Stop picking your teeth, for Christ's sake. It is over!"

"It's not my teeth I'm picking," said Meyer. "It's my brain. This is wonderful news, Egon, wonderful news. I'm so relieved for you, congratulations. But it's also a big story for the *Aufbau*. Don't you see how powerful our petition must have been? That the president took note of us will be front-page news. Can you read me the letter again, slowly this time?"

Egon read it to him, then said, "I am glad I could be of service to your newspaper. I am hanging up now and calling Catrina."

Catrina let out a whoop. "This is the best news! What a relief, finally we can go on with our lives."

Carola was also happy for him, though she could talk for only a minute because she was making Max's dinner.

When Egon told Art the following morning, Art turned darker than his usual liverwurst pink. "Well, the president has always had a soft spot for the underdog. Good for you. I'm sure the letter from your superior at work didn't hurt your case."

"You are probably right. Thank you again for writing it."

Egon told himself that it was human nature for people to place themselves in the center of a story regardless of whose story it was. So what? The fear and anxiety that had defined his days and nights were gone. Now anything was possible.

His joy lasted a little more than a week before he found himself slipping into a different kind of worry. He'd been breathing danger for so long; now that he was back in his routine, the air smelled used. Everything had changed, but nothing had changed. He still went to work at Art's every day and came home to the same apartment every night. He was still engaged to Catrina, and he and Meyer met for coffee and cake on most Sundays. The routine that he'd arduously cobbled together over the past three years suddenly seemed an artifice, an excuse for a life. The smallness of his days and circle of friends now felt suffocating, but he had yet to figure out how to live larger.

Egon's reprieve from the INS was inevitably overshadowed by current events. As Meyer wrote in his July 14 column, *The news from Germany smells like rotten eggs. Two weeks ago in Frankfurt, a group of "scholars" gathered for a conference to discuss the "problem" of European Jewry. Adolf Eichmann, head of the Gestapo section of Jewish affairs, has announced that he plans to restrict Jewish emigration from Germany. Hitler has taken Yugoslavia and Greece, and has repeated his threat to destroy all the Jews of Europe. Is this not more worthy of a cover on* Time *magazine than Bing Crosby?*

Rumors of mass murders were swirling, and every day, it seemed, someone heard of someone back home who'd been arrested. The news came as one blow after another to the Schnabels. Their Germany, the one they'd been certain they'd return to one day, was disappearing. All that remained was what they'd created in America. Their tiny apartment was cluttered with the furniture they'd brought from Frankfurt. They ate only foods they'd eaten in Germany. They played German music and had no American friends. Out of necessity, they bought American clothes, but only when what they'd brought from Germany had worn out.

America, they believed, had spoiled their friends and destroyed their values, but they didn't even see the biggest blow coming.

It was the second Friday in July when Georg's boss, Mr. Harold, called him into the back of the store and pulled the curtain closed. Steam heat from the irons always kept the store hot, but on this humid day, the place felt as if the air had been sucked out of it.

"I won't beat around the bush with you, Mr. Schnabel," said Mr. Harold. "Things are not working out."

Georg felt sweat snail down his back.

"Customers have complained about you. They can't understand you. You don't speak our language." Mr. Harold licked the bottom of his gray mustache as he talked.

"Have I not done a good job?" asked Georg. The steam clogged his throat.

"You've done a fine job folding and ironing, but half of our work is making customers feel we're part of their community, and someone with your . . . ah . . . limited English makes them feel the opposite. Ya know, a little uncomfortable. Maybe even threatened."

Georg wanted to promise he'd work on his English, wanted to ask for another chance. But these things felt like begging, which was something he would not do. So he sat, stiff and mute, he who used to swagger around the courtroom and argue cases in front of top judges.

When he told Kaethe he'd been fired, this was the part that shamed him the most. "I didn't fight back. I just sat there like the stupid refugee he thought me to be."

Kaethe tried to shrug it off. "So I'll take in more dresses. You'll find another job, one where they'll feel lucky to have a distinguished person such as yourself."

But Georg didn't find another job. He didn't even look. When customers came to see Kaethe, he'd go into the bedroom and close the door behind him. He stopped wearing suits and ties, and there were days when he didn't leave the apartment at all.

Daydreaming one morning, Kaethe said aloud, "I wonder if our lilies bloomed this season."

Georg closed his eyes. "There would be dozens of them now. The peach-colored ones; those are my favorite. The pear trees, they must be pruned. The rain has been good for the roses. I can smell them even now." Kaethe saw the strain go out of his face, as if he were being carried by a wave to a safer time.

If this was what would bring him back to life, then Kaethe would ride that wave with him. "The foyer needs painting by now, and we should get someone to tend to the tarnish on the chandelier," she said.

Georg nodded. "Finally, we will repair the lintel over the front door."

It was Kaethe's idea to plan the party they would have when they returned to Frankfurt. They obsessed over the details. Should they serve goose or duck? ("Duck, of course," insisted Georg. "Goose is liable to be overcooked and dry.") He said they'd begin with foie gras, but Kaethe said no, something lighter, salmon croquettes perhaps. Which dishes would they use? Would they set out the linen napkins with their initials, or her mother's floral ones? They wrote down the names and addresses of the people they'd invite, though most of them weren't living in Frankfurt anymore, if they were living at all.

Planning for the party took a week. When there was nothing left to plan, Georg fell quiet again. Kaethe kept straight pins in her mouth as she fitted her customers, ensuring there'd be no small talk. She'd been buoyed by Georg's enthusiasm for the party, but now she could feel the life ebbing out of him. Always a man of proud bearing, he allowed his shoulders to stoop and had a shuffle in his gait. Kaethe desperately tried to pull him back into old memories, but now nothing engaged him.

Georg began the conversation early one drizzly evening. "I'm tired, Kaethe. I'm close to sixty and what do I have? I have no future. I have no home. I've lost everything: my honor, my profession. I can't even hold a job. Can you imagine if our parents were alive and knew I had been fired from a dry cleaner's? I don't know what to do next. I don't know what you should do next. I only know that it is now intolerable for me."

Kaethe looked up from a blouse sleeve she was mending. "You have me. We have each other. What are you saying?"

"*Ach,* it's nothing," he said, waving his hand. "I'm being foolish."

"No, tell me. What's intolerable?"

"Everything. My life. Our future. What's happening in Germany. Sometimes . . . I don't know. Sometimes I think I can't go on."

"Of course you can, you always do."

"Lately, I've been feeling that I can't. I'm so very tired."

"You must rest, then. You're exhausted."

"It's not that kind of tired, *liebchen*. I'm tired in my heart. In my bones."

She put down her mending. "What can I do?"

"You can let me do what I want to do."

"And that is what?"

"Must I really spell it out for you?"

The room was darkening. Kaethe sat in the rocking chair they'd brought from Germany; Georg on the desk chair he'd used in his law office.

Kaethe's voice was hoarse when she finally spoke. "Have you made up your mind about this?"

"I have."

"And what about me?"

"I'm sorry." Georg blew his nose. "I feel I have no choice. Do you understand that? You're still a handsome woman. You have life left in you. You will find some nice American man to take care of you. You'll see, it will be a relief to be rid of your old useless husband."

"You talk nonsense, Georg." Again she reached back in time. "Soon it will be apple season. Remember how heavy the trees get with all that fruit? I'll make a compote. You love compote with fresh cream." She made an *mmm* sound, hoping to carry Georg along.

"It won't work, Kaethe. We will never go back there," he said.

"Of course we will. You're always saying how —"

"It's ruined for us. Who can be sure if our house will even be standing? I have tried, I really have."

They stared at each other, neither willing to say what they both knew would come next.

Kaethe went into the kitchen. On the top shelf, above the stove, they kept a bottle of Drambuie, which they saved for company and special occasions. She poured them each a finger. They drank it in the dark, then drank a second finger before Kaethe finally spoke. "If this is what you decide to do, then I do it with you."

Georg got up and brought the bottle of Drambuie into the living room. He poured them each another drink. Before they sipped, they clinked their glasses together. In the wordless shadow of evening, they could see the tears in each other's eyes.

Georg got their papers in order. They wrote a will leaving what money and few possessions they had to Egon. Despite everything, they still felt affection for the old life they'd had with him in Frankfurt. Kaethe stopped taking in sewing. They polished the furniture, cleaned the floors, folded their clothes, and washed the windows. They spent lavishly on food they'd craved but never thought they could afford: fresh tongue, seven-layer cake, eye of round roast, duck, foie gras, salmon croquettes, raspberry tarts, and pricey bottles of Liebfraumilch.

For eight days they ate and drank whatever and whenever they pleased. They stopped sleeping in any natural order and would doze off after a big meal, then awake to another. On the ninth day, neither could bear to look at any more food. They lay in their bed half-dressed. Georg rolled onto his side and looked at Kaethe. She had gray pouches under her eyes, and her face was bloated. "I think it's time," he said.

They got up and straightened the bed, then both of them bathed. He put on a freshly starched shirt and trousers, she her favorite dress from home, whose side buttons she had to leave undone because it no longer fit. She combed her hair and put on rouge and lipstick; he splashed on some aftershave. He opened the remaining bottle of Liebfraumilch and pulled a glassine bag from his pocket. It contained thirty Seconal, which his doctor had given him when Georg had told him he was having trouble sleeping. "Take one at a time with plenty of wine," he told Kaethe.

She sat in her rocker, he in his desk chair. They held hands as they swallowed the pills and drank the wine.

"I'm sorry," he said.

"We've had a good life," she answered.

As they got drowsy, their sentences dissolved into words.

"Fruit trees . . . piano . . . roses . . . chandelier . . ."

If orderliness can be considered a legacy, that's what Georg left behind. Before he and Kaethe took the pills, he slipped a note under the superintendent's door. Using the old law firm letterhead, he wrote in his cursive hand:

8 August 1941

To Whom It May Concern: By the time you receive this notice, my wife Kaethe and I will be deceased. Our will is on the dining room table under a silver bell. The rent for August is in an envelope next to it. Contact Egon Schneider (LO7-9301) and ask him to tell whoever might be interested about our passing. Mr. Schneider can dispose of our bodies in any Jewish cemetery of his choosing. I have signed a blank check to take care of the cost. It is in the same envelope as the rent money. Should Mr. Schneider inquire about the reason for our death, please tell him that no one is to be sad, that we have had enough, that this is what we wanted, that we are sorry to inconvenience him.

Mr. and Mrs. Georg Schnabel

The call came to Egon the next day. The superintendent spoke quickly, obviously eager to dump Mr. and Mrs. Georg Schnabel into someone else's care. The horror of hearing this news was different from the horror of hearing about someone lost in Germany. The worst thing that could happen to immigrants had happened to the

438

Schnabels. They were trapped. They'd made it to America, but they couldn't adjust to this country, and they couldn't go back to their old one. Their circumstances were of their own making, and in some way, that made their deaths even more grotesque and personal.

Meyer did what he always did when his feelings overwhelmed him: He turned to his typewriter. In his next column, he wrote: *That grand master of hatred and misery, Hitler, has reached across the ocean and claimed two more victims, Kaethe and Georg Schnabel.* He described who they'd been in Frankfurt and how they'd come to New York two years earlier, when they could no longer rationalize staying home. He called their deaths a tragedy. *They brought the old country with them to America and never gave up hope of returning to Frankfurt. As a reminder of the life they cherished, they kept a silver dinner bell on their kitchen table and wore clothes more suited to climbing the Tyrolean Alps than strolling through Manhattan. Their oddness was easy to mock, but their perseverance and deep love of country was something to be respected.*

Meyer helped Egon arrange for the funeral the following day. The burial was at a Jewish cemetery in Fairview, New Jersey. Liesl, the Cohens and their baby, Meyer, Egon, and Catrina stood graveside that morning. The rabbi recited a blessing of peace as the caskets were lowered into the ground. Each person dumped a shovelful of soil onto the coffins. There must have been loose rocks in Meyer's pile because the sound that it made when it hit the wooden caskets was the sputtering of pebbles. He pictured the Schnabels holding their hands over their ears. How they'd hate all this dirt. But there they were, locked in their boxes and help-less, being laid to rest by people they barely liked. What an inglorious end. Meyer placed his shovel down and ran into the woods that butted up against the graves.

Only Liesl ran after him. She found him doubled over, as if he was going to be sick. "It's hard, I know," she said, putting her arms around him.

He let himself be comforted and cried on her shoulder. They stood like that for a few minutes before he lifted his head and wiped his nose with the handkerchief she handed him. "I was so intolerant of them," he said. "I wanted them to want what I did. I wanted them to embrace America. Not give up. I was harsh. With him, especially. That's my way. I don't think. I say or do whatever comes into my mind. I'm sorry. I'm sorry for everything."

"I know you are," said Liesl, rubbing his back.

"I'm sorry for the ridiculous night you and I had. I was so eager. I was confused."

"I know," she said.

"I'm sorry that I still haven't gotten your pearls restrung."

Liesl used her thumb to wipe his tears. "Poor Meyer, your brain is so quick, the rest of you has trouble keeping up. What happened with the Schnabels would have happened whether or not you were harsh to them."

"Why are you being so nice to me?" asked Meyer.

Liesl fingered the single strand around her throat. "I still want them back."

They laughed, and together they walked back to the group.

30.

The old rules were hard to follow. The new ones we make for ourselves are harder still.

— Meyer Leavitt, *Aufbau,*
September 8, 1941

As always, Egon woke as the sun came up. In the two months since he'd received the second letter from the INS, he kept up his habit of going to the park in the morning. These days, he moved with intent and eagerness; his visits with the birds had more purpose. In addition to feeding them, he began sketching again. He sat and listened, and could distinguish the whistles and warbles of the European starlings from the incessant *chirrup chirrup* of the house sparrows. It made him laugh to think they might be saying *cheer up, cheer up.* With the bread crumbs spread around him, he sat so still that sometimes the pigeons would peck at

442

his shoes. They would fly close to his face and stare at him with their doleful red-orange eyes, and he would feel certain that something had transpired between them. He became a young boy again, sitting in the Stadtwald with his mother. He could smell the gooseberry jam she'd eaten for breakfast and feel the smoothness of her skin as he leaned against her arm. The long, slender beak of a woodcock would flow from her pencil, and the bird's sneezy *tsiwick tsiwick* would fill his ears.

He knew what Catrina would say about these moments, that his mother was keeping watch and guiding him, and he thought how comforting it would be if she were right.

On the Tuesday after Labor Day, the sky was so lucid that everything beneath it looked new and clean. Egon felt the same way. It was as if a storm had blown through his head and cleared out all the debris. He was left standing, he and Catrina. Together they would be the Schneiders, perhaps not as successful as his parents but no less remarkable in their possibilities. He searched through his drawer for the blue-and-white-striped Arrow shirt that Catrina had given him for his birthday. He decided to wear his only suit, the navy blue one, and his brown Oxfords. Not so bad, he thought, catching his image in the hall closet mirror. He strode up to the Cloisters like a man about to break into song. At his usual bench, he fed the birds and sketched a starling and a herring gull. When he finished, he tucked the drawings into his pocket and leaned on the stone wall overlooking the Hudson. There was a hint of ocean breeze in the air. A knot of joy clumped in his throat. It was beautiful and magical, this New York City, and it made him sad that the Schnabels would never see it this way. Egon was different from them. He would never let himself give up the way they had.

When he arrived at Art's and pulled open the front door, the odor smacked him in the face: sour and stale, as if sediments of Swiss cheese and ham had sunk into the floorboards. The light was as dim as at four thirty on a winter's afternoon, and the sawdust looked gray and exhausted. His yellowing apron slumped on its hook with its miserable Cheese Man button pinned over its heart. Had he never noticed these things before, or had he just endured them?

He folded up the apron and stood by the door. When Art walked in, he was startled

to find Egon waiting for him. "My goodness, we're all dolled up today. To what do I
owe this special greeting?" he asked.

"I am afraid this is no greeting, but a
farewell," said Egon. "I am grateful for the
work you have given me, but now it is time
for me to leave this job." He handed Art the
apron.

Art held the apron in both hands like a
folded flag. "This is what I expect from
people like you. You think you're too good
for this place, but let me tell you something:
I gave you a job. I gave you respect. I taught
you how to work in America. If you think
you wasted your time here, Mr. Schneider,
you've got another thought coming. And I
haven't even mentioned my letter to the
president. Who did you turn to when you
were in a pinch? Art Able. Who came
through for you? Art Able. I don't even want
to think of what might have happened had
the president not responded to my letter.
Not a pretty picture at all. So tell me, Mr.
Schneider, do you have a new job lined up?
Are you going to be a physician at some
fancy hospital? Have you suddenly inherited
a windfall from one of your relatives in
Europe? What do you plan to do next?"

"I cannot say for sure."

"Well, whatever you do next, you can stay

the week and collect your full pay at the end of it." Art stuck out his hand.

Egon shook it and gave him a strained smile: "Thank you, that is a very kind offer, but I am finished with the grocery business."

"That's your decision, but never let it be said that Art Able is anything but a fair and decent businessman."

"You are a decent businessman indeed. I am grateful for the opportunity you gave me." He made a slight bow, then went behind the delicatessen counter and retrieved his old sweater.

Outside, Egon spread his arms, breathed in the fresh air, and squeezed his eyes shut. "Thank you," he whispered. Then he crossed the street to a phone booth and called Catrina at the ASPCA. "I quit my job."

With all the barking in the background, he couldn't be sure if she laughed or sighed. "Oh my, when it rains it pours," she said. "What are you going to do?"

"Tonight!" he shouted. "We will discuss it tonight."

Meyer sounded impatient when Egon called him. "Very nice, but now what are you going to do?"

"Maybe I will take Georg's place at the

dry cleaner's. How can I know, Meyer, I only quit five minutes ago?"

"Here's what you must do right now," said Meyer. "Go home and sit quietly. Think about what you'd really like to do, and what you must do to achieve that. And for God's sake, please don't call me with any more startling news."

Egon took Meyer's advice. At home, he rummaged around his desk. He pulled out his mother's drawings, his parents' books. He walked around the apartment. He studied his reflection in the bathroom cabinet mirror. His hair was thick but grayer than he remembered. His father's face stared back at him. He opened the cabinet door. The old bottle of Kreml. He rubbed some in his hands and smoothed back his hair, put on cologne, and brushed his teeth. His blue eyes shone; maybe they were still the kind that women could fall into. "I will be all right," he said to the man in the mirror.

Whether out of pity, kindness, or necessity, the old man who managed the ASPCA gave Egon a temporary job. Catrina would overhear him talking to the dogs in the small voice his father had always used with animals. "Eat up now, sweet boy. You give me your paw and we shake our hands."

"You miss this, don't you?" she asked him one day.

"I miss Johnny."

But he did miss them: the brave dogs, the wounded rabbits, the shy turtles. He had shopped around Manhattan for a veterinary school, but the closest one was ninety-six miles away in Pennsylvania. It was Meyer who noticed an ad for a small college in Staten Island that was opening a department for veterinary medicine.

The late October wind spun the first chill of winter as Egon and Catrina boarded the Staten Island ferry. Egon carried his old briefcase filled with his diploma, a record of his grades from the university, and — for good luck — his *Doktor Egon Schneider* brass plaque. They sat inside on benches made out of slats of wood. Egon stared straight ahead at the flat gray water and drummed his fingers against Catrina's thigh as if he were keeping rhythm to a private song.

She watched his hand. "Are you nervous?"

He stopped drumming and looked at her as if he'd just remembered she was there. "Am I nervous?" he repeated.

"Yes, you seem a bit twitchy."

He put his hands on Catrina's shoulders.

"I have not been on a boat since I came to this country. Now I am crossing the water with the woman who will be my wife, hoping to enroll in a school where I wish to learn my new occupation, and some American woman whom I have never met will determine whether this is possible. Nervous? Is that what you call it when you have butterflies in the stomach?"

Catrina clapped her hands over his. "You'll be fine. You know how it is with Americans: First, they're suspicious, then they get to know you and they come around. You'll charm whoever it is, you'll see, you and those big blue eyes of yours."

"I'll do my best."

Catrina laughed. "Egon Schneider, did you just wink at me?"

The school, such as it was, was two blocks from the ferry and housed in an old multi-colored brick building with two gargoyles on either side. Above the arched doorway were carved the words PUBLIC BATH CITY OF NEW YORK. Egon checked the address he'd written down against the number on the building to make sure they were in the right place.

A piece of paper was tacked onto the door with the handwritten words *Staten Island*

University. Egon and Catrina both looked puzzled.

"Meyer said it was new; he did not say I would be going to school in a public bathroom," said Egon.

Catrina laughed. "Before people had plumbing in their apartments, they would take their baths in public places like this."

"So, at least we know it will be clean," he said, trying to sound more lighthearted than he felt.

The heavy wooden door creaked as he pushed it open. Inside, the walls were bare and stripped down to their original stone. There were no pictures or signs. The only light streamed in from the outside and left billowy shadows on the inlaid marble floor. There was a long corridor of closed doors but no people. Egon walked up and down calling, "Hello, hello?" until a stout woman with braids pinned around her head like a halo emerged.

"Ah, you must be Mr. Schneider," she said, extending her hand. "I'm Mrs. Flint." Her grip was firm and she smelled of peppermint Chiclets.

After introductions, Mrs. Flint led Egon and Catrina to her office. They sat in rusting chairs in a small room that still bore the faint odor of bleach. Mrs. Flint must have noticed how Catrina's eyes roamed the empty space. "It's not much to see yet," she said, "but we have ample room, and big plans. My father — my late father —" She swallowed hard before she continued. "He endowed the veterinary medicine department." She pointed out the window. "Our farm was across the way. We had sheep and cows and horses, and though his methods were crude and unsophisticated, my father learned to care for them himself. But he believed that animals deserved to be taken seriously and treated professionally. When they started to talk about this college nine years ago, he said he'd do everything he could to make sure that animal medicine would become part of our college curriculum. And he did. It's my job to make sure it's a success."

Egon was moved by the way the woman spoke about her father. "I too had parents who were interested in animals," he said. "My father wrote a book about birds, and my mother illustrated it. They taught me how to treat animals and how to understand them. They wanted me to follow in their footsteps, but I became an ophthalmologist instead. Since I came to America, I find it is the animals that draw my attention. Catrina and I, we have worked with them together."

Catrina nodded and shot Egon a look that seemed a warning. He took it to mean that if he told Mrs. Flint too much about their experience in Washington Heights and his run-in with the INS, it might jeopardize his chances of going to this school. He stopped talking and began to fidget in his briefcase. As he pulled out his diploma and his immigration papers, the brass plaque fell to the floor. Catrina picked it up and showed Mrs. Flint. "This was on his office door. He was a famous eye doctor in Frankfurt."

Mrs. Flint ran her fingers over the plaque. "So shiny after all these years. We don't have many doctors here," she said. "Mostly it's neighborhood kids who can't afford to go to state schools. You'll have more medical experience than some of our teachers. I'd like to introduce you to Dean Okrent, if he's around. Let me go look."

After she left the room, Catrina whispered, "How are your butterflies now?"

"They are circling."

Privately, Egon worried about whether he would be able to follow the teachers' English. How could he keep up with young people? What if he was too old to learn new medicine? Only when he realized that he'd voiced all these questions to himself in English did he understand that these were old anxieties, that he had already answered them.

Mrs. Flint returned with Egon's papers in hand. A man so flimsy, he could have been made of straw, stood behind her. "Dean Okrent, this is Egon Schneider."

The two men shook hands. "A pleasure to meet you," said the dean. "Welcome to our little school. You can start auditing in November and begin the new semester in January. All things considered, if your grades are adequate, we think you'll be able to complete our four-year program in two years."

Catrina smiled. "His grades will be adequate, I can assure you."

Dean Okrent smiled at her as Mrs. Flint turned to Egon and said, "In our own way, we follow in their footsteps, don't we?"

On the ferry ride back, Catrina and Egon sat outside, the cold air pricking their skin. They held hands as they sailed by the Statue of Liberty. Neither spoke, but Egon kept shaking his head.

"What is it?" Catrina finally asked. "Is something wrong?"

"No," he said. "I was thinking about the Schnabels. How I will use their money to help pay for my tuition. How they will have a toehold in America. I wonder what they would think of that?"

31.

The man in front of the classroom speaks so quickly that his words roll over one another. He is holding a rubber-tipped pointer to an illustration of a horse's eye. "This is unlike any other," he says.

The teacher hurries along: "Horses have the largest eyes of all land mammals. Because their eyes are on the sides of their heads, they can see their surroundings on both sides and detect even the slightest motion. That's why wind makes them jumpy."

Egon is curled into his desk. The old wooden flip-top is ink-stained and carved up with initials. On the desktop he has laid out a new composition notebook and a row of six freshly sharpened pencils. This is his first day of class, and he has purposely chosen a seat in the back of the room so as not to call attention to himself. The teacher is probably younger than he is by ten years, and the students by twenty. Egon is wearing a suit and tie, as was proper when he was in medical school. Here, the dress is more casual: The men wear slacks and sport shirts without ties, and the one woman — a girl, really — wears brown-and-white saddle shoes and a skirt and sweater.

The room is cold, but the air smells fresh. Small black and white tiles in hexagon patterns cover the floor. *They must be left over from the baths,* thinks Egon, and he can imagine the sound of wet bare feet slapping against them. In this room, illustrations are taped onto the walls: the anatomy of a cow, a goat, a horse. The animals are all the same salmon color, but the details are distinct: the gullet of the horse; the sternum of the goat, the rear flank of the cow. Only one drawing is in black and white: a bald eagle in flight. Egon is drawn to the precision of its tail wings and layered feathers neatly stacked up against one another like dominoes about to tumble.

His heart shifts.

The teacher is continuing: "They see out of one eye at a time. Monocular vision. When a horse sees movement using monocular vision, he will usually turn his head to see with both eyes. When they look with both eyes, they can only see directly down to their noses and not straight ahead. That is binocular vision. They can't use binocular and monocular vision at the same time."

Egon doesn't need to write down this piece of information; it will stick in his brain like all the facts he learned about the human eye in Berlin. But the other students are earnestly scribbling in their notebooks. He doesn't want to appear arrogant, so he scratches down a few words: *Horse eyes. Binocular. Monocular.*

The teacher, who has been facing the horse illustration, suddenly whirls around and says, "Can anyone tell me which animal is best at color detection?"

Egon sits up straight. No one has raised a hand, and he considers whether it is wise to do so on his first day. He waits a moment to see if anyone else will answer. When no one does, he takes a deep breath and shoots his hand into the air.

The teacher points to him, and everyone turns in his direction.

"This would have to be birds. They can see many colors," says Egon, horribly aware that he has said "*Zis* would have to be birds."

He remembers his early days at Art's, when people complained about his English and told him to go back to where he came from. He grimaces at the memory of that first Thanksgiving at Catrina's when her awful neighbor Mr. Delaney cupped his ear and asked Egon to repeat what he'd said after he'd wished everyone a "Happy *Sanksgiving.*"

The teacher asks, "Why is that?"

"The extra number of cones in birds' eyes makes them exceptionally sensitive to color," says Egon.

No one laughs. No one asks him to repeat what he said. The students return to their notebooks.

"Excellent," says the professor. "And, you sir, what is your name?"

"My name is Egon Schneider."

So our story begins.
        — Meyer Leavitt, from his book
                In the Free Country,
        published December 1946

ACKNOWLEDGMENTS

Like the characters in it, this book took a long journey before finding safe harbor and graceful direction at Grand Central Publishing. I will always be indebted to Deb Futter for getting me there and to Millicent Bennett for her kindness and good judgment in steering the course. Victoria Skurnick, intrepid friend and agent, I will forever owe you.

I am blessed with fellow travelers who also happen to be great readers: Kathy Robbins, Rachelle Bergstein, and Barbara Jones. It's rare to have good friends with great taste and the patience to read and advise, but Becky Okrent, Oliver Kramer, Linda Eisenberg, Pam Friedman, Ellen Schrier, and Scoop Wasserstein all answered the call.

My writing and reading groups inspire and encourage me: Alexandra Horowitz, Elizabeth Kadetsky, Sally Koslow, Aryn Kyle, Jennifer Vanderbes, Meakin Armstrong, Lorrie Bodger, Bill Glass, Andrey Henkin, Nancy Novick, and Karen Wunsch.

Miriam Brumer, my sister, grew up in the world of Washington Heights and helped me fully realize the places and people in this novel.

The exuberant team at Grand Central — Michael Pietsch, Ben Sevier, Brian McLendon, Matthew Ballast, and Tracy Dowd — made all the rest possible. With her keen eye and precise vision, copy editor Laura Cherkas ensured that dates, places, and commas ended up where they were meant to be. Art director Anne Twomey brought time and place into reality with her gorgeous cover. I am lucky to have publicist Andy Dodds in my corner, and I am grateful to Siri Silleck and Jessie Pierce for their competence and cheerfulness in making this all come together.

Lisa Grunwald writes like a dream and edits like one, too. Thank you, dear friend, for your advice, your ear, and your generous spirit. This book would have never landed without you.

The New York Society Library and its warm staff provided a sanctuary where I could write and research. I am particularly grateful to head librarian Carolyn Waters, who uncomplainingly guided me to answers about everything from bunnies and table linens to Oscar Levant and pigeons.

And always, my husband, Gary Hoenig. Thank you for inhabiting this parallel universe with me. The characters in this novel and I would not have survived without your care, your wisdom, and your unrelenting love.

ABOUT THE AUTHOR

Betsy Carter is the author of the novels *Swim to Me, The Orange Blossom Special,* and *The Puzzle King,* as well as her bestselling memoir *Nothing to Fall Back On.* She was the founding editor of *New York Woman* magazine and has worked at many other magazines, including *Newsweek; Harper's Bazaar;* and *Esquire.* She lives in New York City and is the daughter of immigrants.

NRTH